Entrys

INTERSECTIONS

ASIAN AND PACIFIC AMERICAN
TRANSCULTURAL STUDIES

Russell C. Leong
General Editor

Entrys

« PETER BACHO »

*University
of Hawai'i
Press
Honolulu*

*in association
with UCLA
Asian American
Studies Center
Los Angeles*

Printed in the United States of America

11 10 09 08 07 06   6 5 4 3 2 1

Library of Congress Cataloging-in-Publication Data
Bacho, Peter.
Entrys / Peter Bacho.
    p. cm — (Intersections)
ISBN-13: 978-0-8248-2945-2 (pbk. : acid-free paper)
ISBN-10: 0-8248-2945-X (pbk. : acid-free paper)
1. Vietnamese Conflict, 1961–1975—Veterans—Fiction.
2. Racially mixed people—Fiction. 3. Veterans—Fiction.
I. University of California, Los Angeles. Asian American Studies
Center. II. Title. III. Intersections (Honolulu, Hawaii)
PS3552.A2573E58 2005
813'.54—dc22
                                     2005010032

Designed by Liz Demeter

Printed by Versa Press, Inc.

For Mary, Fred, and
my two Mandan daughters

TALL AND TAN and young and lovely, she passes, and Rico watches her, but not in Ipanema. Has she somehow lost her way? Why is she here in dreary, overcast Seattle? Twenty-three, twenty-four, max, with Audrey Hepburn's narrow, high cheekbones, a timeless face that makes makeup redundant. Only the one he is watching, Audrey *redux*, is younger, maybe even within reach. Long-limbed and graceful, she is stunning in her white cotton dress—glamour for the masses, a prima ballerina for the poor.

Miss Andrews, she says, in a way that isn't from here as she continues gliding along the floor, moving up one aisle and down another, touching heads and shoulders, smiling as she goes. She declares, but not in so many words, that she wanted this landfill of minds already wasted, a class full of earthtone faces, of blacks and browns, earthbound boys and girls born without wings or hope.

In this class, there are no other hues, no Japanese or Chinese (Confucian order took care of them—made them well behaved and polite, burdened them with books, made them future dentists). There are no whites, at least on this day. Bobby Ray is white, but he isn't present. He hangs with the brothers, makes love to the sisters. He's missed a few weeks, having been shot in the back by his occasional lover's husband. As a white guy, Bobby Ray doesn't count.

In a larger sense, the other students don't count either. For the school district, they are academic slag, and this class (remedial English) is the district's asshole which, after a term's digestion, pops out colored human turds.

Still, Miss Andrews wants this high school. She wants this class.

Why? Her interrogator is a young black boy, a skeptic full of young black boy snarl and attitude. She answers first with a smile, amped even brighter now; it narrows and bores into the boy, its heat melting his will to doubt her. She thanks him for the question, then poses a question to his question.

"What's your name?"

Bug-eyed, he stares, like he'd just seen Easter Jesus smiling smugly and strolling out of his tomb. Maybe he was blinded? Seeing the stigmata has that effect. The boy doesn't, can't, immediately reply.

Rico, impatient, awaiting her explanation, wanting to hear her voice, reaches across the aisle to nudge the boy.

"It's Delbert, you dumb motherfucker," he whispers, but not so discreetly that those nearby don't hear. They chuckle.

"Huh?" he screeches, and begins to sweat. "Ah, yeah, uh, what was the question?" he asks, to a chorus of derision growing louder and just starting to crest.

"Fuck you, Rico," he adds, before mumbling to himself.

"It's Delbert, Miss Andrews," Rico says, after the laughter subsides. His tone drips white schoolboy sincerity.

"Then you, ah . . ."

"Rico."

"Rico, thank you," she says, as her smile shifts from Delbert to a new, fully appreciative target.

Miss Andrews begins walking toward her desk. She then turns and casually sits on the edge and faces the class. She slouches ever so slightly, relaxed, like she is visiting old friends. But old friends wouldn't stare at the hem of her dress, which has hitched an inch above her knees. Rico does.

To get a better view, he has to clear an obstructing Afro more high than wide, so he leans slightly to his right. The hair belongs to Muhammad Kenyatta who, for his first seventeen years had been known as George, as in Washington—a slavemaster, a slave name. That's why over the summer, he changed his name, as did others, even Delbert, who became Ali Karenga, a name that growled more than poor Delbert did. The name is fierce; Delbert isn't. By the end of summer, he'd become Delbert again.

Rico adjusts to the new sounds and looks, but frankly, he has trouble recalling the African-sounding names, and liked it better when the bloods got haircuts, but that was before Stokely and Rap had made all of that political. He can't help it if he likes the old look—Diana Ross straight hair for women, tight (covatis) cuts, like Sonny Liston's, for men—but hair in 1967 is a black *thang,* which means, by definition, it isn't his. Besides, big hair and *baad-*sounding names make cops and teachers nervous, like hair and names could start a riot. Rico being Rico, he likes that.

Afro cleared, Rico's target comes into focus. Tanned, he thinks, and wonders where the tan line stops or, better still, if it does. He smiles. She is clearly not from here.

She is getting ready to speak, to stir and challenge. She sighs and as she does, Rico memorizes her form, toe to head to just above her waist as he follows the movement of her breasts—inhale (nipples up), exhale (nipples down).

Thirty-four B, he guesses. Firm and just right. Composed now, her smile reappears.

Hard now, Rico smiles at her smile. Oh sure, he'd had lovers, nasty, stank-filled one-night party stands, even rumors of a kid or two. But hey, prove it, okay? What was my name, my out-of-town one-night alias? Oakland? My hometown, my brother. He'd even had girlfriends, a few long-term (more than a month), but he'd never had Audrey Hepburn.

She is serious now as she begins explaining why she'd come

to Adams High. She begins talking about JFK asking what you could do for something or other—"He spoke to me," he thinks he hears her say—and how she'd sobbed on that deadly Dallas day. But Bobby is still here and Martin had a Washington Monument dream of a better America, which triggers Rico's own dream of being invited one day to trace that tan beyond Miss Andrews's hem to discover where, or if, it ends.

American, he thinks—for beautiful, for spacious brown thighs on which God has shed his grace—a place of wonder, of endless potential. As Miss Andrews tells her story of hope and faith, Rico smiles at her.

He has his own set of hopes.

He hopes to fuck her; he is feeling patriotic.

Chapter One

March 23, 1967

Miss Andrews says shes gonna make us look into ourselves and dig deep and find some sorta rough hidden dimond that no one else can find. She says were gonna surprise ourselves (Yeah right me and them bloods that aint goin nowhere nohow ceptin maybe jail or the army, same fuckin dif) Thinkin back though, Mrs Papachalk (4th grade teacher) said I had lotsa talent and that I should develop it. That I was reel smart and such but that was eight years ago, a boy to man gulf of time (draft board says what I already know and thats that Ima man). For a while I tried it and liked the idea of telling stories with happy endings and too bad 4th grade had to end.

Yeah me Rico Divina a Pinoy. Well actually half a Pinoy, a Filipino-Indian, Indipino; dads from the islands and moms from Yakima. Me and them bloods over there too, we needs our ejucation and writin this diarys spose to get us that but I don't see the point. Is it gonna make us better mailmen or grocery store clerks or whatever. Bein Filipino and Indian I don't know what part makes you pissed and poor.

Miss Andrews tho she just keeps talkin bout college like its real, like its even any of us heres gonna go. We spose to write every day from now til the end of school—its called ENTRYS— Language Arts 4, then shes gonna read it and give us a grade.

Shes pretty in a rich white girl sorta way—and like I thought shes not from around here. LA a vista and I aint never done a vista so shed be my first. I like her legs myself. Lean and got nice shape and she got titties, medium and firm and pretty nice, so yeah for you Miss Andrews Ima dig deep into myself and write into this diary and when I do all I sees this hardon which of course I think bout puttin in you . . . Oops forgot shes gonna read this. Gonna have to rip it out befor I hand it in but okay for now cuz I like writin bout her.

And another thing Miss Andrews is is just nice, nothin fake so I don't give her no attitude, not like Delbert, that big lipped brother that aint got no sense. Almost got into it with him over that but he backed his butt down cuz he knows I box and like to fight and Ida beat him just for fun and Ima look for a reason to jack him which he knows and when I get that way I don't care much bout livin or dyin and he knows that too.

Speakin of which just signed my papers day I turned 18, USMC badass motherfuckers. If Ima die Ima die a marine. My ace Buddy —another Pinoy—says whatcha go do that for? And I says armys gonna draft me anyway. Then he goes and gets all upset and says armys a bigger place man, more slots to avoid the infantry and maybe even get outta Vietnam. Like Germany. His cuz just got back and said it was fun. And I says shutup man and fuck the army and fuck the draft cuz the army can take that retarded mother-fucker Delbert and his brothers and can even throw in his sadsack momma for all I care . . .

May 24, 1967

Never did make it to writin every day. Had other stuff goin.

Told Buddy I left school and was leavin for boot. Coulda waited but what the hell? A month or so aint gonna make no diff.

We grew up together me and Buddy. His dad and mine go back-aways back to the Philippines. Same village and came over the same boat I think. Hes a little younger so hes got time to plan and avoid this shit. Goin to catholic school, got good grades from what he says. So I says to finish up and go on to college and avoid the shit Im about to do. Said Id write back. I love Buddy like a brother but right now Im kinda jelous . . . Shit Ill get over it.

Then I swung by to see Miss Andrews to say goodby. She musta guessed I was up to somethin cause I aint been in class for the last three weeks. Caught her up by the teachers parkin lot. She smiled and asked if I needed a ride. Fuck yeah I says. She smiles and looked good. Got her tan back cuz its been hot here lately. Then I told her what Id done and she was quiet for a second and lookin really sad like she really knew me . . .

Damn I was thinkin maybe I shoulda kept goin to class.

I lied and told her that even though I left school I kept writin in the diary just like she said and she smiled at that. Then I kinda fuckup and say what I really think and say damn woman you a fine ass girl. And then I catch myself and apologize and say well, you know like pretty, and she just blush but then she smiles dead at me and she just keeps gettin prettier.

And we just keep on drivin and talkin and I was right: shes a Vista, a recent graduate from some rich school back east and I said I hope us knuckleheads didnt discourage her cuz shes a good teacher and she said we dint and she says she believes the US is at a crossrodes or somethin, and that folks gotta help each other out, gotta help the poor and shit. Then I says Im poor and she smiles again then says in a real low sexy voice that she wished Ida stayed in school and I says I do too now that I think bout it.

Shes twentythree next month. Happy birthday I say. Sorry Ima miss it. She says somethin bout the war, says its no good and that only poor boys go and that she got friends who could get me out and I say its done. Then she gets quiet again and we just drive and before I know it were down there right by the lake over by Seward Park. Its one of my favorite spots that and Puget Sound cuz my dad was a fisherman back home. He was on the water every day. He seen it all storms and shit. Magic, he said, thats what the water was to him. Bury me there on that beach in the Philippines he told me.

I wish Ida gotten the chance.

I tell her she was the only good thing bout school and that I could tell the truth because hey I was outta school and in a year it could all be over anyway. She says not to talk like that and that what I said (about her bein the good thing bout school) meant so much to her. Then I get quiet and shes just starin at me. Shes got nice eyes (green) and they begin to get wet and I touch her face. Run my finger right over a tear thats just startin to get fat and fall. Then she grabs my hand real soft and we just sorta come together and start kissin and lucky for us the parks empty. And the kissins just the start. I mean we do it right there in the front seat of her corvair . . . man I didn plan this but whos complainin.

Woke up at her place, shes Toni now and we go one more time til its time for her to go. And man then it really gets wild. For starters I eat her then she turns round and gets right on her belly and she makes me eat her there and man I aint never done THERE befor. Man that chicks to much. Wonder if she got cousins or somthin . . .

Then I tell her Ill remember her and she says the same bout me but I gotta write first. Then she says I got talent. She says its a raw intelligence—says she got an instinct on these things. Damn aint herd that in a long time, least not used for me. Then she says I should start thinkin bout what Ill do after the marines like college or somethin. Said I wanted to show her my diary but Im scared cause the mistakes and all. That plus what I wrote bout her. Besides I say Id already packed it away. She says she wants to see it when I get back. I say okay. She says writins no secret. You get good just by doin it. It aint math and thank you lord for that.

Writins hard but its better than math. Toni then hands me some books (3) and right away I find out I been misspellin the dam word (writing) of what Im spose to get so dam good at. Shit this aint a very good start. After my first letter shed write back right away. She says expect a letter a week. I says cool and then she makes me promise to read the books. I says I will and Ill write too. We kiss one more time (sweet). She goes one way and I go the other.

*   *   *

DEPARTURE LOUNGE. SAN FRANCISCO INTERNATIONAL AIRPORT. JANUARY 2. 1968

The teen Marine sits quietly in a corner. The room is jammed with others like him, just killing time until the charter loads them up and deposits them in the middle of a savage, ceaseless war half a world away.

Some of his comrades are sleeping. Others are talking about girlfriends who promise to wait, hot new gas-eating Detroit machines, and other postcombat tour dreams. No one dares talk about dying or about not returning, or returning without a mind or a limb, or two limbs, or more.

Some of his comrades sleep, trying hard to be tired, or trying hard to be interested in sports magazines or skin rags, the materials of choice. No one is reading a newspaper, at least not the front pages, where reports of engagements and casualty tolls are daily, dreary bold-letter fare.

The Marine in the corner is also a reader, but, unlike his peers, he hasn't learned that the aging Celtics seem to be through or that Miss January studied Latin and is learning to read ancient Greek. Instead, he seems to be focusing on each word of a small, thin paperback volume, the title of which has no meaning to anyone else in the room. As he reads, his eyebrows sometimes furrow; sometimes he underlines words or sections or sentences with a red pen; other times, while reading other pages, or even other paragraphs of the same page, he might frown or whisper a barely audible "damn." Resting against his right thigh is another book with a smooth blue leather cover and a ribbon page marker; this book is larger than the one he holds in his hands. So intent is this reader he doesn't see Jerome approach.

"Rico, hey partner, whatcha readin'?" Jerome asks, in his rural Oklahoma drawl.

Jerome King is his closest friend from boot camp, a whip-thin redhead Oklahoma country boy. Jerome walks slowly, speaks even slower. Rico had told him that when he talked he was like some poorly dubbed character in a samurai flick, where the lips would stop moving but the sound would go on. They are an odd match —Rico is not inclined to liking white guys (until the Marines, he just didn't know many)—and Jerome loves Conway Twitty, loves America, hates Commies, and misses the palomino he left behind.

One night, in a Mexican bar in San Diego, Rico, his Indian half acting badly, had declared, a bit too loudly, that all Mexicans were tame Catholic Indians who spoke bad Spanish. He wasn't, he screamed, a tame Indian. Loudly, he cursed the Church and goddamned holy Jesus—not a good move since even the meanest, drunkest Mexican—with "life" and "death" tattooed on his knuckles—might be bearing his savior's name. Rico, though, couldn't be stopped; he was half Filipino, he said, which made him tougher than any Christ-kissing wetback in this bar.

That, of course, triggered a cultural and religious dissent that included flying chairs, swinging fists, drawn knives, and the business end of a Cuervo bottle upside Rico's shaved head. He'd awakened in a cab next to Jerome, who'd carried him to safety. "Man, what the hell you say?" Jerome had said then. "You sure made them Mexicans mad." Rico hated country music (sung, he'd often tell Jerome, by poor toothless white folk), but he understood backup.

Jerome clears his throat, then repeats his question. "Hey partner, whatcha readin'?"

Rico doesn't bother to look up.

"What's it about, man?"

"'Bout writin'," he says flatly. He is hoping his friend will take the hint and disappear. For Rico, being friends doesn't mean having to be polite.

Jerome, who'd grown somewhat immune to Rico's hints and insults, verbal and otherwise, just shrugs. "Huh? But I don't see . . ."

Rico sighs and places the Strunk and White on his lap. He stares at his friend. "Man, I can't write worth a good goddamn, and I'ma fix it. Simple as that."

"Man, what's that other book?" Jerome points to the blue leather volume. "Looks like a . . . "

"Diary, man," Rico says, as he returns to Strunk and White.

"A diary? Man, ain't that somethin'," Jerome exclaims. "But we're Marines. We're about fightin', not writin'."

"Maybe," Rico replies calmly, eyes still focusing on a page. "But the war's gotta end sometime, and when I get home, my first priority's gonna be to stop bein' like you."

"What's that?"

"An ignoramus," Rico said. "You cowboy, John Wayne motherfucker."

Even for one as patient as Jerome, there are limits to abuse. The ignoramus part he doesn't much mind; Rico'd called him that, and even worse. But using *John Wayne* to modify *motherfucker* is too much. Rico, as he'd sometimes done, has again crossed the line. "Sure," he sniffs, trying not to sound wounded—an invisible Choctaw arrow through his heart—as he retreats to the opposite side of the room.

"Got the point, I'll catch you later."

For a moment, Rico watches his friend. "Next time, leave me in the bar," he mumbles, and turns to the next principle, which declares that "The number of the subject determines the number of the verb." He studies the examples that follow. Eyes squinting, lips moving, his face becomes an image of almost painful concentration. He fumbles to his side and reaches for the diary, turning the pages to an early entry, the first one, in fact. He scans the page and finds an offending sentence. "We needs our ejucation," he'd written then.

"Damn," he whispers. "Ignoramus."

"We need our education" it quickly becomes in the Departure Lounge, San Francisco International Airport. At least of the effort, the recognition, either Strunk or White, maybe even both, would've been proud.

* * *

November 1, 1968

Got a few days off in Hue, a chance for cold beers and a hot shower, a clean bed. Life's good (okay, too much), but it's better than it's been. It's okay for now, and that's all that counts. I'll trade an okay now for a good tomorrow any day.

I haven't made an entry in a long time because I knew I didn't know how to write. But I'm readier now. Everyone needs their safe little spot and this diary gives me mine.

I studied the books Toni sent me and practiced writing, mostly in my letters to her. Always the teacher, she'd send my letters back corrected and explained. She still writes every week, just like she promised, and I write back. I live for those letters—her terms of affection. Her words promise me tomorrow.

But with Toni, first things first. She taught me how to use an apostrophe. Ignorant, I was so ignorant, and I look at those earlier entries here, and I was so embarrassed I stopped writing for awhile, stopped doing entries (not "entrys"). I just practiced and practiced on loose leaf.

Imagine, "shed" for "she'd", just basic things I'd never picked up. What was I doing in school anyway? Clearly, not too much (sentence fragment, I know). She (Toni) asked me if I read the grammar and style books. Read and reread, I wrote back. I told her I liked Strunk and White. Simple, clear basics (another fragment).

She said she could tell from my letters that I was getting better at writing, becoming more polished, and that I improved with each letter. She said the improvement was "dramatic," "remarkable," that I could handle college, that I wrote clearly and with a "certain flair" (her words) that showed "natural" talent. It would be easy for me to handle the essays in college because college was mostly about writing. She said my letters intrigued her—they were "descriptive and bold, gripping" (her words again).

But here's the truth. I tone them down, every one of them. It's horrible here, I can't tell her everything.

I know I'm getting better. Just read those first entries again. Damn, maybe I should rip them out. No, I'll keep them—reminders of distance traveled. I wonder though what's in it for her? She could sail or play tennis, marry some rich college deferred white guy...Why write to me? I'll have to ask her, but only when I get back.

Ah hell, even if it all ends with Toni, I can still thank her for this little diary that I've come to like. I open it whenever I can. It's just me and my thoughts and this empty page.

I can remember and record events, tell a story, even change an ending if I want. These are my thoughts and words. In that sense, I'm like God, at least as far as this little book goes. I control it all. I like that. In this goddamn place, I can't control too much of anything else.

November 20, 1968

Damn, "everyone" is singular, "their" is plural. Probably some other mistakes too. Keep writing, keep learning.

Now I'll have more time. I'm finally out of the shit. The docs say I got hit a week ago, but I don't remember...

It all happened so fast. We were on patrol just north of here (Hue) and I remember counting down, thinking that I'd be out soon and that maybe the worst was over. All I had to do was keep low, stay calm, keep writing, keep counting down. Maybe the lieutenant will cut me a break, pull me out of the bush. That thought kept me going . . .

Then they hit—NVA regulars, some bad, bad boys—and all I remember is pointing and shooting, sometimes not even that. Then it gets louder and faster, a blur, and I can't remember the sequence, except that I began feeling light, beyond caring. I remembered someone saying, "He's lost a lot of blood," and me thinking dude must be talking about someone else.

I woke up in a hospital bed. A nice young doc said, "You're lucky, Corporal Divina, you're going home. Nasty, yeah, some muscle damage, but no vital organs. A frag just missed your heart . . ."

Doc was wrong. I don't have a heart, not now, anyway. "The others," I asked.

He was a nice doc and he looked at me, like maybe that's something I shouldn't have said. "You're lucky," he said and turned away.

* * *

THE NEW HUE BAR

It was Friday night at the New Hue Bar. In this faraway, violent place, the New Hue had become American territory, if not by geography, law, or logic, then by occupation. Starting at dusk, teenage GIs began to gather, settling in small groups at tables, or lining the bar where they slammed beer-chased shot after beer-chased shot and declared that back home, they couldn't legally buy a drink. Here, they weren't carded, and thank God for tiny blessings. Some of them, the bolder red-eyed ones, would whisper slurred "I love you" words to rouged-up bar girls who never bought the line, but always kept the change.

As night fell, the music would crank up and, from up to a block away, an evening stroller-by just might hear Beach Boys' harmonies or a Jagger snarl, or maybe, if the place was packed with poor white boys from Selma or East Texas, old Minh (the owner) might put on Patsy Cline or Conway Twitty, at which point, black soldiers, or Mexicans, or Filipinos—if they weren't too drunk—might hear the twang and jump up and leave for the soul bar two blocks down.

That night at the New Hue, Minh had made his call. He knew foreigners, starting with the French. He spoke their language and believed in them, had served them in fact and, at nineteen, had lost his leg trying to parachute into the doomed French garrison at Dien Bien Phu. He was so small that when he jumped, a strong wind blew him miles off course, and his chute got caught in a tree. A Viet Minh soldier spotted him as he dangled, trapped, helpless. The soldier took his time; Minh watched him nudge his comrades then point to him. Minh heard them laugh at his plight. He heard one of them say that the soldier who spotted him should at least finish his cigarette. He saw the soldier take one last drag, then flick the butt. He saw him take aim, fire. He felt the bullet rip into his left thigh and saw his lower pant leg slowly change color. He heard himself scream but not so loud he couldn't also hear his tormentors laugh again as they walked casually away from him and toward the battle, but not before the one who shot him lit another cigarette.

Eventually, Minh was captured and, after the French quit Vietnam, eventually released. In 1954, Minh had volunteered for the jump; he was an idealist, but that was fourteen years and one leg ago.

After that war, he'd bought the New Hue—then just a little noodle shop—cheap and on speculation. He was beginning to understand politics and knew the French would be replaced, that the Americans were just around the corner, so he studied them, made efforts to talk to the fresh-faced advisers and functionaries that were trickling into the country. And when the new war finally came in 1965, the now English-speaking Minh was ready with a quickly remodeled, air-conditioned bar and every greeting from a toothy "hi" and "howdy" to "say, brothaa." The variety of Americans amazed him—from black to white, to Indians, Mexicans, and Filipinos. Tonight was a howdy sort of night; Minh had a keen ear for language and inflection, and that night he had heard an awful lot of twang spoken, which meant Roger Miller or the Statlers or Conway Twitty amped up loud. Twitty, whom Minh didn't really like, would likely keep blacks away but would spur these sons of the South to dance and drink more, to mourn why their fellow Americans failed to understand them, or better still, to eventually come to rest with their foreheads and faces on the bar or a table-top, their wallets open and their cash soon gone.

For that night, Minh knew the South would rise again, which is why he was surprised, later that night, when Mel walked in the door. It was near closing and Twitty had given way to Patsy Cline singing ballad after ballad of lost love and fading pictures and cheating hearts; most of the young white GIs had already stumbled out the door, leaving just a few on the dance floor, a handful at the bar. Mel was a big man—over six feet and a rock hard 230 —who looked every inch the airborne master sergeant that he was. He was also a black man from Chicago, where twang was seldom heard, either spoken or sung. About half a year ago, Mel had first walked into the bar; it was a quiet night and he and Minh had struck up a nice conversation that became a friendship, an air-borne sort of bond.

"Heard this was a good place to drink," Mel had said then.

"Say, brothaa," Minh answered in his best black English. "You heard right." His pitch was high, almost falsetto, like Smokey Robinson had suddenly walked through the door, changed colors, lost a leg, and was working the bar in the New Hue.

Mel blinked at the odd mesh of sight and sound. He paused and smiled. "Heard you don't cut your drinks."

Minh smiled back. "For you, sergeant, baddest of the bad, never. But for the rest of these sorry-assed grunt mothafuck-aas . . ." His hand swept a room full of drunk teenage soldiers. "Not until after the third round when they can't notice." Minh paused. "Want pussy?"

Mel shook his head. "Jack Black straight," he said. "What I've seen, pussy ain't gonna fix."

Minh grabbed a fresh bottle and that first night they just sat together at a corner table, and talked airborne to airborne— Minh's Dien Bien Phu, Mel's high, cold Korean ridges and his Vietnam bush—the horrors they'd seen, the comrades they'd lost. A full on the house fifth of Jack baptized that night, and over the next few months, several more fifths repeated the ceremony. They'd just sit, the two of them, the big black sergeant and his pale little friend half his size—drinking, smoking, talking—usually past closing, often until dawn.

This Friday night, though, was different. Minh could tell. They were drinking more—at least Mel was—and talking less. They'd already gone through one fifth and it was still an hour until closing. Minh then left the table and brought back another bottle. He slowly unscrewed the top and filled both glasses.

"Ice?" Minh asked.

"No."

"Mel," Minh said slowly. "What's really up?"

"Nothin'," came the soft, slurred reply.

"Mel."

"Fuck it all," the sergeant mumbled and fixed a squinty, bloodshot stare on his friend. An index finger wiped the corner of an eye. "Look at these kids, Minh," he whispered. "Drunk tonight, maybe dead tomorrow or the next." He paused. "And the survivors, Minh, even if you get outta here, you're fucked. I got kids, Minh, boys, like the ones I'm tryin' to keep alive. They're in Oakland, you know, the Bay Area? My oldest, that's Reginald, he's sixteen. Told 'im to get his ass in college, grab that deferment, but he's a knucklehead, not too good in school."

Mel sighed, then leaned his huge frame back in his chair. He raised the glass and took a sip. "Know what that means?" he asked quietly.

Minh shrugged. He didn't.

"Two years, no college, baby, Uncle Sam wants his young black butt, more meat for this fucked-up war we ain't never gonna win," he said. "I'm outta here, Minh, five more months, second and last tour, just seen too goddamn much."

"Mel."

"Almost twenty years this man's army," he whispered as if alone. "Seen horrible things, but this was the worst I ever did see." His eyes were glazed, unfocused, wide open but unseeing.

Minh didn't know the image replaying itself inside his friend's head. But he knew it was there, this snapshot of hell. He knew the signs. In the days and nights after his capture—as he watched his leg turn black, then disappear—he'd visit often this driftaway land of vacant stares where only his mind could see. His friend was there now. "Mel," Minh said softly, and shook his friend's shoulder.

"Damn," Mel whispered.

"Mel."

"Last week, it was last week," Mel began. "We went in." He was speaking softly, slowly, like each word was an effort to form, a greater effort to say.

"Go on," Minh said.

"A Marine platoon got hit just northa here," he continued. "Hard, NVA regulars, fierce fighting, close quarters, hand to hand . . ."

Mel then buried his face into his huge black hands; he shuddered and took a deep breath. His lips began moving again, but just barely. Minh inched closer to his friend.

"We got there in time to save maybe some, a handful, maybe, dependin' on who survived," Minh heard him say.

Minh then reached across the table to grab his friend's thick wrists. He then stared at him, hoped to catch his eye; he didn't, but he still wanted to say words that he knew wouldn't heal, but just might help to lift this horrible moment or, later, help him through this night. "Listen, you did your best, Mel," he said calmly. "In this business, men die, boys, too. It's war, my friend, something we both know too well."

Suddenly, Mel dropped his hands to the table. This time he was the one staring, his focus so fierce that Minh, who'd hoped to heal him, found himself retreating nervously into his chair. His smooth, black face appeared calm—a classic African bust, its stoic surface marred only by a single tear that was beginning to form in the corner of an eye. Minh watched as the tear gathered itself and paused, as if maybe by sheer force of will, its owner—this brave, powerful man—might suddenly recall it, deny it permission to fall. The tear fell anyway.

"There was this one Marine," Mel began. "He was in a gully, off on the edge, so we didn't see 'im right away, not durin' the fight anyway. Then after it was clear, we check it all out, tend to the wounded, and I just come across 'im, at first all's I can see's this blade, risin' and plungin' down, again and again, and I slowly approach, and this kid, he's maybe nineteen, small, wiry, dark brown—Filipino, nah, Indian, maybe Mexican—he's there in that gully just covered with NVA bodies—maybe eight or ten—and he's hackin' away, and he's screamin' and singin' callin' for some dude named Jerome, his partner I guess, and I tell 'im to stop, and he don't hear me." The words were faster now, a purgative rat-a-tat-tat.

"And me and some others is watchin' and someone says we should stop it—the screamin' from his victims, at least from some of 'em that's still alive, is just gettin' too much—and I says there's no way we can, unless we wanna shoot the boy. We can see he's wounded, upper chest, left shoulder, so I says it's just a mattera time . . . "

"What then?"

Mel sighed. "We just back off and wait, and soon we can't see the knife and it gets real quiet, so I go up and he's lost enough blood and, sure 'nough, he's weak, almost out and I talk to him real slow, tell him he's gonna be okay, we're friends . . . " He looked away and cleared his throat.

Minh studied his friend; he knew that this was the end, all else was just prelude. This last scene—the one so horrid that lingered in this hard man—words, even swiftly spoken ones, could not leave behind.

"Man," Mel mumbled. "That gully, I mean, ah, 'scuse me." He cleared his throat. "It was, ah, fulla heads, fingers, ears, eyes." His eyes began to water again.

"Stripped like an old Buick, man," Mel said softly. "That youngster took parts."

"Did his friend, that Jerome, did he survive?"

"Don't recall, but probably not."

"What about the kid, the Indian? Did he make it? Did he survive?"

"Him? Yeah, I 'spose he did, medics said he'd live, get his ticket back home." What should've been good news wasn't spoken like it was. Mel's hands then opened to form a cup. And into that cup he poured a melancholy gaze that saw beyond his own flesh and bone.

"But did he survive?" Mel whispered without looking up. "Did the Indian kid . . . " He paused, unable for the moment, to finish the question. He stretched his thick neck back to look at a point in the ceiling directly above them.

"Nah," he finally said. "Not really."

Chapter Two

It was one of those odd Seattle February afternoons that the city would get every decade or so. The sun—often gone until the spring—had fooled the weatherman and had made a surprise call. It was still cold, around zero, but no one was complaining. On such days, one of the better places to be was on Capitol Hill where, depending on the exact spot, both the Olympic Mountains to the west and the Cascade Range to the east could be seen— stunning snow-capped ranges both. It was the perfect time for a stroll, and Capitol Hill, with its broad, tree-shrouded boulevards, was the perfect place—perfect for sweethearts and for families, perfect even for walking alone.

At such a glorious moment, what could possibly go wrong? For one young couple who, just ten minutes before, had been walking on the Hill hand in hand and stealing deep kisses, apparently everything.

The woman, a pretty young brunette, was standing away from the cluster of cops and medics who hovered over the prone body of her companion, a young white man. After that last kiss, he was suddenly attacked, the victim of a vicious, unprovoked assault. It

had come from nowhere and had lasted—witnesses were saying—
less than a minute. The young man was clean-cut and well dressed,
even handsome, a description some would have used before his
smooth, well-defined face had turned into a porridge full of welts
and open wounds—a pulpy bloody nose, two blackened eyes, deep
eyebrow cuts caused by his pair of shattered glasses, and a boot-
inflicted cheekbone fragment breaking his skin. He hadn't yet
regained consciousness; blood still dripped from a fractured jaw,
mouth that couldn't close.

The woman was sobbing into the shoulder of a passerby. Her
lover was still motionless on the concrete. A detective in a light
blue sports jacket busied himself interviewing possible witnesses.
The young brunette was so distraught, he put her off until last. He
quickly reached the end of sketchy impressions and inconsistent
memories. "Rashomon," he sighed and motioned for the passerby
to send the victim's companion over. He'd seen it all before.

"Miss, I'm sorry, things like this don't usually happen here, it's
usually very safe," the detective began. "But what happened?"

She took a deep breath and glanced at her friend; he was now
on the stretcher and just beginning to stir. Weakly, he waved in her
direction. She smiled and waved back, then dabbed at her eyes as
she turned her attention to the detective. They were just walking
along, she said, when this man suddenly appeared and began beating her friend. No, she wasn't sure where he came from, but thinks
he might have run there, to a winding park trail. Or maybe there,
to a neighborhood tavern. She apologized. She does remember
screaming and trying to pull him off, but not before he'd kicked
her friend twice in the face as he lay sprawled on the ground.
Much more than that, though, she just wasn't sure.

"Any description?" the detective asked.

She shuddered.

"Take your time."

She nodded. "Dark, short hair, medium build, kinda tall,
maybe five-ten or so," she mumbled. "Older, maybe thirty."

"Can you recall anything else?"

She paused. "It was like a flash, so sudden, I . . . "

The detective placed his hand gently on her shoulder. "This is important," he said softly. "Try to recall."

"He looked like an Arab," she said finally. "Maybe Middle Eastern, crazy."

The detective paused and checked his notes; he flipped back a few pages and paused before speaking. "Are you sure?"

"Pretty much, but it was so fast, I . . . "

He reached into his coat pocket and pulled out a cigarette. "Do you mind?" he said as he lit up.

She shook her head. "No."

As the detective took a long drag, he studied her. "One of the witnesses said she'd heard you screaming," he said evenly, "then you looked up and saw who she thinks was the suspect. After he'd knocked your friend out, he reached down and picked up something, maybe a small book, that fell from his coat. Color, she wasn't sure, could've been black, maybe blue. Then the suspect ran right by her. He was carrying the book—she was sure of that. She said he had long dark hair—black, she thinks—and looked like an Indian, maybe a Filipino, wiry, not too tall . . . "

She began to shake and covered her face with her hands. "It's just so horrible . . . "

"It's okay, it's okay now," he said, his tone soothing. He knew he had to calm her down; he knew enough not to press, at least not now. Twenty years on this job had taught him that. He'd return to her later. "Miss, ah . . . "

"Toni," she said. "Just call me Toni."

*   *   *

February 15, 1970

I know, I know, it's been a long time since an entry, more than a year, in fact. The stay in the hospital was rough, all that down time with nothing to do but think and remember and dream. In the VA I dreamed of Jerome, that ambush, of him being overrun and calling out to me, and me freezing just a second before getting there, and in that second, I got there too late. And in the dream, I try explaining, and he always shakes his head sadly and says that back in that bar, he never waited, never delayed that night when the bottles were up and the knives were out and aimed at me. In the dream, I always say I'm sorry, I'm sorry, but he still just shakes his head and says to tell that to his family.

I told the nutcase docs and social workers about it, and they all joined together to sing, like some damn gospel chorus, that such a dream was normal, these feelings of guilt for surviving when close friends die, and that eventually, it would stop. So far so good. I've been back home since August, and Jerome's gone back to Oklahoma, or at least stayed out of my dreams. Maybe the nutcase docs were right. I'm away from the VA now, away from the wounded, the double amputees, the suffering and hopelessness—reminders of this fuckin' war.

I'm out, and that's better, but I'm not quite clear yet. There's still my left shoulder, and the body docs all saying it would be fine and me not believing, thinking they're lying. For months I couldn't move it, not without a lot of pain. I just watched as my upper arm started to shrivel up. I didn't want to write then; I couldn't think straight. I was too mad, madder than I'd been in Vietnam. Maybe it was because I had so much time to think, to fester... The only thing good about this time was that I fell into the habit of reading—books on anything, magazines, newspapers, all of which the staff was happy to provide me with because if I was reading, I wasn't complaining. My friend Sammy helped me. He was in the bed next to mine; the docs managed to save his leg, but he'll limp from now until they put him in the ground. Twenty-one, a smart man, an English major in college. He lost his deferment when he cracked under the pressure of having to stay in school—that and having to work 30-40 hours just to afford tuition. He just dropped out right before finals and took his chances. He'd recommend books and we'd talk about things that in the military are never heard, like writers and structure and meaning.

When I was a kid I'd sometimes read a book (not too often), but I'd just stay on the surface, never dig deeper. I never understood the use of symbols, but that's changed now.

Some days at the VA, if I was awake sixteen hours, I'd be reading for twelve of them, sometimes more. The later I stayed awake, the better, like I was avoiding sleep, running from dreams. A book a day for some weeks—history, essays, politics, fiction, trash, whatever. I began to read not just for the substance, but also for style, how certain writers put certain sorts of words together. How some words fit, others don't. I also learned that although I was fucked up, there were others a whole lot worse off than me. Hell, all I had to do was look at Sammy. (Cool, eh? I recognized that verb tenses in the same sentence should usually be consistent.)

After awhile the shoulder started coming around. The therapy began to take hold, and my shoulder started getting more range of movement without pain. I began squeezing a handball with my left hand and lifting small weights, and slowly, my arm began to look better. I was released not fully healed, but good enough and glad enough to leave the VA. I took the first flight back to Seattle.

I'm a civilian now and I'm back home, growing my hair long, a luxury. It's nice just staying at my mom's and hanging with my sisters. Mom just cried when she saw me; who says Indians are stoic? Not Mom.

Dad? I sometimes wonder where he is, but hell, I've wondered that for years. He said life here was too hard. Maybe he did go to his little grass shack in the Philippines—somewhere close to the water. I don't know. It's been too long to care, or so I remind myself.

There's still a little pain, a little reminder, but all that's left are the scars on my left shoulder and a bigger one on my back—entry and exit points. No big deal. The docs said there was no permanent nerve or muscle damage, and eventually I'd get full movement back.

Jumped in Mom's raggedy Buick and cruised the old neighborhood; most of the guys my age are gone. A few to college—like Buddy, who's in his first year—but most are in the military. The good thing is that this war's been going on so long that the younger brothers know what to expect. Some are getting smart and taking steps to avoid what I did. They're going into the reserves, or the National Guard, or the Coast Guard, or even the Navy or Air Force or ROTC—no Army infantry, sure as hell, no more Marines.

Saw Buddy for a hot minute; he was at his folks' place, just down for the weekend. It was nice seeing him; we just talked about old times, what we both planned to do. He said he wanted to teach, to work with young kids—he's calm, good natured (unlike me), smart. A perfect fit. Me? I don't know yet, but the worst part is over. I can decide tomorrow or the day after—no big rush. After Vietnam, just breathing or talking loud is good enough.

About noon, I swung by to see Toni. She was glad to see me and I, of course, was glad to see her. She was as pretty as always. I thanked her for the books; she said that judging by my letters, I'd learned very well. She asked if I'd thought about college. I said we'll see. We spent some nice time together—that first night I slept over—then I had to spring the bad news. I told her that I was leaving town for a few months. She cried, but I promised I'd call her and stay in touch. Told her I'd be back in June when the weather improves. She said she'd wait.

I don't know if she will. But no matter—because she'll always matter. She taught me to write and to love the power and beauty of words. She taught me to think, not just react. For all of that, yeah, I'll love her forever.

In Vietnam, I thought I missed Seattle, and sometimes I did. But the Seattle I was missing was the one with the nice summers and soft, pretty falls, those beautiful snowcapped mountain ranges, Puget Sound, the nearby lakes and rivers. It wasn't like I was a great outdoorsman or anything; hell, I'd barely been outside of the city. But even as a poor kid, I knew what beauty was like; this was beautiful and, better still, nobody owned it. At least the views were free. In my worst days in the bush, I prayed that when, not if, I was killed, there'd be enough of me left to identify and bring back and bury. An arm, a foot, a jaw, whatever. Just enough to be buried. After what I'd been through, I figured at least part of me deserved a break.

In Vietnam, I'd almost forgotten that living in Paradise carries a price that must be paid in January and February of each and every year. These are the dark days of constant cold, rain and snow. (I know, I know, got a bit of sun today, but that's just a tease; we won't see it again until June.) This February Seattle—this dreary, suicidal place—I didn't miss at all, and hell, now I'm plopped back right in the middle of it. Got some old buddies down in California, around Stockton, went to boot together; called them last night and they said to come on down. There's a Greyhound leaving at midnight; I've picked up a ticket and I'll be on board. They said it was warm. Man, I can't wait to get there.

Chapter Three

April 20, 1970

I've been here more than two months and, for me, at least, it's a nice change from the Northwest. For the first few weeks, I stayed with my friends outside of Stockton, but they're hustling to make it, so I found a job—working days in a grocery store—then got an apartment in the city. The money's not great, but it's enough to pay rent. Got a room down on El Dorado, where the old Pinoys still hang out. A couple of them knew my dad—they'd worked the same asparagus crews in French Camp—and one of them said he saw him before he left for the PI; so I was right on that one. The oldtimer said Dad wouldn't be returning—got his little hut down by the beach. Got his teenage bride, hell, that asshole's set; he probably didn't even know I was in Vietnam.

These old guys, though, are pretty good to me. They tip me off on jobs, and tell me to stay out of the fields, work's too damn hard. Get an education, they say. Maybe, I reply.

We shoot pool, drink coffee; sometimes they even feed me if I'm short before payday. I like it here; they remind me of my dad, at least the good parts I remember.

Got this one old Pinoy I really like. His name's Constantino, an ex-boxer. He didn't have to tell me that; I could tell by just looking at his face—the scars around his eyes, the flattened bridge. It's the map of the profession. One Sunday in the pool hall, we were talking, and I told him I used to box amateur. Had a good record, but never took it too seriously because only the fighting part was fun. The problem was I just hated training and loved to party, and you can only go so far on talent alone (which the coaches all said I had). So, I lost some fights I shouldn't have and sometimes I wondered what it might have been if I'd really applied myself. A good pro career? Maybe a championship shot? Damn, if I'd have done it right and had a big enough amateur record, I could've pulled duty on the Marine Corps boxing team, instead of getting my young ass shot at. But hell, I'm still young, twenty-one's not too old.

Constantino then asked me to shadow box, so I did, right there in a corner of the pool hall. He looked at me closely, studied me, as I threw combinations and did quick pivots. Some other old Pinoys gathered around and watched—other old time fighters, longtime fans, a tough crowd. Out of the corner of my eye, I could see them whispering to each other; some were smiling. I guess they liked what they saw.

So, Constantino told me about this gym, and two days later, after I pay my fees, I started working out after work. I have to admit, I didn't look too bad either. I was still moving well, the rust was coming off fast. Even my left shoulder was cooperating. It's beginning to feel strong, less stiff. Good thing I'm a southpaw, though, and do most of my work—jabs, hooks, uppercuts—with my right. My left hand, my power punch, I just save for certain spots, like when the sucker's groggy or leaning against the ropes, and I'm real close.

I've been at the gym a week or so, and I'm really starting to get back into the feel of it. I'm still quick, and I'm starting to pick up notice. I worked three rounds with this pro, a young guy, and made him miss. Every time he threw his left jab, I countered with a right hook and did it so often, he stopped throwing the jab. Joey

Keefe, this old Irish guy, walked over and said he wanted to train me. Fine, I said. That was three days ago. He thought we could make some money because I moved well, and being lefthanded, a southpaw, made me awfully hard to hit. There's a card in Sacramento at the end of the month. He thought he could get me a preliminary, a four rounder, which would be my first pro bout. I told him to go for it.

I'm much more serious now than I was as an amateur; I'm running in the morning, working out after work, getting a lot of sparring rounds in. The other fighters like working with me, even though I'm hard to hit and make them look stupid. I'm the only southpaw in the gym, and that makes me valuable. A right hander never knows when he'll be matched with one.

When I'm not at work or in training, I look up Constantino, and we just talk, mostly about fighters and fighting. He showed me some moves, I picked them up and tried them out in training. He taught me how to spin a man who's got me pinned against the ropes, and later that afternoon, I tried it against this tough Indian kid who thought he had me trapped. The spin worked. He came in hard. I pivoted away to my right, and he just dangled on the ropes and looked like a chump. I then nailed him with two hard shots for good measure.

Thanks, Constantino.

*   *   *

SACRAMENTO CIVIC CENTER, APRIL 28, 1970

Every fighter has to stare down fear. Whether he's honest enough to admit it is another matter. On the eve of his first pro fight, Rico was no exception. He knew fear personally, his ace boon coon from his days in the bush. But this was different, with the spotlight on him alone.

How long had it been since his last amateur bout? Was it five years ago? Six? Would he get hurt?

Worse, would he get embarrassed?

The old days were fun—big headgear, big gloves, safety-first bouts packed with friends and family cheering him on. Fun. But pro fights were different. No headgear, small gloves, blood-lust expectations shared by fans and fighters alike.

In the dressing room, old Joey and Rico sat facing each other on a bench. Joey slowly taped his fighter's left hand, then his right, a ritual performed thousands of times before.

"Make a fist," the old man said before grabbing Rico's left hand to inspect his handiwork. Satisfied, he grunted and let it drop.

Without being told, Rico closed his right hand, holding it tight for Joey's inspection.

"Scared?" Joey mumbled as he straightened Rico's wrist and patted that section of the tape covering the knuckles. He grunted again, a sign the inspection was over.

"No."

"Good," Joey said as he rose slowly to his feet and began walking toward the door. "No reason to be."

"Where ya goin'?"

"Grab a smoke," he said as he opened the door. "Back in ten. Warm up, shadow box, you know the drill. Relax, kid, ya got nothin' to worry about."

Rico knew the drill: dance, loosen up, and throw punches. Drown the fear in sweat and imagined in-the-ring movement. In his mind, he'd be swift, slick, unhittable—a smaller version of the great Ali. He began moving in a tiny circle, feinting here, dipping there, flashing tight five-punch combinations.

Rico did it for a minute, maybe less, until he felt his belly push upward and both hands reflexively rise to cover his mouth. He had, he guessed, ten seconds to make it from where he was standing to the nearest toilet. If he moved fast enough and in a straight enough line, he figured he could make it.

*   *   *

SACRAMENTO UNION, APRIL 28, 1970

Clearly, the best action of the night came from two young light-weights in a four-round affair between Luis Flores, the highly regarded Mexican amateur champion and Mexican Olympian, and Rico Divina of Stockton. The bout was the heavily favored Flores's fourth professional fight (all KO wins), but his first north of the border. This was the unheralded Divina's pro debut.

The pace was set early by Divina, who defied ringside experts by taking control from the opening bell. Using his long right jab (Divina was a southpaw), he continued to keep the more aggressive Flores off balance. Like most Mexican fighters, Flores was an "action guy," and his go to punches had always been his left hook—another Mexican staple—and his strong right cross. Through the first round, though, Divina simply stepped away from the hook and, by moving to his right, didn't allow Flores to get in range for his right cross.

In that first round, Divina's southpaw style seemed to confuse Flores, who was always just a bit slow or out of position to punch effectively.

Beginning in round two, though, Flores seemed to adapt to Divina's right-hand lead. He was much more aggressive and began to follow one of boxing's basic rules—he moved forward and threw punches. More important, at least in terms of fighting a lefty like Divina, he began putting his lead left foot outside of Divina's lead right foot. This forced Divina to move to his left and within range of Flores's dangerous right cross.

It was the right cross that almost did Divina in. Once in the second, Flores staggered the local boy with a cross that landed flush on his jaw and knocked him into the ropes. But surprisingly, Flores didn't immediately follow up and finish the job. Maybe it was because Flores expected Divina to fall—others usually did—but Divina didn't. He seemed to be cut from tougher cloth. Flores's brief delay was enough for Divina to clear his head and survive the round.

Again, in the third, Flores hit Divina with another right cross on the point of his nose, the sound of which could be heard throughout the arena. This time, though, as Flores moved forward, Divina, now bleeding badly from the nose, met him with a furious five-punch combination, all of which landed and forced the Mexican back on his heels. That flurry broke Flores' momentum and stole the round for Divina.

With one round left, Flores knew he'd need a knockout to win. To this point, the action had been furious and many fans were standing in the aisles roaring approval. No one would have expected, though, that the last round would be far and away the best of all.

At the bell, Flores rushed to mid-ring looking to brawl. That was expected. The surprise was that Divina—whose better boxing skills had served him well—went forward to meet him. For the next three minutes, both youngsters stayed close to each other and just threw leather. Each fighter landed his share of power punches —for Flores, the left hook, for Divina, the straight left—but somehow the action never ceased.

It was even through the first two minutes, then Flores finally uncorked his best punch, a tight left hook, that caught Divina over the ear and wobbled him. He collapsed into the ropes; his mouth wide open and bleeding, Divina looked finished. Flores quickly moved in for the knockout, but not quickly enough. Divina suddenly sprang to life and caught Flores with a nifty right uppercut that landed on the jaw. Divina then followed with a right hook to the temple. This time Flores was staggering back with Divina in pursuit. Lucky for Flores, the bell then rang before Divina could do further damage.

The result was a close but unanimous decision for Divina, who won his debut in most impressive fashion. Less impressive were the actions of some hooligans—apparently enraged fans and friends of the beaten fighter—who booed and threw debris into the ring, and then tried to storm it. Before security officers were able to react, one member of this little mob actually entered the ring and went straight at Divina. He was screaming loudly and advancing when the fighter, who'd already removed his handwraps and gloves, decided to go an extra round. Divina stepped up and nailed him with a bare-fisted right hook. The intruder fell face down and had to be dragged away by his friends.

Divina was then escorted from the ring by Joey Keefe, his veteran trainer, and by four burly security officers. Although neither he nor Keefe was available for comment after the match, it's clear that this young prospect's talent would enrich the local fight scene.

*   *   *

May 1, 1970

Right after the bout, the doc said my nose was broken, and I said I didn't need a doc to tell me that. He said he'd take care of me after the card was done, and gave me some painkillers to hold me over. I told him I'd be there, but then I took two shots from Joey's flask, gulped a painkiller, and left.

When I woke up this morning, I looked in the mirror—swollen nose and two black eyes—and any fool on the street would swear that I'd just lost a fight. Badly. I woke up not really sure where I was. I vaguely remembered collecting my money, packing my stuff, and catching a bus for Frisco. Then I opened the window and felt the cold air. Frisco. I must've checked in last night.

I cleared $200 bucks for that fight; blood money and it wasn't much, but it's still two bills more than what I had. Before leaving Sacramento, I told Joey it was over; I'd never fight for him again. He just sat there and shook his head. He didn't say anything. He must've been worrying about what might happen to him.

That pissed off Mexican who climbed into the ring? Even though I nailed him hard, he had a right to be pissed. A day before the fight, Joey told me I'm supposed to fall in the fourth. I told him no way, then he flashes five bills at me (I don't know what the Mexican paid him, but five bills were enough for me). So, I thought about it a bit—about two seconds—and figured that it was only

one fight, and $500 would come in handy. So I took the money, and
told Joey to go tell his Mexican to bet heavy on my fourth round
flop, that I'd make it look good for three rounds then go in the
tank, no sweat.

Well, there's a difference between intent and action. If this was
a fixed fight, someone forgot to tell Flores. That boy sure can hit,
and he didn't pull a single punch. And when we clinched, the second round I think, I cursed him, told him to relax, to lighten up,
we knew the dance. And the fucker grunted and pushed me off, so
he could hit me some more. He tried to nail me with this wicked
uppercut, aimed right for my chin. I pulled back and he missed,
but just barely. A clear case of failure to communicate, I'd say.

Maybe he didn't understand English.

I was still in on the scam up through the fourth round when
Flores nailed me and I flopped into the ropes. I was hurt and dizzy
—that was no fake—and I could've sat down then and no one
would've complained.

It was only a prelim fight after all. Those Mexicans in the
crowd would've gotten their money's worth.

Then I looked up at Flores, and the bitch was laughing at me,
calling me names, like maricon. And while I don't know a lot of
Spanish, I've known enough Mexicans to know the word means
faggot, which I'm not. So now, he makes me mad and just a little
crazy, and all of a sudden I don't really care. I figured right there,
we were going to have to change the script. I knew he'd be coming
in for the kill, and I also figured he thought I'd either flop before
he got there or fall with the next punch. He was almost casual as
he approached—his arms were open—and I snuck my right uppercut between them and, bingo, hit nothing but chin. I'd hit him so
hard, I could feel the jolt through my forearm and elbow.

Then I followed with two hard hooks to the head and some
other shots. It was all kind of a blur from that point, but I remembered winning and standing over Flores while he was looking up,
and I said, "Who's the maricon now, bitch?" He didn't answer or
get up.

And then I saw the Mexican gambler—Jorge, I found out—and his pals trying to swarm the ring. Now that had to have been the dumbest thing I'd ever seen—to try and beat someone in front of hundreds of witnesses. Jorge made it in, and it was a bad move for him. With his buddies, I'm sure he's pretty tough, but alone, he's just another Mexican, and worse, a Mexican who can't take a punch.

Still, since I showed him up and caused him to lose money, probably lots of it, I figured that Sacramento wasn't the best place for me. I can't fight there for awhile. I'm sure old Jorge won't forget me, and he and his pals might try to bump me in an alley, or nail me when I'm walking down the street. Stockton's no better; it's smaller than Sacramento, too small to get lost in, at least in the neighborhoods I can afford. I hope Joey—scumbag that he is—figures out the same thing and leaves town. There's this huge river, the Sacramento, same name as the city it runs by. And if Joey's not careful, he could find his wrinkled white ass floating downriver into San Francisco Bay.

Which reminds me, if the morning warms up, I think I'll play tourist and check out the wharf. I hear it's pretty there and, for a change, I've got some cash in my pocket. Besides, old Joey might just resurface, so to speak.

Myself, I'm feeling pretty good, like my stuff's finally coming together, like I'm back on track. At the fight right before my introduction, I saw a guy in the audience who looked like Jerome, the same goofy looking face. He was a few rows back from ringside. He was smiling, just like Jerome used to, like he didn't have a care in the world, and I'm sure that's mostly because he was so sure he didn't. I blinked twice, and then the referee called me forward for the instructions. In center ring, I snuck a peek but he was gone. He was smiling, though, and that was different, not like those last moment images of pain and doubt that were fixed on me. Maybe he was telling me that he'd reached where he was going, and that he was pulling for me to whip this Mexican's ass.

Chapter Four

May 3, 1970

It was a good day. The sun came out about noon, I had money in my pocket, and the breeze wasn't too strong. Perfect. Better still, no dreams, no Jerome.

I had my shades on, which at least covered some of the bumps and cuts on my face. For much of the time, I just sat there near the wharf, sipped on coffee, read the newspaper and smoked. I wasn't worrying too much about tomorrow, or even later this afternoon. When it started to cool down, I met this girl, a Filipina, but not like most of the ones I knew back home.

Before I left for boot, I met a couple of these new immigrant girls from the Philippines. I was at a party somewhere in the south end, at Buddy's cousin's house. They all came from money back in the Philippines, and were in the States on student visas at this or that college. They were different, that's for sure—refined, educated, very impressed with themselves. Back home, I'm sure the nuns had them practice penmanship and tactical giggling. Snobs, I thought, too much damn effort to get a taste. I just didn't have the time.

Still, I figured I'd check it out, but after some polite chit-chat, I decided hanging with them wasn't my scene, although a couple were pretty, more Spanish than Filipino. Maybe if I hadn't been thinking so much about getting drunk and worrying about what might happen in Vietnam, I might've spent more time and gotten over on one of them—Lisa, the tall prettiest one—asking why I sounded so funny, so black ("Negro," her term). She looked offended when I talked.

Buddy then pulled me aside and said they're trained to sound that way, to ward off lower class sorts like me or my asparagus cutting old man. For women like this, Buddy said, they married white or light and always for money, lots of it. These chicks were high yellow, Filipino style. He figured it was a Spanish and American colonial thing, a hangup from the past where white's always right and hooking up with some pasty motherfucker improves the race. Since I'm neither—actually, I'm darker than most bloods— and always broke, he said to forget it.

So I did. Besides, Stephie, another of Buddy's cousins, was giving me the eye; she's pretty fine and she'd been dropping hints for the last year or so, but I'd just put her off because doing her would've seemed awkward. But hell, she was American born and didn't have any problem with the way I talked; she came from the same place, the same neighborhood. Next year she's going to beauty school, not Harvard. So, that night, with me that drunk, I remember saying I could be dead in eight months.

Damn, I said, you're patriotic. Fuck me, I'm a Marine. So she did and it wasn't awkward at all.

Marites—the girl I met at the wharf—was working at a little shop that sells tourist stuff. I caught her out of the corner of my eye as I walked through the square, just looking at all that overpriced junk. She was in an aisle stocking coffee cups and plates covered with the city's image—the cable cars, the hills, the downtown silhouette. It was trinket heaven for idiot tourists from Arkansas or Oklahoma; only they'd buy this junk, folks like Jerome. I used to tell him he was clearly a product of fourth gen-

eration incest, but that he shouldn't worry because it was a long
established cultural trait and besides, God loved retards.

I miss that dude. Old Jerome would've liked it here, Gomer Pyle
that he was. He'd have blown a full paycheck, and wouldn't have
even blinked . . . Damn, he'd be twenty-two now. Wherever he is,
I'm sure it's better than being in the bush.

So, back to the store and the start of this operation . . . Being
the slick street devil I am, I walked over and asked Marites where
the beer mugs were, and she stood up, smiled and pointed to the
next aisle. Then I carefully stared at her. Immigrant, I could tell—
high cheek bones, light, tall, looked a bit Chinese with all that
Spanish. Family has money, I could tell that, too. I made sure she
noticed me scoping her out. Then she asked innocently (daintily)
if there was any other assistance she could provide. Confirmation
as soon as she opened her mouth. High born immigrant women
from the Philippines have this delicate sounding voice when they
speak English, you know, "The rain in Spain . . ." Their tone rises,
dips and rises again like they're all following the same music
sheet. Another dead giveaway.

So I cleared my throat and went through a checklist, number
one of which was I shouldn't sound like a brother. "Pardon me,
Miss," I said in my slowest and best rich white boy English. "Are
you from the Philippines?" I listened to myself talk. I sounded like
I was speaking to an idiot . . .

"Yes," she sang, then smiled that lovely polite rich Filipino girl
smile. "Are you a Filipino?"

Yeah, I wanted to say, just another nasty jungle brother,
straight up, baby . . . Got all the gear, too, wanna see? But I didn't.
I smiled back. "Why, yes," I said, acting surprised. "You must be
one, too."

Her smile got brighter (if that's possible). "Ah," she said. "You
must speak Tagalog."

Damn, I thought, she got me, had to think fast. Growing up, I
never heard Tagalog, the language of Manila and the elite. In the
community, most of the oldtimers came from the provinces; they

spoke Ilocano or Visayan, like my old man, the language of country folk. Back there they were poor; over here they stayed poor.

"Ah, no," I said. "My father came to America in the 1930s to
practice medicine. Now, he spoke beautiful Tagalog, but unfortu-
nately, he died when I was a young child, so he wasn't able to
teach me . . . "

I know "fuck you," "fuck your mother," "fuck your dog" in
Visayan, would you like to hear it? If so, which one? Or, my old
man, the now suddenly esteemed Dr. Divina, had a thriving practice among gamblers, pimps, and camptown hos up and down the
West Coast. Surely, you must have heard of him. I was staring
hard at the floor, happy I was wearing shades, otherwise the scam
would have been up. Marites, bless her innocent heart, thought I
was sad.

"I'm so sorry about your father," she said, and put her hand on
my shoulder. I inched closer.

"It's okay," I said earnestly. "It's just sometimes . . . "

She began patting me. Another inch closer. Damn, I could feel
my heart race. I knew I was going to get some just on sympathy.

"It's hard," I said. "Being fatherless." I was into it now; I could
hear my sincerity. I was even thinking of sobbing, but I stopped
myself. That might have been too much. Goddamn amazing. Dad,
that son of a bitch, was finally useful.

Now the other hand on the shoulder, double pats, this time I
edged two inches closer. She'd be hugging me soon. Would licking
her tonsils be far behind? My dick started to grow.

"My name's Marites," she said softly. "My own father, he
almost died last year, burst appendix, but thank God he made it."
She paused and I nodded sympathetically. "Maybe we should have
coffee and just talk, I'm off in ten minutes. Would you mind waiting?"

I glanced up. "You needn't," I said, thinking that "needn't"
sounds nicely Caucasian.

She smiled. "It would be my pleasure, ah . . . "

"Rico."

"Ten minutes, okay?" she sang. "Don't go away now."

June 1, 1970

It's been awhile since I've written here, and so much has happened since, especially between Marites and I. It turned out I was right on the rich girl thing. She comes from sugar money, lots of it, on the island of Negros. Her father sold part of his holdings and took the proceeds and bought a textile plant that exports cheap clothes throughout Asia, parts of Europe, and the U.S. A smart move. They got richer as a result, just swimming in American bucks. Marites had gone to the best private schools in Manila, one of those Santa what's-her-name convent school sorts of places where all the rich girls go. Her father had visited San Francisco after World War II on some kind of post-graduate fellowship; he decided that if she (Marites) continued to insist on coming to the U.S. for college, it had to be here in this city.

Courtesy of Daddy's cash, she's taking business classes at USF, a nice Jesuit school that dependable Daddy picked out probably because he figured that going to a Catholic school would keep her safe and holy (read: virginal).

His loot set her up—the youngest of three girls and the only one still single—very nicely. She's got a big one bedroom on Nob Hill, a sweet little Triumph sports car (last weekend, I gunned it on the Bayshore at 4:00 AM), and enough spare change so that she really doesn't have to work. The working part was her own decision, just enough hours to break the boredom of school and study. Then I pop up, take away her boredom, and cut back her work schedule.

Folks say beer and wine are bad for young people like me because they lead to hard liquor, which leads to cigarettes, which leads to marijuana, which leads to continuous unemployment, harder drugs, a drain on the public dole, cootie filled hair and a short life, then a violent, pain wracked death with no one claiming the body.

They've got it all wrong. I'm hooked on this girl and the first link on the chain leading to my addiction began with a substance as innocent as caffeine. Our little coffee date started at four and lasted till sunset, which led to questions of dinner and sweet Marites' suggestion that we go to her house (where she said she had a marinated chicken ready for the oven, no problem she said), which led to a bottle of wine, more conversation, louder laughter, a second bottle, and then to her bedroom.

I never saw the chicken. Hell, it might still be marinating . . .

Lovely, refined Marites is just wild in bed. For starters, she made me enter her standing up, even before our clothes were fully off, and we went on from there.

"Hmm," I said, "where'd you learn that?"

"Santa Anita," she whispered. "I watched my best friend, ah, oh, do her boyfriend, aah . . . "

"At the convent school?" I stopped and just looked at her. Her ankles were wrapped around my calves.

She kissed me and smiled. "Oh yes, inside the chapel."

"At the convent school?"

"You'd be surprised," she said in that song-like voice. She then grabbed me tight and began to grind. "Continue, please . . . "

Politeness—another convent girl trait. Standing sex was just the start. We were on each other all night. Doo-dah. When we finally stopped, it was near dawn. So much for convent school girl stereotypes. A plus, I'd say, for cultural understanding.

As the sun broke through the window, she saw me without my shades for the first time. She saw my cuts and bruises; she touched them oh-so-gently and asked me what happened, and I told her. "I'm a fighter."

I was looking at her; she looked confused. I guess girls from convent schools don't sleep with prizefighters. I explained. "A fighter, Marites," I said. "A professional boxer, it's how I make my living."

"Ay, pobrecito, such a hard life," she said, as her fingertip gently traced the shape and direction of each bump and cut. In the light she also saw the scars on my shoulder and back and touched them as well.

"How . . . "

"Vietnam," I said.

"You were . . . "

"Just a stupid young boy." This time I couldn't look at her. I turned away and stared at the ceiling.

"Hush, you're not stupid," she whispered. "What, ah . . . "

"I can't tell you, babe, too recent." I shook my head and tried not to sound hard or impatient. I couldn't tell, though, I was still not looking at her. I was hoping I hadn't blown the mood, but Marites fixed that by climbing on top of my chest. We're eye to eye; she smiled and said that I was a dangerous man.

"Not to you, baby," I answered softly. "Not to you."

June 14, 1970

Marites and I have pretty much worked it out. Love? If it isn't, it's pretty damn close. During the day, I'll be doing something, maybe waiting for the bus, and I'll see her in my mind. She makes me care . . . She makes me forget. The crazy war dreams are gone.

We talked about living together, but decided against it. Daddy probably wouldn't approve. I said that was okay and that I'd get my own place just in case the old man swung by unannounced for a drop in visit. So, a week ago, I got a third floor room in the Tenderloin, about a mile closer to downtown, but several lifestyles away.

Damn, the Loin's a trip: junkies, addicts, cops, pimps and their hos. Yesterday, I had to step over two dudes who'd nodded out in my hallway. But it's no big deal, I've seen a lot worse. Besides, I jacked this big black guy who tried to give me attitude right in front of the apartment building. Dude was so big, his shoulders looked like shoulderpads. It was daylight and a lot of street folks saw it. I hit him with a three punch combination, and other than hearing him grunt and fall and crack his thick head on the cement, all I could hear was the crowd going "oooh." News like that travels fast. Yeah, it's a rough place, but I don't expect any more trouble.

I've still got cash from the fight, but that won't last forever, so about a week ago, I got a job at a supermarket up by Marites' place. The pay's low, but I can get full-time work stocking shelves and carrying groceries for the old Italian women who come by here.

A couple of days ago, I had a day off, so I just walked around the neighborhood, and came across this boxing gym. It was early afternoon—Marites wouldn't be back at her place for an hour or so—so I just strolled in. It's funny, my ring career started fast and, I guess, it ended fast, too. Besides, Marites doesn't like this idea of me fighting, so one night I told her I'd stop. Still, there were a couple of guys working the bags, and two guys sparring. I couldn't pass it up. One of the guys in the ring was a Mexican kid, a light welter, about my weight. He was working against this black kid who was holding his own. I was sitting by the wall, just watching the action, and the Mexican kid—at least that's what the oldtimer sitting next to me said—was scheduled to fight for the California State title in two weeks.

"For four thousand bucks," he said.

Nice, I was thinking, more than I'll make in four months of stocking shelves. Second round, and I walked closer to the ring. Hey, the blood's just an amateur, raw, but he was pretty quick. His quickness made the Mexican look awkward, slow; the Mexican was getting frustrated. He started missing with his left hook and getting nailed with right hand counters. His corner was yelling at him. Damn, I'm faster, better than either one. I watched the action through the round then I just got up and left. The temptation was too strong to lace up right there. I'd made a promise to Marites.

As I was leaving the gym, the oldtimer asked me if I was a fighter. I guess I was still a little tender and puffy around my eyes. I just smiled at him.

"No," I said.

June 15, 1970

I had dinner with Marites yesterday, then spent the night. As always, it was very nice and a good break from the Loin; living in this dump can get on a man's nerves. But I have to stay here a bit longer because it's all I can afford.

At dinner, she suddenly said Daddy was coming to visit. Got the phone call earlier in the afternoon. She said it calmly and dropped that little bit of information between other regular daily items and events, somewhere between her Spanish Literature class and the brush fire near Golden Gate Park. No big deal, at least that was what her tone tried to say, and I let it slide and played along for a bit. But later, after a glass or two of wine, I began probing deeper, and she admitted that Daddy was a big fan of status and blood lines, neither of which I have. He also fully believed—or wanted to believe—that Marites was still a virgin (hey, can't pin that one on me; she hadn't learned to fuck standing up by just watching). To be honest, she was worried how he'd take to me. Whether he'd be so disturbed he'd pull the chain and yank her all the way back to some convent in Manila.

She wanted to introduce me, but she wasn't sure how. Maybe a quiet dinner over at her apartment (not mine, since all it's got is a hotplate). Maybe as a classmate? A fellow worker? But surely not as someone who makes love to her at every opportunity. No, no, no . . . While Daddy was in Frisco, she said I couldn't stay overnight, and had to pick up anything that was a sign of cohabitation, i.e., spare toothbrush, extra socks, my underwear, etc.

And, oh, one other thing, could I dress up, maybe trim my hair? Sure, I said, wouldn't want to make it hard, fuck up our future.

Daddy, that motherfucker, my competition. Marites loves him, admires him, has his foot high picture beside her bed. (Where's mom? I once asked. Oh, in New York, she said. They live apart, no divorce allowed. He bought her off.) And Daddy, of course, loves her, the unmarried, virginal baby of three. When she speaks of him, he sounds like Kennedy or Einstein or one of the better popes . . . the brightest, most ambitious, most athletic, most handsome. She said he built a church and an orphanage back in his hometown. She said it solemnly, like it was a big deal for a multimillionaire to part with pocket change.

You know, here, you legless leper, have a peso. The church's name? St. Daddy, I bet. I wanted to ask, but didn't.

A few nights back, she was really off on one of her I love Daddy riffs and said he'd be most disappointed if . . . and she didn't finish but I did, at least in my head: if he found out his beloved daughter, his lovely, refined, destined-for-better-things-pet, was shackin' with some grocery packin', no college goin', shot-up half-breed. For a moment I was pissed, but I caught myself when I glanced at the clock. It was late, we were going to bed, getting horizontal. I smiled. The feel, the sweat, the taste, all stronger than words. They're just words, I kept telling myself.

June 20, 1970

As it turned out, dinner with Daddy wasn't too bad. Daddy was already there when I arrived; he was seated at the table. Marites had dinner ready, and she seemed a little tight at first. She introduced me as a friend and a fellow Filipino. I smiled, he smiled back, but I watched him checking me out, looking for flaws. I'd tried not to provide the old fucker any first impression ammunition—I'd pressed my jeans and shirt, damn, I'd even trimmed my hair. My impression? Tall guy, at six feet, mid-fifties, sat erect, thick, wavy brown hair, looked mostly Spanish, like the dude who played Zorro, or maybe Ricardo Montalban. In his eyes, there was a trace of Filipino, just a hint, a tiny slant, buried in each corner.

Marites and I sat down. He said something to Marites in Spanish, and then caught himself, looked at me, and said, "We'll speak in Tagalog, so your friend, ah . . . "

Marites blushed and leaned over to whisper in Daddy's ear, my guess, that same bullshit story (as yet, unchanged, Marites—bless her heart—takes it as gospel) about my status-heavy "doctor" dad.

Yeah, my old man probably worked one of your Daddy's plantations for less than a buck a day.

"Ah, of course, of course," Daddy finally said. "In that case, English, we wouldn't want to be rude."

I was thinking, no, you wouldn't you pompous old fart, at least you've got manners. The rest of the dinner went okay. He asked what I was doing, and I told him in slow, precise, Caucasian English that I was working at the grocery store where Marites shopped, and that's how we met. She was always so gracious, I added, a true, caring friend.

I told him I was saving for college because I knew (stress "knew") that a high school diploma (not that I had one) wouldn't be enough. (I made sure I was furrowed brow serious when I dropped that line. I glanced over at Marites, damn girl almost fainted.) Didn't mention I was half-Indian, didn't mention prize-fighting, the Marines or Vietnam. Daddy's a stranger; he means as much to me as some bum in the Loin.

Besides, I'm fucking his daughter, not him. The way I figured, he had no need to know.

Over coffee, I dropped my best bomb. The main branch of the

public library is a great place to find out stuff from all kinds of sources—journals, international papers, magazines. Turns out old Daddy's pretty prominent in Philippine and Southeast Asian economic circles. He's part of President Marcos' kitchen cabinet, which means he doesn't have papers or rank, just access to under the table cash.

Armed with this information, I started talking about him, about his holdings and interests—the world price of sugar for starters. How I thought diversification into textiles—especially with this American trend toward diets and artificial sweeteners—was very smart, but that more could be done if American laws weren't so protectionist. I said that dramatically expanding free trade was the wave of the future. It was inevitable. I smiled and looked at him, then raised my cup and calmly took a sip.

Daddy blinked. Bingo, dead on shot in the eye of the pig.

"Could you please pass the sugar," I said.

In my mind, I heard the blood dripping out of the wound, heard the breath grow shallow. Leave on a high note, I said to myself. Let the villagers carve the meat.

I glanced at my watch, then stood up. "I should go now," I announced.

"But it's so early," Daddy protested. "Not yet nine."

"I would love to stay, but my shift starts at 5:00 AM." I paused. "Hope you understand."

Marites was just a walk-on in this little drama. This was between Daddy and me. I thanked her, bowed slightly and kissed the back of her hand. I turned to Daddy and firmly shook his hand.

"Pleasure to meet you, sir," I said with a smile. I could still see the blood.

"Ah, Rico, the pleasure is mine. Another time, perhaps. If you're ever in Manila . . . "

"Ah, perhaps, but only after school, sir." I paused. "I have my priorities."

I walked out the door. Damn, at the end I was sounding like him, the perfect Eddie Haskell con. I learned this trick talking to officers, especially if they weren't inclined to give me something I wanted. Flattery and imitation. I guess my time in the Corps was good for something.

Semper fi, dickhead.

*   *   *

NOB HILL APARTMENT, JUNE 20, 1970, 10:00 PM

The newspaper ad said the apartment was spacious and elegant, with hardwood floors and a fireplace, a territorial view. For once, an ad didn't lie. And its occupant couldn't have been happier, a safe lovely haven away from the guaranteed protection of her rock-and-cement-walled Manila home. She'd moved in a year ago, and had taken a full month to make it just right—the right wallpaper and furniture, the right paintings, the right silverware. If money could indeed buy comfort and security in a foreign land, she would gladly pay any cost.

That evening she was entertaining a guest, a handsome older man. The two weren't lovers, although upon seeing them together, a casual friend of one or the other might have thought so; in truth, they were closer than that. They faced each other at the dinner table—a mid-sized and lovely piece of thick glass and black metal—and as she sipped coffee, he leaned back in his chair. He then lit a cigarette and inhaled deeply before finally pushing the smoke out. For a moment, he followed the trail as it lifted slowly toward the ceiling, then shifted his gaze toward her. She seemed anxious. Casually, he flicked ashes into a nearby saucer turned temporary ashtray.

"Hija," he said. "Seems like a nice boy. Bright."

She blinked quickly as she sipped from her cup. "No te pre-ocupes, Daddy, he's just a friend, he's nice and he's disciplined and so busy, demasiado ocupado para mi . . . " She wondered if her words, her lie, sounded rushed, artificial.

He listened quietly, then raised his hand. She stopped talking and studied him; he wanted to believe her.

"Well and good, hija," he said. "But even as a friend, how well do you know him, how much do you know about his family?"

She lowered her eyes, and placed the cup on the table. "Not much," she mumbled. "Only what he told me."

"Just what he told you?" he said slowly. "And what was that?"

"That his father, the doctor, died when he was young, and . . ."

"And his mother?"

"He said once she was Indian of some kind . . . "

"Bombay?"

"No, American Indian."

He looked at his cigarette and inhaled a final time before crushing the filter on the saucer; he then pushed the saucer away and leaned forward. "Ah, an Indian," he began. "Your friend's not really a pure Filipino then, but an Indian. No wonder he can't speak Tagalog. I've been here to the States, hija, and I know about Indians. They're poor and, by God, no wonder he's so dark, I mean like a common fieldworker or even a Negro, and, umm, what was his name?"

"Rico."

For a moment, his gaze turned away from her. "I knew there was something about that boy," he mumbled.

"Papa?"

"Ay," he said with a wave of his hand. "No es importante. He's just a friend, you say?"

"Si, Papa, just a friend."

"Good, carina, friend only," he said softly. "Yo te creo."

He wanted to believe. She smiled. "I wouldn't lie," she said slowly. "Especially not to you."

He reached into his shirt pocket and pulled out another cigarette. "You don't mind?" he said. He then lit it before she could respond. "Ay, America," he said. "So grand, so different, so obsessed with civil rights, ideals of equality. But that's all they are, ideals, not reality, no?" He paused. "And I'm glad you haven't changed."

"I haven't."

"Good, good, carina," he whispered. "Just remember who we are, our blood, our long distinguished line which is now almost pure Spanish. Remember that class and wealth and blood do count . . . "

She'd heard this all before. Still, her demeanor was calm, accepting. "I know," she said softly.

"When it comes time, to marry, I mean, you'll consider these things," he said evenly.

She nodded.

"And that means your friend, ah . . . "

"Rico."

"Ah yes, Rico, well, he just doesn't qualify," he said. "A nice enough boy, true, bright, too, but poor and he's part . . . "

"But he's only a friend."

"Indian."

"Don't worry, Daddy, Rico's still just a friend." She sighed and hoped he couldn't hear the desperation she was just beginning to feel.

Chapter Five

January 3, 1971

I took Daddy up on his offer of visiting him in Manila and, as I'm writing this, I'm sitting on this small liner on my way to Zamboanga on the island of Mindanao. In the Marines, I'd heard so much about Mindanao. About the American suppression campaign, about the fierce Muslims who lived there and who fought anyone —Spaniard, Filipino, American soldier—brave or stupid enough to venture south and claim their lands. Marites was in Manila for Christmas and I went to join her. She's there now, but should be back in San Francisco by the end of next week.

All in all, it was a great time to be in the Philippines. Festive, even the poor, very happy. Daddy—I found out his real name was Alfonso, Don Alfonso, folks call him out of respect—seems to have gotten used to me. Or at least he was polite.

Of course, we didn't sleep together at Daddy's place; the closest I got to her bedroom was staying one night (the day I arrived in Manila) at the guest house on the other side of the tennis courts (two courts/swimming pool area). Marites told me that as far as Daddy knew, I was still just a friend, and that maybe it would be better if we acted that way for a bit longer. So I put on my friend face, and refrained from fingering Marites as we sat together at the dining table (damn girl—cotton dress and spread legged, she put my hand on her bare thigh).

Daddy was cordial. He asked about work (fine, I said), school (registered at junior college). He seemed surprised about me actually signing up for classes and asked which ones. Economics and poetry for now, I said, maybe creative writing later. I lied about the economics part.

Poetry? He said more with a raised eyebrow than with words or even tone of voice. Can an eyebrow be condescending? His was. I stopped the bitch dead in his tracks. A well rounded man, I said, knows the arts. That knocked that eyebrow right back down.

The old shit then got friendlier; that was when he even invited me to stay over—mandatory Filipino hospitality, more so than any particular joy at seeing me. Daddy made a big deal of welcoming me. He was smile-fucking me, I'm sure.

Pretty impressive spread, though, if I do say so. Staying there for more than a night would've been too much. Instead, I rented a room in a small hotel in Ermita, close enough to her Banyan Park neighborhood. Then I created this story about going down to the Visayas to visit some relatives with whom I'd been corresponding, etc.

I added that my Uncle Tirso (I made up the name) wanted me to meet the niece of the mayor. She was unattached and very pretty, a recent college graduate.

I wanted to say more about this make-believe niece. I was blowing major smoke up Daddy's constricted asshole. I just might've said it all, but Marites was scowling at the image—of me meeting (and eating) this woman who doesn't exist. The story allowed me to gracefully leave Daddyland Acres and check into a little room here at El Caballero.

It's close to this shopping center, and each day I was there, Marites would have her driver drop her off and pick her up in three hours or so. Carefully, she'd walk from shop to shop, making sure she seemed leisurely, buying a little trinket or book or piece of clothing just in case one of Daddy's spies was watching—and, if it was clear (it always was), she'd walk over to my place and we'd make love till the walls turned hot and began to peel. The last afternoon we were together, her period started. Not heavy, just blotches. We were both kind of relieved. Sometimes, we'd been careless, but no unexpected blessed events, at least not yet.

Safe for one more month.

As we were lying there, we began to make out and then, as it always does, we got into it, into each other and she told me to eat her, and I did. She came and then I came in her, and she came again. She got up and got a towel, and wiped the blood from my nose and mouth.

"You do love me," she said fiercely.

Despite the obvious, it was a first-time declaration—a statement of faith in me, in our future. But the moment was too precious, too once-in-a-lifetime. And the muse of mischief whispered play it out.

Timing is everything. Casually, I licked a speck of blood from inside my upper lip.

"Missed a spot," I deadpanned.

She looked startled. It wasn't what she expected to hear.

Still in character, I shrugged. "Hey, I ate you, didn't I?"

"Rico," she said, in a tone so plaintive it pulled at my heart.

I cupped the back of her head and pulled her to me. "Of course, Marites," I whispered. "I love you now and till the end of days."

She sighed. "I love you, too."

Admissions all around. Oh yeah, we'd known it all along, but saying it made it harder, like it was recorded and the world was in on the conversation. Couple that with the problem of Daddy, and how I didn't fit his profile of the proper mate. I asked her what she was going to do. Marites was flustered; she loved me, she loved Daddy. What to do? She just didn't know.

"Maybe I should kill him," I suggested.

She gasped.

"Shit, think of it, dead daddy, we could be rich . . . "

More gasping.

I chuckled. "Joke only, darling."

"You and your humor." She sighed and patted her heart. "It's a problem."

"Yeah, it's a problem."

January 4, 1971

We're getting closer to Mindanao now; the captain of this slow, smelly, overloaded tub said we're only three hours out of Zamboanga. But the fresh air cleared my head, despite the stench of humans, livestock and such.

I thought back to my last image of her, of Marites, as she walked away from the room. Her shoulders sagged. We still hadn't figured out how to handle Daddy, and for the sake of avoiding suspicion—we'd seen each other four afternoons straight, she looked much too classy to be in El Caballero, and besides, how many of the same trinkets and books could a shopper buy?—we'd stop seeing each other in Manila. I told her my plane didn't leave for a week and, since I figured the Philippines was a bigger place than my room and the bar of this dump, I'd better get out and see at least part of the country. That's why I'm on my way to Mindanao, or at least one of the reasons.

I also needed to think this Daddy/Marites thing through more clearly. It's hard when you're wrapped around and sweating on the woman you're supposed to think calmly about.

One thing's clear, though, Marites will just have to tell him. She's going to have to choose. In a moment of detachment—yeah, I have some of those—I was figuring out the odds. She loves Daddy, naturally; he loves her back, wants the best for her, supports her. When he dies, she'll inherit a good part of his multimillion, maybe even billion dollar estate. On the other hand, she loves me and I can barely support myself. If she tells him, Daddy will likely cut off the money pipeline and force her back to Manila, maybe even disinherit her.

Hard choice, huh. Damn, if I were Marites, I'd tell me to go fuck myself . . . If this were a fair world, it shouldn't have to be that way but, then again, if there was such a thing as fairness, I'd have never gone to Vietnam.

Late last night, I started thinking that maybe over the long haul, she and I would never make it. Love aside, maybe we're just too different. My heart hurt when I thought about it. But say we push on—for love or just out of spite—maybe one or two kids later and living in a basement apartment, she'd start resenting me, asking me why I couldn't do more or be more (like Daddy, of course), telling me she'd given up this or that for me. Damn, thinking of that, I just started to shake, and left my cabin, took a walk on the deck and just stared at the sea.

When I returned, I picked up a pen and started to write what I felt. It was rough, the writing didn't flow, not at first, but after three or four drafts—and two hours later—it came out okay, at least I think. I stuck it an envelope and addressed it to Marites, to the apartment in Frisco. This is what I wrote.

To Marites, On a Boat to Mindanao

The southern sky,
A rocking ship,
The freedom of the wind.

Once you and I
And now, just me
Enchantment lures me in.

Alone, alone.
To be, alone . . .
My life can now begin.

But softly, Love,
And gently, please,
Become a memory . . .

Encapsuled in
A single tear
That falls into the sea.

Maybe it's no masterpiece, but what the hell. It said what I felt. I guess I'm getting ready for whatever . . .

Okay, I addressed the envelope, but will I send it to Marites? I'm not sure. Just heard the captain say Zamboanga's half an hour away. I can see Mindanao off starboard. The city's got to be close. When we dock, I think I'll kick around town for a day, see the sights, visit some bars and drink dark rum. I'll head back to Manila tomorrow. Maybe I'll decide whether to mail it by then.

Chapter Six

"I have to say something," she said softly. Her long, narrow fingers tapped the stem of her wine glass.

"Um," he said, not really hearing. "Babe, pass the butter, huh?"

"He's coming."

He looked up. "Who?"

"My father."

"When?"

"Next week."

"No sweat," he said lightly. "I'll just go back to my place, pretend, make myself scarce, you know, just like before. Three days, a week at most. No sweat. Oh, yeah, the butter . . . "

His smile was smug, her tone was impatient. "No, darling, you don't understand."

He stared at her, trying to read her face for a clue. "No," he said slowly. "I don't."

Her eyes roamed wildly—over him, over the room, over the table, back to him. "He's coming to stay, not to visit." Her breathing was short and shallow, very fast. "To stay."

His hands flew to his face, covering it. He slumped in his chair and pondered "to stay." He marveled at it—to stay, an infinitive— such a simple little two-word phrase that in this case meant the end of something, maybe the end of it all.

*   *   *

CRIME SCENE, NOB HILL APARTMENT, APRIL 4, 1971

The bloody shards of what had been a priceless Ming vase were on a rumpled shag rug that now only covered part of the foyer's smooth hardwood floor. On the rug a severed earlobe and splotches of blood could be seen.

The scene told a story of fear and struggle and finally, of flight, as drops, and handprints—left and right—tracked from the foyer through the living room and, finally, into the kitchen, where more blood smeared and streaked the white tile floor. Fortunately for the victim, critically injured but still alive, his loud, losing struggle had not gone unnoticed. A neighbor called the police who arrived at the scene to find one man, the younger one, about to plunge a knife into the exposed neck of another.

The victim had grabbed hold of the knife hand wrist, so stale-mate, at least for a moment frozen in time in the lead officer's memory. But the blood loss of the victim, the inching downward of his own shaking hands toward his clavicle, the strength and fully tapped fury of the younger man, told the officer that death was seconds away, if that.

The lead officer was an older man but new to the force; he could have shot him. Such a shooting—to save the life of another —could have been justified. The incident would've been open briefly to perfunctory review, then quickly shut and buried in a one-inch back-page story in the morning paper. Justifiable, any board of inquiry would have stamped, a clean shoot.

But in the back? the lead officer thought as he came upon the scene. He had a clear line of fire and had shot men in the back, but that was before, in war, a memory he was trying to bury. He screamed for him to stop while, at the same time, reaching for his revolver. In that moment of choice, his hand felt the butt, his finger stroked the trigger, but the gun stayed holstered. The young man, engrossed in the deadly task at hand, couldn't hear the command over his own wailing—a garbled mix of song and chatter—just as minutes earlier, he couldn't hear the screams of a young woman who begged him to stop, to please stop. Failing that, she fled from the scene and ran down the hallway, pounding on doors and yelling for someone, anyone, to open.

The lead officer then flung himself across the kitchen floor, like a linebacker going for a loose ball. He hit the young man with his shoulder against the back of his neck; he hit him so hard he launched his much smaller target forward and toward a refrigerator door. The loud thud of bone against metal, of blood gushing from a forehead cut and a body going limp before falling to the side, were reasonable signs the drama was finally over.

And the lead officer, who was prone on his belly, closed his eyes and sighed; he knew adrenaline well, knew its role and value, but had grown to welcome its leaving. He sighed. It was gone now, and he relaxed too much.

Too much, almost too fatal, as he heard too late the warning of his partner—out of position and slow to his gun—that the young man had somehow come to and was lunging, knife in hand, toward the unprotected back of the prone officer. He pushed himself forward just as the young man lunged and pierced a seam of a blue polyester pant leg. The point of the blade ripped fabric and struck the floor, but drew no blood.

With surprising quickness, the lead officer spun around, gathered his legs under him, and leapt at his assailant. He landed on the back of his attacker's head, then with his hands—huge, powerful, and black—he grabbed his hair and slammed him face down into the hard tile again and again until he could see blood rush from his nose, then from his mouth. He felt the young man's body go limp and turned slightly to see his fingers finally release their hold on the knife.

The lead officer then rose slowly and turned toward his bug-eyed partner who'd finally drawn his gun and was sweating more than him.

"Cuff him up," he said softly.

* * *

WARD D. SAN FRANCISCO GENERAL HOSPITAL, APRIL 7, 1971

Even without a uniform, the stride and carriage of the tall, muscular black man looked like what he'd been or was now, a solider, maybe a cop, maybe both. In the hallway, he quickly passed doctors and patients, hospital police, and a handful of laughing, chatty nurses just glad to be off shift. One of the doctors knew him.

"Mel," he said. "It's a day off, what're you doin' . . . "

Mel smiled and waved, but just kept walking. "Gotta check something out," he said, as he jumped into an elevator, destination Ward D for the criminally insane, East Wing, Sixth Floor. The zoo, his colleagues had called it. In his year on the force, he'd been there once before and had hated it.

Still, he was here again, off duty, on his own time. He sighed and signed in at the locked entry, then took out his wallet and showed his star and ID card. The attendant buzzed him in and, as he entered, his nose began a familiar twitch: ammonia—old and thick—that seemed to have coated wall paint and floor wax.

For a second, he stood still and surveyed the room. A television commercial enthralled most of the Ward's residents. In one corner, two young women clasped hands and sang a medley of sorts, each one singing her own song, and in another, a young man had pulled off his pants, squatted down, and smiled as a companion, a wiry little man who moved like a monkey, screamed, "He's doing two, he's doing two."

Mel sighed, lowered his eyes, and shrugged. Even war made more sense. He wished he was somewhere, anywhere else. Too late. A young attendant, cheerful and smiling, stood in front of him. "This way," he said, and motioned to Mel.

"You're new, huh?" Mel asked, as he followed.

"Yes, almost three weeks," he replied. "How'd you know?"

"Just a guess," he said, as they passed a man who was leaning forward while he sat on his haunches and tried to catch flies with his tongue.

"How's he doin'?" Mel asked.

"The docs think he's borderline, worse than others, but not as bad as some," the attendant answered. "With the right meds, he could maybe function outside."

Finally, at the end of a long corridor, the attendant pointed to a room. "He's the only one in there," he said. "He's coming out of sedation. Shall I wait?"

"Not necessary," Mel answered and entered the room.

Not only was he sedated, he was handcuffed to the iron railings on both sides of his bed. Slowly, as quietly as possible, Mel studied him, his arms and chest and legs. He was young, boyish, and not very tall, 5'7" max, or heavy, maybe 135 lbs., and, for a moment, Mel marveled at how someone so small, so harmless-looking, could generate such power. He walked around the bed, looking at him from different angles, trying to get a clue, make a connection to a time in the past. He stepped back; except for the long hair, he looked just like that Indian or Filipino kid he'd pulled out of the death trap north of Hue.

Suddenly, the body in the bed began to stir. First, one eye, then the other opened. Surprised, Mel stepped back. "Goddamn," the young man growled, as he strained—puffed chest, wild-eyed, arched back—against the metal restraints. The bed shook and clanged, a ruckus so loud it brought a small party of attendants who stood at the entry.

Mel, who was used to command, turned toward the entry and issued his latest order. "Stay back," he whispered.

"What the hell," the young man screamed, as he gathered himself to try again. So furious was he, he didn't notice that anyone else was in the room.

Mel moved forward to calm him. "Son," he said slowly, calmly. "Just easy, take it easy now, no one's gonna hurt you . . . "

The young man, eyes blinking, stared at Mel. He suddenly stopped thrashing and slowly tilted his head from one side to the other. He then quickly inhaled and tried to sit up, but couldn't.

"It hurts so bad, Sarge," he whispered.

Mel's stomach dropped and roiled and although he'd never run from anything in his life, he wanted to run from this. He wouldn't, though, and told himself to stay calm, and if he couldn't do that, to appear calm. The kid was there, in the shit, like so many of his boy soldiers who never came back. The distance between there and home couldn't be measured. Still, Mel figured, he owed this kid a try.

He took a deep breath and told his hand not to shake, then put it on the young man's shoulder. "It's okay," he said softly. "It's okay, I've seen worse."

"But Jerome . . . "

"It's okay, Marine."

"Jerome," he repeated, this time louder.

His eyes scanning the walls and ceiling, Mel was playing for time. "Ah, well, he didn't make it," he finally said, as the young man began to cry and mumble Jerome's name and the names of others—his pals, the old sergeant knew—who didn't make it.

"You're going home," Mel said evenly, his hand still on the young man's shoulder.

The young man stared at him. "Where's home, Sergeant? Where you're born, or maybe raised? Is that too long a distance now, too far away? Or maybe it's here, in this shithole where your heart's been cut and wounded, covered with blood? Have we given too much of ourselves here? Has this become home?"

He paused, his eyes starting to fill. "Gimme the shithole, Sarge. Just leave me there." Then he chuckled bitterly and on Mel, he refocused his deathmask stare. "Next time, just leave me in the bush," he said, and paused. " Just curious, Sarge, you dream?"

"No," he mumbled, and turned slightly away.

"You're lying, Sergeant," the young man said. He then chuckled, the sound hollow and mirthless. "Sarge, you can write me up, you know."

The old sergeant wasn't sure what to say, what to feel or do, other than to withdraw his hand. Without a word, he turned and walked toward the door with a concentrated calm, as beads of sweat began forming on his brow. He entered a small sea of attendants who parted as he passed. He was leaving, but not quickly enough.

"We died there, Sarge, all of us," the voice from the room said. "I know it." The voice paused. "Only problem is you don't, but you just go on now, keep thinkin' the way you are. I understand, really, I do. You dream, man, just like me, I know it, brotha Sergeant, but you doin' whatever it takes . . . to get by."

*   *   *

California Medical Facility, Vacaville, June 16, 1971

Oh man, I must be getting better. They're allowing me a ballpoint pen, a gift from Buddy who came down with my mom a couple of days ago. It's a sharp object, and crazy folks can't have sharp objects. But the attendants have seen me with it, and haven't taken it away. Good thing I talk to these guys. I don't give them any trouble, no drooling at the mouth or flailing my arms, no reason to throw me down and nail me with a needle to sedate me. We just talk, sometimes in the building, sometimes on the grounds, oh, about the usual things—sports, mostly, that's pretty safe.

A couple of the guys, the attendants, were in Vietnam, and I ask how come they're not patients. They just laugh and say they weren't Marines, but if they talk long enough to nuts like me, then maybe they'll just up and join the other side. Still, the bottom line is that those guys were in the bush; they understand, like a brother to brother thing. They cut me some slack.

I've been able to remember almost everything since I've been here, at least from those times when I was conscious. I remember the sessions with the nutcase docs who said I'd repressed these experiences, these horrible memories—that it was normal, the mind's survival trick—and that I needed to bring them all out into the open.

Not much hassle, here. Peaceful. The dreams? They seem to have disappeared. Maybe the nut docs know what they're doing.

Before I came here, there was county jail, the news, the prosecutor who wanted my head. The fracas became famous, a bona fide international incident because of Daddy's connection to Marcos, our strongman in the Orient. His government, through its consulate, "expressed its concern" that justice be done. Then, as soon as that got out, the lefties wanted me as their anti-imperialism, antiwar, political prisoner poster boy, kind of a Filipino-Indian Huey P. Newton, but darker and not as pretty, and all of a sudden I was all over this town—tv, the papers, local mags, everywhere.

Even a literary agent stopped by to chat.

In other words, for awhile I meant something to everyone. I kind of liked the celebrity and was actually looking forward to the trial, to see who or what popped out of the woods, and besides, I was getting tired of my all jail, no bail life, and I figured that sitting in a courtroom, dressed in a suit, was better than sitting in a cell.

As it turned out, the show never made it to Broadway. For that little brawl, I was facing a list of major charges, two of which were for attempted murder. A week before the trial, the prosecutor caved in; he agreed to my insanity plea in large part because of holes in the state's case, like victim one (Marites' dad) leaving for the Philippines and telling the cops he wouldn't cooperate, and victim two, Officer Mel, telling my attorney what he'd seen me do just north of Hue, and that he'd be willing to testify to that if called by the defense.

No trial, no more celebrity. The lefties lost their interest. The agent stopped returning my calls.

Oh well, it wasn't so bad. Instead of Folsom or San Quentin, I get to rest way out here in the country and write in my diary and have the docs treat me like I'm some fragile but resilient little valley flower, still capable of recovery.

Buddy's been down a few times. He's still my ace. Same stuff with him, he's getting near the end of school. Mom and my sisters have come down. Even Mel visited once. The last time, I thanked him for helping me—twice now. Imagine.

Then, there's Marites, who's written regularly and come up from San Francisco at least once a month, especially since her lobeless daddy has gone home. She told me she'd wait, and I believe her, although for her, I know, it was a big choice . . . Guess I won for once.

I've got another session with the doc in ten minutes or so. She likes Indians—anthro undergrad, my guess—so I think I'll play that part up, talk about traditions I know nothing about. Have to get myself together. I miss Marites; this session I'm going to show some real improvement. Any more improvement and they'll have to let me go, then it's back to San Francisco, back to Marites.

*   *   *

BANYAN CORNER JACARANDA, BANYAN PARK, MANILA, PHILIPPINES, JULY 14, 1971

Banyan Park is an island fortress of wealth, extreme and conspicuous, surrounded by endless waves of poverty—just as extreme, just as conspicuous. The residents rest easy at night, their treasure protected by guards and gated checkpoints, and by a high stone and concrete wall that envelops the mansions and estates therein.

An observer standing outside would see, at most, green tiled roof-tops or the tops of tall banyan trees that grace the enclave's wide, spotless boulevards, and gave the settlement its name.

To further discourage the curious, huge, thick shards of broken glass are embedded deep into the concrete of the enveloping wall's top layer. Upon closer inspection, an observer might also see splotches of red, some quite large, on the shards and along the wall.

Over the years, the splotches remained, dimmed by the elements but otherwise untouched. The residents could have had them washed or painted over, but didn't. The outside world of the rest of the Philippines needed a warning, a sign that Banyan Park was reserved—try to enter, the splotches said, but only at a price. Deals, mostly unwritten, were made here over midnight martinis and bottles of aged imported wine. Handshakes, nicknames, and smiles controlled the country and divided up its wealth.

In the open air dining room of the largest house—it, too, surrounded by its own walled gate and protected by its own armed servants—an older man and a much younger woman were sitting down to a mid-morning breakfast. As the older man sipped coffee he fingered the lumpy bottom of an ear, oddly incomplete, while reading the financial section of one of Manila's many dailies. The young woman, sitting across from him at the dark mahogany table, picked gently with her fork at the fringes of a single fried egg.

The man lowered the paper and peered at his companion. "Carina, you should eat more," he scolded. "Anding," he then said and snapped his fingers. "Bring some more pan de sal and chorizo for both of us, por favor." Anding, the ancient white-haired servant who was hovering near the table, nodded and disappeared into the kitchen.

Within seconds he reappeared, laden with his master's request, which he then placed at a point equidistant between the man and his companion. He turned and walked toward the kitchen, but paused by the kitchen door. He turned to look backward, ever so slightly, and sighed. He knew the young woman well, almost from childhood. It hurt him to see her so. His eyes blinked. What she really needed for this hole in her heart, chorizo and pan de sal piled high would never fill.

"Ay, querida," the man said. "You need to eat more, you're getting so pale, so thin. You've been here, what . . . "

His tone was crisp, matter of fact, like an order to his broker to sell this or that stock because the price was just right. In his world, he spoke, things happened, things got done.

"Three weeks," she mumbled.

"Yes, Marites, three weeks already, and you barely eat."

"It's just the heat, Daddy," she said softly. She fanned herself limply with her hand. "Hot, so hot, that's all."

He wasn't convinced. "Well, you've been away for awhile, but you're young, you were born here, you'll readapt." He paused, smug, as if saying it made it so, then shifted his sight toward the kitchen door.

"Anding," he bellowed. "Mas café tambien, por favor."

"Daddy," she began.

He knew the tone and peered at her over the top of the paper. "I did it for your own good," he said, and returned to the business news of the day.

"Hmm, it says here that Hong Kong investors are looking overseas, and that the Philippines is their prime target. Hmm, very good, very good for us . . . "

"Daddy."

With a sigh, he put down the paper and stared at his daughter. They'd been over this topic before, too many times, in fact. How often did he have to explain? It was, after all, his money, in truth, his apartment, his car, his expensive Jesuit education. She hadn't been truthful about that boy, that Indian boy—"Injun," he called him like the Hollywood cowboys he'd loved so well. Sometimes, at night, when he'd been drinking, she'd join him and sometimes, he'd even do war whoops and regale her with what he'd learned about Indians. "They're useless, drunken, defeated," he'd told her.

He was cruel; it was purposeful. He'd told her he hated him, her lover; he'd told her she'd chosen that boy, that "Injun" over him. At his cruelest, he'd say that sometimes he'd hated her, too, then smile slyly and add, maybe he still did.

But she took it, silent and half drunk, because in some odd way, his words and insults created an image in her mind of the only man she'd loved.

She was a liar, he knew. Just a friend, she'd said. Some friend; he'd cost him an earlobe and almost his life. Daddy had asked her to come back on her own; she wouldn't. So he'd pulled the plug, and still she didn't return, preferring instead to survive on her own. But surviving in San Francisco is never guaranteed; for awhile, though, she'd managed. She'd dropped out of school and had lost the car, but she'd paid the rent by working two, sometimes three jobs, hustling between them courtesy of late running buses or long, lonely walks up and down hills.

Sometimes she was so tired, she couldn't sleep the three, four, or five hours that were left in a cycle of twenty-four that was so full of motion, constant and meaningless. A shot of gin, she found, would do the trick, two or more, she also found, did it better. Drunken sleep and fast-moving days, she wondered when it would end.

It ended one late, fog-shrouded evening after her waitress shift at a teriyaki joint on Kearny. She'd just missed the last bus and, after fishing around in her purse, found she didn't have enough for a cab. She sighed; life had suddenly become like that, full of hills, like the ones she had to walk just to get home from a waitress job that paid subminimum wage. She didn't make it.

As she neared Grant, the entry to Chinatown, a voice in her told her to stop, to turn back. She wished the voice had been a bit more clear, and that she hadn't sat in the bar for an hour smoking cigarettes (a habit she'd picked up) and drinking two straight shots on the house. She shrugged and cursed (another new habit) and figured it was just some boozy whisper. She'd heard it before— harmless, she thought—and kept walking straight into a car full of drunken young men parked along the curb. One rolled down his window and catcalled; another sprang onto the sidewalk, grabbed her arm and pulled her in, and when they dragged her out, she was on her back in the middle of a damp, fog-shrouded field.

The police report said it was a meadow in Golden Gate Park near the horse stables, and that the victim had been found by a maintenance worker who'd just started his shift. He'd reported he'd almost run her over with his truck. She was unconscious and stripped. Blood had caked around her mouth and nose and vagina. Her body, from her neck down, was a quilt of scratches and deep bruises.

Daddy got the call the next day. That evening, he and two of the best physicians that Philippine money could buy were airborne to San Francisco. His rescue gave him a chance to reassert control, and to vent a bulging chest of "I told you so's" he'd been carefully hoarding.

How could she, his daughter, argue now, after all that had happened, after all of her errors and stupid actions, after all their deadly consequences?

"Daddy," she said.

"Carina." His tone made no effort to hide his impatience. "Look, we've already . . . "

"You should have left me there," she said quietly.

"But you would have died there." Daddy was surprised. He hadn't heard that before.

"Living, dying," she said calmly. "Either one, it just doesn't matter."

*   *   *

SANTO TOMAS CATHOLIC CHURCH, DECEMBER 20, 1971

It was one of those churches that marked its time in centuries, not decades or years, and unlike many of Spain's enduring monuments to God, this one was not in disarray. Its well-heeled and devout congregation, many from nearby Banyan Park, saw to that.

On this morning, it was filled, but not for any pre-Christmas celebration. The purpose was far more somber—the burial of a beautiful young woman, and not just any young woman. She was the youngest daughter of the most powerful man in the Philippines after, of course, Marcos himself. Suicide, some had whispered once the news of the death was known. The whispers had grown so loud that two days earlier, they'd forced the archbishop of Manila to intervene. Physical evidence notwithstanding, it had clearly been accidental—she was drunk, the razor had slipped, she had weakened and drowned (water in the lungs and loss of blood) in a tub that soon overflowed with warm, red water.

The good man, having read the police report, had said that Anding, the servant, had heard her scream, but he was old and was working in a distant corner of the estate when he'd heard this last mournful cry. He moved, he'd told the police, as quickly as he could, but not quickly enough. This showed, said the archbishop, that even if she'd wanted to die, she'd retreated, in her last conscious moment, from exercising the power of God—an acknowledgment that only He could take a life. She'd retreated from arrogance.

Tragic, he tsked in solemn conclusion. But not suicidal, or at least not suicidal enough to keep this poor soul (of this prominent, powerful family) from the solace of Christian burial.

And where was Anding, the faithful, loving man who'd known the young woman since birth? He was missing, a fact not escaping the notice of some in attendance.

"Ay," whispered one, after scanning the front rows of the church where immediate family was seated. She was rumored to be the mistress of the Minister of Finance. "That servant, that, ay, ah, what's his name?"

Her companion, an older woman with interests in casinos and shopping malls, fanned herself as she leaned closer to reply. "Yes, of course, I can see him, always at the estate as long as I can remember, an old man, white-haired . . . "

"Ay, what's his name?"

"Andong, no?" said the older woman. She made sure her fan was strategically placed to cover her face and her friend's ear. She then turned and whispered, "Anding, that's it. Anding."

The younger woman smiled. "Anding, ah." She paused. "Odd, he shouldn't be here."

"Oh, querida," the shopping mall lady said. "Tsk, so tragic, at least that's what I heard . . . "

Her friend's arched eyebrow urged her to continue.

"He died."

"Died?"

"Heart attack from the sorrow and stress," the older one whispered. "So sudden."

"He died?"

"Yes, heart attack," she said, and paused. "Or something."

"Or something," her friend repeated.

*　*　*

December 24, 1973

Thank God for budget cuts, or the nuthouse docs would have kept me in Vacaville forever. All this year, they kept changing my meds and dosages, trying new forms of treatment—claiming it was all so very good, that it would all pay off outside. I was so fogged up, I don't remember too much of anything.

It took a long time, more than two years, but the nutcase docs figured I was finally good to go—or that there were others worse than me who needed a bed. They told me I needed to stay on my medication schedule, then handed me some Prolixin and sent me on my way.

Thank God for budget cuts.

I headed back to the Loin—new apartment, same old shit. I recognized some of the junkies and the ladies, and a few I didn't even know asked when I'd gotten out (I guess they remembered all of the publicity). Three weeks ago I started a job working the morning shift at a Safeway over in the Castro. It's a little bit far-ther away than the old gig—a concern since I don't have wheels —but still close enough.

Yesterday, I signed up for a poetry class next term at the com-munity college. It's in the evening, it's advanced. But the schedule had a "staff" designation for the teacher. I just hope it isn't that raggedy assed free verse fraud—who knew someone, who knew someone who once had coffee with a very minor poet—I had the first time around. Damn, she almost killed my love for the art.

I've been a pretty good boy, taking the meds, staying on sched-ule—for the most part anyway. When I'm medicated, I'm under control, Citizen Rico—or so society says. I go to work, attend class, get my assignments in on time, stay out of jail.

I watch television—a lot of television. It's nice to wander through a wasteland where no one's shooting at you. A few nights ago, I caught a Bob Hope Christmas special. Bob Hope? Now that's a profoundly unfunny man. I saw him in Vietnam. He was there, I suppose, to remind us of every anti-commie "Leave It to Beaver" thing we were supposed to be fighting for. Myself? I was too high to get the punch line, not that the dude had anything to say to me anyway. I signed up because I knew war would be something I'd be pretty good at—no other reason. During the show, I was sitting next to some black Marines and they were high on some serious shit, talking loud and carrying on. One of the bloods rolls his eyes and says, "I see this pasty motherfucker one more time, I'ma join Uncle Ho."

Speaking of pasty, I've been seeing a lot of the Beaver lately, courtesy of syndication. That's when I decided not to take my meds for awhile just to understand what was really going down. No one could be that perfect—or that dumb. One night, I finally figured it out. Old Beav and June had a thang; that's why the little twerp was always coming home after school, on time, all the time. Had to be.

I was off schedule for a day or so and during that time, the dreams came back, complete with stereophonic sound and a cast of thousands—with me as the star. I know it's not healthy, but sometimes it's nice to be free of routine and convention—of expectations. I dream—or daydream—and when I write I can feel my pen fly and merge the realms of cadence and prose. I feel—no, I know—that in those moments, I can hit the high notes. But then something happens, a realization that a work shift or a class assignment is just hours away, and I have to get straight. So I do, but sometimes I just hate the tyranny of those little fucking pills.

I was straight when Marites called this morning from Manila. I was surprised; I'd just gotten the phone two weeks earlier. She said I was listed. It was exciting just to hear her voice. She was crying and said she missed me, and that she'd do everything possible to get back to the States, to Frisco, to me. Daddy's taken away her passport and has made it be known that a new one shouldn't be issued. Imagine that, someone having that much power over his adult daughter. As badly as I miss her, it made me feel worse to hear her that way. We talked for an hour—thank God, her nickel—and I spent most of that time telling her I still loved her, hadn't replaced her.

"Yeah, right," I told her. "I found a nuthouse sweetie, she's gorgeous but she's afraid to leave her room, so that means you and I can still live together as long as it's not at Vacaville." That made her laugh. Just the sound brightened my day. I need a lot of that right now.

I'd do anything to be with Marites, but I can't. If I went back to Manila, I'm sure Daddy's goons would have me killed. She, on the other hand, is going to have a hard time even leaving the country. I thought about going home, to Seattle, for a few days, but I just can't afford the time off. So I'll just sit here, sit tight, work when I'm scheduled, eat when I'm hungry, watch the happy shoppers, ignore the happy drunks, and just count down the days until the end of this not-so-happy time.

Chapter Seven

Rico sat at the end of the bar, a half-empty bottle of Bud and a full
shot glass the marks of his bar top domain. His time was marked
by three butts crushed in a black plastic ashtray. That told him,
without having to look at any watch or clock, that he'd been here
an hour, three sticks per. Three more sticks to go until he had to
hop the Muni to go across town to the community college and
take another class in poetry, with the teacher saying the best work
would be submitted to this or that journal—he couldn't recall
which—for publication. He spent his weekday afternoons this way
and, when he didn't have class, his weeknights as well.

On weekends, he'd drink a bottle of bourbon or two while
locked in his room or, if he felt like it and the wind wasn't too hard,
he'd pour the bourbon into a thermos and go sit by the wharf
where he'd first met his love a forever ago. At the wharf, he might
try to write or just remember, or drink the last drop of this brew
that brought him relief.

He'd stare at the water and let his mind drift to things long
forgotten, or purposely put aside. Like the time his father brought

home a box of plastic soldiers. He came to love each soldier and gave each one names and ranks. Everyday, he'd line them up, ready to storm this or that corner of his bedroom where imaginary enemies lurked and threatened all he held dear. At nights, his dad would sing him a lullaby about "playing a soldier" and the battle having been won. Eventually, he outgrew his little army and the lullaby and returned the soldiers to their box, never to take them out until the day he knew his father would never return. He took out his favorite soldier—a grenade-tossing sergeant named "Vic" —and brought him to the lake where he threw him in.

Vic was on a mission. He was to ride the waves from the lake through the canal to Puget Sound, where the current would sweep him through the strait and into the ocean, to be taken at last to the Philippines where Rico hoped an old fisherman would find it and remember for a moment he still had a son who loved him.

At that moment, he wished he had another soldier he could drop in the bay. This one for a woman in that same distant land.

On that and other afternoons, he would stay until dark when the wind would begin to whip, or the fog would roll in, or both in concert would arrive and seem to target him, their victim.

Just him, he would think as he watched families and lovers walk by.

He'd take it as his sign to leave, and so he'd rise and retrace his steps back up the hills he'd walked down hours earlier. On his return journey, he'd always pass her old apartment on Nob Hill, and there he would pause and look at the glass-encased list of tenants, and try to imagine her name still being there. And of course, it wasn't; a "Johnson" had now taken her place. Without fail, he would kiss the tip of his index finger, then place it where her name used to be, before resuming his trek—this time downhill—to his home in the Loin. There, he'd drink himself to sleep.

Alcohol put him to sleep faster and took him away from his thoughts, his nagging regret. He would sometimes remember those dreams in Vacaville, where he dreamed only of the dead, never of the living.

The longer he stayed at the hospital, the worse the dreams became. Near the end he saw not just his friend from Oklahoma, but others as well. The anonymous little men and women, and yes, one child—a little girl killed by accident in a firefight.

Their faces—his dream eyes tracing their wounds to open sternums and jagged, gaping jaws—all mouthed the question, why. Because, you sons of bitches, he answered defiantly in one dream, because most of you tried to kill me.

Not me, the little girl said. That was an accident, he answered. And besides, he added, why just me? Others killed, did far worse things, like the fliers, those pretty, clean, college white boys who brought death from a distance and then flew back to showers and hot meals. They never had to distinguish, to make the finger on the trigger moral choice of friend or foe.

What about fliers?

Because they're hopeless, their god is technology, the girl answered. And besides, you're Indian. You believe in dreams; the others don't.

Rico's defiance changed nothing; he continued to dream, but at Vacaville, he told no one, especially not the nutcase docs. He was cured, he lied, careful to smile, careful to seem upbeat. He kept telling the docs the dreams feared their white-smocked therapy; the latest developments in integrative white guy hoo-doo made the dreams go away.

On the radio, Buddy Miles sang about dreams to remember. Rico was haunted by dreams to forget.

Rico just wanted to get out; temporary insanity meant temporary, not one day more. Hey all, he was healed, he kept saying. Get out of jail, collect two bills, go back to the city where your lover is waiting.

But she wasn't. And he tried to find her, but couldn't, and he feared for the worst and somehow knew it had come to pass. For awhile, he'd taken the pills, and for awhile, he even got refills. But he liked booze better—no walking down to the pharmacy, no waiting, no hassle. He drank because he found that alcohol diluted his dreams and took away his fear of sleep, and that if he drank enough, her image wouldn't appear.

He drank most on the weekends. This afternoon, though, his thoughts were elsewhere, like whether he should order one more boilermaker and whether—he couldn't recall—he was one or two assignments behind. Was the current one due today, or the next session?

He wondered if he'd make it through class and instead of nodding, as a classmate read drivel, he'd just nod off. Bad poet move, he thought.

What if the teacher asked him for a reaction? What would he say? Probably the staples, he figured, and pulled out a pen and a piece of paper, just in case he'd forget: "I loved its cadence," he wrote. "It spoke to me."

Could he, should he? Or was the issue of one more round irrelevant? Fuck it, he thought, as he gulped the shot and what was left of the Bud in quick succession. He nodded to Freddy, the bartender, who nodded back and soon returned with another cold bottle and its brimming shot-glass companion. He put the note to himself in his shirt pocket.

"Say, brother," a deep voice said as its owner moved onto a stool next to his own. "Man, hope you don't mind."

"Free country," he mumbled as, out of the corner of a bloodshot eye, he tried to size up the man sitting next to him. He was large, he was black. He seemed vaguely familiar. The rest of the bar was empty. Why was he sitting next to him? His shoulders tensed.

"Saw you writin'," the big man said. "You a writer?"

Rico relaxed. The question was innocent. "Kinda," he said. "Write in my diary, good practice. Thinkin' of writin' fiction sometime, New York Times best fuckin' seller, you know? But that's for down the road."

"Man, that so?"

Rico laughed easily and took out a cigarette. "Want one?"

"Gave 'em up, you know, bad for you'n shit."

Rico downed the shot. "Freddy, one more round."

"You write anything else?"

"Kinda," Rico said. "Right now, I'm tryin' to do poetry."

"No shit."

"Yeah, I like it, you know, poetry'n all. Just do the shit, bam, it's done. I like that now, need it, in fact."

"No shit."

Rico nodded and downed another shot. "Hmm, bit of a buzz on that one," he mumbled and paused. "Hey, brother man, how come you ain't drinkin'?"

The black man shrugged. "Hey, man, tell me a poem, you know, one you wrote."

"Ah, man . . . "

"Come on, brother, I know you can," he said, smiling.

Rico smiled back. "Hey man, alright, my brother, my public." He looked up at the ceiling, then turned toward his audience of one and bowed deeply. "Ah, here we go, ah, 'The southern sky, a rocking shit,' I mean, ship," he slurred. "Ah, fuck it, do it later." He started laughing.

"I'ma write," the black man said.

"That's good," he said, and turned toward his beer. He was beginning to nod out.

"Yeah, motherfucker," the black man snarled. "I'ma write how I kicked yo' gook ass." He then threw his huge right hand in the direction of Rico's jaw. That fist, broad and thick, steamed like a predawn semi, full of speed, and snarl, and bad intent.

Was it luck or training? No matter. Its target just leaned back, not far enough to get away clean, just enough to save his jaw. The blow caught the upper part of his shoulder, the wounded one, and was strong enough to hurl him off the stool and into the wall. Oddly enough, the shoulder didn't hurt, but other parts of him did. Guess I'm healed, he thought, as he lay on the ground.

Rico shook his head. He remembered him now; this was the guy he'd jacked in his first days in the Loin. He was a bit smaller now, especially in the shoulders, but still larger than him, and big enough to cause damage. He'd forgotten that incident, forgotten him. It was obviously not mutual.

"Remember me now?" he said, as he stood over his foe.

Rico grunted, and tried to get up; a stomp to the chest kept him pinned.

"I'ma take my sweetassed time," he said. "But I'm still gonna kill ya. Been waitin' a long, long time." He raised his foot to stomp him again but Rico, seeing his opportunity, somehow willed himself to roll away. The sole of the big man's boot crashed down on two cheap floor tiles.

Crashing down as well was a pool cue, the fat part breaking around the right temple of the big man's head. He stumbled, crossed, and recrossed his heavy legs, then fell forward. As he did, he banged headlong into a concrete wall, before crumbling to the floor.

Rico was so drunk, he couldn't see who'd saved him; he'd figure that out later. He needed to leave a card of some sort so that this faux fan of poetry would forever leave him alone. He hovered over the big man's face, trying hard to focus, to gather his bearings, like a bombardier over Dresden. He spotted his target. Bang, he thought, as he kneedropped right into the middle of two full lips, leaving behind a bloody gap where a full range of top and bottom teeth had once been.

Job done, he turned to search for his savior, who found him instead.

"Wynona," she said, and extended her right hand. In her left, she was still holding the broken shaft of the pool cue. She laughed. "Just in case he wakes up."

"Rico," he said, smiled, and reached for her hand. "Thanks. Pretty good with that stick." She was small and thin, a hundred wiry pounds max, much of which was poured into a tight pair of blue jeans. He then looked at her face—narrow, well-defined features, very pretty brown eyes, framed by long, flowing black hair. A mix of some kind, he concluded, but what?

"Had lotsa practice back home," she said.

"Home?"

"North Dakota."

"You Indian?"

"Mandan. How 'bout you?"

"Kinda," he said.

"Kinda what?"

"Kinda Indian," he said.

*   *   *

SANTINI'S COFFEE BAR, NORTH BEACH, SAN FRANCISCO, MARCH 10–11, 1974

She was here, she said, because she didn't want to be there.

"There?" he asked.

"It's too hard back home," she said in a monotone rat-a-tat, so different, he thought, from Marites' lyrical voice. He wanted her to elaborate. She just shrugged. "Tell ya later," she said. It took him awhile to adjust to her brevity, her way of talking; he decided he liked the sound.

Since Marites, other women had made their play to collapse the bourbon bottle fence he'd built around his heart. A couple had even spent the night, but to him they were first-name-only shadows in the fog, more fiction than fact. I'll call you tomorrow, he'd say, more out of politeness and their expectations, but he never did.

This one, though, was different. She was pretty, but that wasn't it. Anna (or was it Juanita?), he thought, was prettier; she was a Mexican girl he'd drunk with at a bar downtown and bedded sometime last week. Actually, he didn't remember having sex, just that she was there in his apartment lying naked and next to him when he awoke. He was shocked; she wasn't.

"Call me tonight," she breathed, as she rose to leave. Of course, he never did.

Sure, he thought, Wynona was pretty, but it wasn't just that.

He inched forward a bit and back, then to one side and the other, hoping with each fraction of an inch movement to maybe get a different view, an insight as to what about her drew him. He didn't look at her face, didn't have to; that part of her, the most obvious part, he'd already memorized. Pretty enough, he knew, but not the whole answer. He had to look elsewhere.

Maybe it was her hands. They were the parts of her closest to him; both were curled around her oversized coffee mug in mid-table. The hands, he thought, looked strong, like they'd lifted and pulled for a lifetime. He smiled. Jerome's hands were like that. She had long, unadorned fingers that, for a woman, were surprisingly thick. And, eyes darting left to right, he followed those fingers from their tips and close-cut unpolished nails to her wrists and well-defined forearms.

He stopped at her forearms. "It's just hard right now," she continued and stared at her coffee. She then leaned across the small table and stared at him. "May go back, though, it's home, got family there, for better or worse, it's home." She paused. "What about you?"

He tried to match her, but couldn't. His eyes drifted upward as he rolled his neck in reply. "What about me?" he mumbled.

"What's home?"

He glared at her. "Whatcha think? I live in a box?"

She chuckled softly and shook her head. "Not what I said, not what I meant, you should listen," she said. "Where you from, what's important, whaddya believe?" She paused. "Your Indian side, whaddya know?"

"Not much," he said. "Yeah, my mom's Indian, but she was raised in the city, not around Indians. She was a foster kid and didn't know much about her tribe and, except for when I was real young, we never went back there."

"Where?"

"Yakima rez."

"Your grandmother."

He began to fidget. "Long dead."

"Your aunt."

"Jesus," he said, again irritated. "What is this, some kinda survey?"

She shrugged, and looked away and, in his opinion, paid too much attention to the artwork and photos on a nearby wall. He feared that was the first step, that she'd soon stop talking, that he'd lost her. She took her time as her eyes roamed the walls before finally returning to him.

"You done bein' mad?" she asked flatly.

"Who said I was mad?" he answered, and immediately regretted it.

She shrugged, pushed her cup away, and got ready to rise. "Okay, you're not mad," she said. "Good coffee, thanks."

In the past, he'd wished for many things, most of which had never been answered, so he'd learned to stop wishing, to keep going and just do without. It was a matter of pride to just keep going; he knew it was pride, not hope, that kept him alive. The hard lessons had taught him not to care too much—keep going, the lessons said—and he'd taken those lessons to the center of his heart. But just now he caught himself caring that this woman whom he barely knew was leaving.

"Ah, look," he mumbled, as his fingers and hands moved and danced. He wished, through some twist of evolution, they could suddenly sprout lips and vocal chords to say what seemed to be stuck in his throat. Like Lamb Chop, he thought.

"I'm, ah . . . "

"Sorry?" she said.

He nodded his head; she sat back down.

"For bein' a prick?" she added.

Both hands began churning again. He looked down at the table and nodded his head. "Yeah," he finally said.

He looked up in time to see her smile ever so faintly. There was no sign of leaving. He sighed.

"Your mother got sisters?" she asked.

"My aunt," he said calmly. "But she died when we were kids; that's why we went back to the rez for a month or so."

"You ever ask her?"

"Who?"

"Your mother."

"About what?"

"About your Yakima side."

"Ah, Mom don't know," he protested. "She's been in Seattle all her life, went to Catholic schools."

"Still practice?"

"It's all she got," he said.

"Too bad."

"Whatcha mean?"

"The priests taught Indians to hate themselves, that's all," she answered. "You one?"

"What?"

"A Catholic."

"Baptized," he said. "But I stopped believin' in too much of anything."

She smiled. "Maybe there's hope for you, at least you don't hate yourself," she said. "Gettin' back to your mom, d'ya ever ask her?"

His head dropped slightly. She had him—he knew it; she did, too—neat and trimmed and tastefully boxed. "No," he finally said.

"Maybe you shoulda," she said.

"Maybe."

"Maybe you still can," Wynona said, as she slowly drew the cup to her lips. She savored the coffee's aroma, felt its warmth. "Ask your mom."

Rico leaned back in his chair, careful to shift his eyes away from her. He fixed an unfocused gaze on a black-and-white photo of a young Joe DiMaggio on the far wall as he pondered his reply.

"Maybe," he mumbled.

Chapter Eight

The Loin, March 22, 1974

It's my birthday, twenty-five years, a full quarter century. It's also the first time I've ever written on my birthday. I used to think that if I did, I'd somehow jinx myself and die the next day. I think I learned it in the bush—draw attention, bingo, your pals begin whispering about you in the past tense. But I'm no longer in the bush, and I figure reaching this point in time is special, so I'm defying the jinx and writing an entry.

There were some days when I never thought I'd make it this far, but damn, here I am. As a kid, I used to think being a teenager was old, and that being twenty-five was a step away from a freshly dug hole in the ground. I've seen the hole and seen friends fall into it. I haven't joined them and, if I'm lucky, I won't for a half century more.

Buddy called this morning; Mom did too. Those two are special, like clockwork, every birthday without fail. Even when I was in Vietnam or in the hospital, or later, in the psycho bin, they'd never forget, and they'd talk or write to me like nothing had happened, nothing had changed, like I was still a kid back home.

I remember one year, Buddy and I had snuck some wine after a party; I'd just turned fourteen. We went back behind the house into the alley and drank good wine in a paper sack. For dessert, he brought some cigarettes, my first ones. We just sat and smoked and talked about dreams, about friendship, how we'd always be brothers. He told me that even if I ever really fucked up and everybody hated me and I died, he'd still claim the body. He said he'd make the arrangements and bury me, say a prayer, light a fire, ceremonial stuff that he must have picked up from the movies or television, or maybe even from reading National Geographic.

He said that even if he was broke or I died broke (both likely possibilities), he'd just dig a hole in his backyard and put me in the ground (he was pretty drunk by then). He said that doing that would make me easier to visit, and that he could even dig me up when he felt like it and we could just hang on the corner.

Relax, he said, he'd do the talking. We laughed and shook on it.

That Buddy, he's got it going. Getting his degree, his teaching certificate; the Seattle Public Schools wants to pick him up. A good job, a future, maybe he can make a difference in a new generation of kids like me. Buddy's got a reason to stay home, to never leave.

Me? Maybe I just don't have the same reason. Thinking back, I was a throwaway, wasting time in public schools. I knew it, my teachers knew it—too much pomade, too much attitude—good only for auto shop, or a tour of Vietnam, or both. Buddy, though, lucked out. His mom worked another job just to get him into Catholic schools, where no one got tossed away, and guys from the same neighborhood as me learned to read and write, apply to college, get deferments, and believe in the future. His mother was religious, kind of a talk-to-the-saints sort of woman, and for her, public school was out of the question. But she had a vision for Buddy, who'd wanted to be with me in public schools, and that's something my mom never had.

There were times when I resented Mom because she never thought of the future, and just kind of went with a flow that swept me into a corner that started shrinking when I turned eighteen. I thought about that in the bush, and later, in the hospital and then in the nut bin—how one event leads to another, and if you look back far enough you can see the beginning, and make out the connections in a life that's going nowhere.

But then, I thought about what Mom had to face with raising me and my sisters. After Dad left, cutting hair was never quite enough, so she added second and even third jobs—cleaning houses, damn, she even tried a paper route once.

Sometimes I halfway expect Dad to call, or maybe drop by, just out of the blue, but he hasn't yet and I expect he never will. I don't know why I think this way; I haven't heard from him since he left and it's likely I never will. More confusing is why I feel this way, why I still have this tiny drop of affection for someone who didn't care, or might have cared, but not nearly enough. Maybe it's that damn polaroid that Mom's still got around the house of me and him and some giant department store Easter Bunny. I must've been about three, and it's been so long ago, I don't remember the shot. But there we are in black and white, that big assed rabbit on one side, Dad on the other, me between them looking confused. Dad's dressed like he always was in public—dark suit, white shirt, and tie, Borsalino hat he's holding by the brim.

Damn, he looked like a banker or attorney or some robot who worked at Safeco, instead of a man who canned fish. He's smiling a that's-my-boy sort of smile. In my cynical moments, and there were many, I'd ask myself if the smile was fake. But I don't think so. There were other times, father and son sorts of times, then one day he just left. Not a word. Nothing. But the picture said he loved me then, I felt it. I wonder why he stopped?

Hell, maybe the picture was faked, or some other little kid who looked like me slipped between the rabbit and my smiling old man.

Mom doesn't know why he left either, or at least she never told me; we've never talked about it. I figured it was just too painful.

She called this morning, right after Buddy, and we covered a whole range of other things. My sisters are fine. Tammy, the youngest, just started a course in "cosmetology," Tammy's term, and a fancy word for becoming a beautician. My older sister Kitty found a nice guy, a Filipino from San Diego who's doing graduate work at the U. He met her in the college cafeteria where she was bussing tables. They're in love, Mom said. She moved out and it's just Tammy and Mom at home.

Mom said the house seemed so empty without me. That was real hard to hear. I didn't know when (or if), but I was hoping to grab some vacation time and come visit. That seemed to make her happy. I told her I was working and taking poetry classes and she said that's good, like it was my life and as long as I was alive and not killing anyone or getting killed, whatever I did was fine with her.

Then I told her I was hanging out with an Indian girl, and then she got real quiet for a second, like she knew I'd ask what Indians were like—the culture, the beliefs. I asked, and was sorry I did because I felt that whatever she'd say—"This is what we believe, but I didn't tell you because" or "I just don't know"—would embarrass her. She's my mom and I got her off the hook by switching quickly to the rising price of gas. I added I'd send her some money because I knew her old Mercury guzzled premium worse than before, and that she needed to get around. Sometime I know I'll ask the Indian questions again, but only when we're face to face. It's too cruel otherwise.

Wynona called just an hour ago, and said she was coming over. We've been hanging out together, mostly over coffee, sometimes over booze. Maybe it's an Indian thing, but she doesn't talk much, except about booze, and that's mostly to warn me. When we're at a bar, she watches herself and says she's seen too many good Indians messed up by alcohol—and then cites herself—so she cuts herself off after one. She tried going cold once, but gave it up. She was in Minneapolis—her first big city before coming here—and attended an AA meeting, but couldn't stand the other drunks, mostly white guys trying to get sober. As she left her last meeting, she told herself that from that point on, she might have a drink or two, but never to the point of losing it again.

I admit, I'm probably a drunk, but I'm a functional one. Hell,

I told Wynona the state patrol could pull me over after three shots and I could walk any line, touch my nose with my fingertips, and recite the alphabet backward.

I liked booze even before the Marines. Dad and all of his Pinoy buddies drank a lot—mostly sweet wine and hard liquor—and I remember one summer when I was fifteen and he and I were the only ones in the house; he filled a big glass full of port for himself and a smaller one for me. "You're my boy," was all he said. We just sat there on this ragged old couch and watched the baseball game, neither one of us saying a damn thing. About the fifth inning, the bottle was empty and he opened (and we finished) another one before the ninth inning. I drank through high school. Then I suppose the stuff in Vietnam just gave me more reasons to continue.

So I figure I'm hooked. But I like being hooked, and I really don't want to stop. I love the taste, enjoy the feeling. I suppose if I got it all together and cut the booze, I could go a bit further— maybe get serious and go over to Berkeley, or buy a suit, or maybe even get a new place outside the Loin. But I like my life and I like the structure I have—work's boring but predictable and brainless, poetry's fun and not too taxing. All of that, and I still have time to hang out, to talk and drink. All in all, I really can't complain.

When Wynona and I do drink, we have to first figure out where we're going. That's always the first skirmish. She says beer and wine, I say full service. Sometimes she wins, most of the time, though, I do because I'm willing to leave her and go drink alone. I drink a bit more than she does, wine sipper that she is—okay, okay—a lot more, and when I do I have to endure her lectures about me not becoming another Native American DOA.

I once answered, I'm sure with a slur, that my Filipino side was doing the sucking and my Filipino kidneys were doing the processing, so forget the Indians and booze lecture.

Wynona wasn't quite sure how to answer that. She huffed off to play pool, and I told her not to nail anyone. I gulped one more boilermaker and a Bloody Mary (counted as a vegetable), then dashed off to class.

Despite our clashes, I like being with Wynona. I'm attracted to her and, I think, it's mutual, though this relationship is an odd one. How long have I known her? Less than two weeks—not quite forever—but I've slept with others in less time (two days, two hours, two minutes). With her, though, it's different. She's real strong, and I just stay back—no groping, not much touching, not even a kiss on the cheek. She's been a bit tight lipped; I don't know that much about her, and I wonder what she looks like under those tight jeans. That thought makes me smile, and hey, it's my birthday, so maybe I'll find out.

*   *   *

THE LOIN. EARLY EVENING. MARCH 22, 1974

"Good wine," Wynona said evenly, and took a sip from her glass of Chablis.

"French," Rico said. "Courtesy of my employer."

"I miss my baby," she said.

He hadn't expected this revelation, not from her, who'd said so little the other times they were together. They were sitting on the floor—too far apart to be lovers, too close together to be friends—with their backs against the tattered front of an old couch that he'd found abandoned on the street. Before them were the signs of a recently finished meal—scattered paper plates and plastic spoons, portions of a store-bought chocolate cake, and half-empty bottles of top brand wine and bourbon—bounty lifted from his place of employment. The chance to steal was an added benefit of working in a large grocery store. He ate well and, more important, drank well, too, with a cabinet full of bottles of wine and hard liquors—whatever was available and would be missed the least.

Rico was staring at the wall, glass of bourbon in hand, when she mentioned her child; just a second before, his thoughts had been free and happy and roaming the lovely, meandering corridors of possibility and seduction. He'd imagined the subtle, teasing start, their first light touch that would trigger the ascending line leading to a passionate, sweat-drenched climax. He'd imagined her unclothed, not all at once, but slowly, discarding piece by unbuttoned piece.

Just a moment before, he'd been happily wondering if she was thinking the same way, too. Now, he just didn't know. He wasn't even sure, at least at first, what to say. Did she have another child? What else was she hiding? Was this her caveat, her warning to him to keep the space between them—roughly a foot, he'd figured—intact? He still didn't know how to respond.

"Got a picture?" Rico managed to ask.

"Yup," Wynona answered, and pulled one out of her wallet. She handed it to him and he raised it to the light. It was a color photo of a smiling little brown girl with straight black hair and dancing eyes. She was wearing a headband and looked about three.

"Pretty," he said dully, as if "pretty" was what was expected. He handed it back. As he turned toward her, he forced a smile. A child, he knew, complicated matters. He sighed. "Yeah, pretty."

"I really miss her bad, she's almost four now," she said, as she returned the picture to her wallet. She took another sip of wine. "Sometimes, I miss my husband, too."

"Your husband?" he gulped.

"Yeah, Frank, he's the father, a Washoe, " she said.

"Washoe?"

She nodded. "Yeah, California tribe, a small one . . . He was good, except when he drank, and he began drinkin' too much. Think it started in the army; he's a vet, Vietnam."

"Your husband?"

She nodded again. "One night, he came home really drunk and tried to tune me up, but I was sober and quicker than him. So I took a frying pan—one of those thick, cast iron ones—and just busted him hard, knocked him out, thought about killin' him right there," she said evenly, then paused and looked at him.

"He deserved it, but I guess I felt sorry for 'im."

He emptied his glass and nodded, too drunk to be affected. She continued. "Smacked 'im once more for good measure, right across the jaw and mouth. Knew it was time to leave, so I did. Thought I'd come here, check out school, or maybe work, then start a new life and send for my baby."

"Where is she?"

"With my mom."

"What about him, your . . . "

"Back home," she said. "You know, sometimes I think of him, wonder how he's doin', whether he's mothered up, and halfway hopin' he ain't. Kinda feel sorry for 'im. He's a bit slower since I beat him. On the side that I hit, his eye gets teary, like he can't control it. Don't talk real good either 'cause I fractured his jaw; ain't never set right. But he ain't a bad man and he knew he was wrong, and he never tried to hit me again. We had some good times, and he gave me a beautiful daughter, so we're tied that way. Filed some papers, but they ain't final yet, and then I saw him two months ago. Got along good. Wanted another chance, said he'd come out, a change of scene. I said we'd see."

Wynona sipped her wine. "Thought you should know that 'bout me, 'bout what I'd done. He's the father of my daughter, still part of my life." Her eyes slowly scanned the room before settling on him. "But he ain't here now," she whispered. "You are."

Red-faced, Rico laughed loudly and rolled his eyes, like he'd heard the words but missed the tone and intent. "Well, yeah, I guess I'm here," he said, and reached for the bourbon. "This calls for a toast." He shrugged. "Some sorta toast, anyway."

"No need," she said, as her hand stopped his. "You drink too much, you might even be a drunk, and I seen that before, but the difference is you don't get mean, and when you're sober you're okay." She paused.

"Noticed that."

"Hell yeah, drunk or sober, I'm a nice guy," he said, and marveled at the feel of her hand touching his. Her palms and fingertips were hard, harder than his. He smiled and wondered about her softer, hidden parts.

"And from where I've been, that's a good thing."

"Let's hear it for good things," he said, his tone vaguely mocking.

"And I like you," Wynona said, as her index finger lightly traced circles on the back of his hand.

Rico chuckled. "Now, that's somethin' we can toast." He then moved again to reach for the bourbon, but his movement was stopped by another movement, this one much quicker, that turned and reached and closed a gap, last thought to be roughly a foot. She straddled his thighs and with her arms extended, pinned his shoulders to the front of the couch.

"I like you," she said again. "I know you like me, too. I can tell."

Faced with this, an obvious truth, he felt himself blush. "Yeah," he said quietly. "But your life, your daughter, your . . . "

"Just figured you should know," she said. "And besides, what's that gotta do with two people likin' each other? I'm not talkin' 'bout love, darlin', it's less serious, like tonight, when sometimes, things just kinda happen."

"Tonight?"

"Honey, our meetin' here in this city, our gettin' together, there ain't no accidents in life," she said, smiling. "Just signs— and these are pretty good ones."

"What about me, don't you have questions?"

"You're also a chatty drunk," she answered with a laugh. "You don't remember what you told me, but you told me a lot."

"Oh," he said, as he wondered just what he'd said. "Ah, hmm, just what did I . . . never mind. And you, other than tonight, you don't say much about yourself."

"Told you enough," she said. "And the rest, maybe I'll tell you later."

Wynona leaned forward to kiss him and with that kiss she led him through the corridors of possibility and seduction. The two soon slid down and onto the floor, one body then the other, top-pling bottles, crushing plastic forks, mashing the remains of a chocolate birthday cake.

"Never mind," Rico whispered as they tipped over a half-filled bottle of expensive bourbon. "It's stolen."

In different states of dishevel, mess, and undress, they eventually rose and began walking slowly toward his mattress that served as his bed. En route, she ran her fingers up and down his spine, her fingers racing like a cellist's to hit exquisite high notes. He sighed and arched his back.

"Had a buddy, Okie cowboy named Jerome," he managed to say. "And he once told me that for every human situation, there was a country song that covered everything and that's why he never listened to nothin' else. No need to, he claimed."

"He's right."

Rico stepped back slightly to hold her with both hands at arm's length. "So, tell me what singer covers this, what song, 'Your Cheatin' Heart,' 'Help Me Make It Through the Night,' Hank, Crystal, Conway? What? Who?"

She didn't answer at first. Instead, she inched closer and began biting and licking first the top, then midpoint, then the base of his neck. She paused at his breastbone. "Hmm, s'pose that depends," she murmured.

"On what?'

She looked up at him and smiled. "On your point of view, darlin'."

*   *   *

March 23, 1974

It's the day after my birthday, and I'm just lying in bed, nursing a hangover (damn, even my knees hurt, a bad sign) and thinking about what's just happened.

Wynona just left. Part of me says I shouldn't go so fast, that I'm on some sort of rebound and that the best time to move is only after I've come to a full stop. That's good and probably wise, and it's easy to be so full of wisdom the morning after. But last night, when we made love, and she was on top and arching her body, I saw the stretch marks, not big, and the little pouch—the signs of past inhabitation, her prior (and current and complicated) life—that told me to slow down, blind spot ahead, only fools rushed in. Danger signs, I knew then and know now, but knowing they were there didn't stop me from staying hard and thrusting up as she grabbed me and pushed back down. We then talked a bit more, little things she hadn't mentioned before (she's working temps downtown, taking a class at Berkeley on the side). Thinking back, it was odd I'd never asked. Hell, I've never been to her place, don't even know where she lives other than it's someplace in the Castro.

Early this morning, maybe two, two thirty, she woke me for a second, kissed me on the forehead, and got up and got dressed. "Kinda busy," she said, as she walked out the door. "Call you later." Just like that.

I asked how she was getting home; the busses weren't running. She had a car, she said, which was also news to me. I didn't even know that about her.

That's just the way she is. I guess I'd better get used to it.

*   *   *

CHURCH STREET APARTMENT, CASTRO DISTRICT

Standing in front of her poorly lit doorway, the young woman fiddled for her key, which was quickly inserted into the door lock. Wynona had wanted to stay longer, but the two of them greeting the dawn seemed to her a form of surrender.

A jiggle and a quick turn to the right opened the door that led to her home, a ground floor studio in the heart of the Castro. It was a neat quiet building in a quiet district and, given the violence and anger of her past, she welcomed the change. Her neighbors, mostly gay, greeted her with a party and dinners and, in the beginning, even tried to set her up with other women.

"Look at you, honey," an old queen, the party's hostess, told her. "You're a perfect dyke, those muscles, umm, and I know you're into denial because I know there aren't any dykes in North Dakota. But I've got a leather vest that just might fit, it'll highlight those biceps and, oh God, those triceps. I'm panting for you and I don't even like women. You'd make such a great little man, you know, like one of those cuuute little Mexicans or Filipinos. Cuuute."

The old queen paused. "You know, it's got zippers and everything."

Wynona giggled and blushed, then flexed her bicep, which was leaner and more defined than those of the men in attendance. "I like dick," she replied in her Great Plains monotone.

"Me, too," the old queen said with a flick of her wrist, at which the other men joined in a "me, too" chorus, followed by a toast led by the queen. "To dick, then."

Wynona loved the Castro, loved her gay friends, and knew from grandparents and other elders that such people—double blessed, they were called—were special. The missionaries changed that, and young people her age now viewed them with derision. She didn't, though, because she'd listened to the elders; she'd heard the legends and the stories, and knew that in the old days, women, or men who wanted to be women, were holy. They played a role, an important one in the well-being of the tribe. In her tribe, women made the rules; they invoked the spirits. At least that's how she lived and was taught in a home where the old ways, tradition, still counted.

Her friends, though, weren't as lucky. She'd heard the talk at school or around the youth center, the common knowledge, how someone's dad tied one on, and "tuned up" someone's mom and, in her childhood, what had once been unthinkable, had become commonplace. "Indian love," they called it.

She understood the ideal, and its modern alcoholic and Christian patriarchal reality and corruption, a contrast driven home by Frank's blind, drunken rage. In the past, she'd have killed him and suffered no consequence. But that was then, not now. The tribal cops—all male, all Christian—would've been called, and everyone knew him. They'd have said old Frank, who wasn't even Mandan, didn't deserve this. He was a man, and his cop brothers and prosecutors and judge brothers would have banded together to hunt her down.

She knew if she'd stayed she'd probably have to kill him—she was traditional, it demanded no less—his recent good conduct aside. That would've unleashed the pack. So she came here—in part to spare him, in part to spare herself—to this city praised by all, where she should've been happy to be away from that past. Yet, despite the city's beauty and her comfort and peace in the Castro, neither was Indian. She dreamed of Indians; she daydreamed of home.

That's what drew her to her half-Indian lover, who knew so little of the side that mattered most to her. Still, she sighed, he wasn't brutal, even when he drank, and he fucked her well and somewhere in the back of his modern muddled brain, she imagined his grandmother mouthing words of advice in a language he'd never heard. At least that's what she hoped. Maybe not, at least not now, she sighed, but smiled at the thought of an act more immediate: more sex, great sex, maybe as soon as tonight.

In the dark she reached to turn on the light, but stopped. The room was warm, and she remembered turning off the heater. The dead air carried the scent of alcohol and cigarettes. The hair on the back of her neck stood up, as she fumbled for the door handle.

"I've been waiting, Nona," said a voice from a shadow seated near the window.

"It's you. How'd you get in?" she said, trying to keep her tone even.

"Open window," the shadow said as it raised a can to its lips. "Thought I'd surprise you, got in today. Where you been?"

"Out."

The shadow rose and took a tall male form. He walked forward and embraced her, smelled her scents, kissed her neck. "Been a long time," he murmured.

She didn't resist, but didn't surrender either. Her arms stayed stiff at her sides. "Frank."

He stepped back. "You, ah, smell funny, kinda feel funny, too." He paused. "Who, ah, who you been fuckin'?" he slurred.

"Better leave," she said calmly. Wynona reached for the door but was stopped by a slap that twisted her head and launched a chorus line of stars dancing only for her. She felt her legs give and knew she was falling.

"You fuckin' bitch, you dog in heat," he snarled, as he approached. "I come all this way . . . fuck you, just fuck you."

In the dark, her hands searched the table top and found their target, a half-inch thick glass ashtray. Suddenly, she stood up and rammed the ashtray upward and straight at the outline of his head. She turned quickly into the blow, a gift from her dad, a former boxer.

Nona felt the impact. She heard the crunch of bone. She was happy the glass didn't shatter. Frank grunted and fell backward.

Nona walked to the wall and turned on the light. He was dead, and she knew it, even before turning to look at his tear-filled left eye and at the blood dripping from the gash opened in the soft, sweet spot above the nose and between his eyebrows. Once, not too long ago in a cowboy bar just off the rez, she'd seen one man punch another, his thick strong right hand landing between the eyes. The victim died before he dropped. That night, she'd fully intended to do the same.

What next? Call the cops? All men, probably all Christian, she thought as she sat on the floor and filled her lungs with smoke. She reached for the phone. Her ashtray, her former deadly weapon, had returned to its intended use as she flicked ashes onto a spot now covered with blood.

She dialed a number she knew by heart. "Hey, darlin'," she said. "Gotta shovel?"

*   *   *

ROAD TRIP, SAN FRANCISCO TO MARKLEEVILLE, CA

It turned out he didn't have a shovel, but his manager did in the storage room. She didn't explain why she needed one—especially at that hour—such an odd request. Still, he rose and dressed warmly and walked down the three flights of stairs into the unheated basement and then, shovel in hand, he walked sleepy-eyed into the predawn chill. He shivered as he turned up his jacket collar and—shovel at his side, small knapsack at his feet—he watched his breath turn to vapor. He knew he must've looked odd, the sort that might attract a wandering cop.

Pack some clothes and bring some cash, she felt like going for a ride, she'd told him. Be by in twenty.

Nervously, he glanced at his watch. Fifteen minutes down, five to go, then four, then a glare of highbeams flashed on and off, on and off, and an old gold Pontiac slowed to a curbside stop. An automatic passenger's side window rolled down.

"Get in," she said.

Quickly he opened the door and slid in. "Damn, Wynona," he managed to say through chattering teeth. "This thing got heat?"

"No," she said, as the car crossed Market Street heading east. "Got coffee in the thermos," she said with a turn of her head that pointed at the back seat. "There."

He reached for the thermos, which was sticking out of a small duffel bag. He unscrewed the top and warmed his hands and lips on the escaping heat before pouring the coffee into the small plastic cup balanced between his knees.

"Better," he said, as he took his first morning sip. He turned to look at the driver. "Ah, where we goin'?" he asked.

"Headin' east," she said.

"Why?"

"Gotta take Frank home," she explained. "His tribe's in Nevada."

Gripped by a sudden panic, he quickly turned to look at the back seat. Maybe there was something he'd missed?

She chuckled. "Don't worry, he ain't there."

"Huh? You gonna pick him up?"

"No need."

"Well, whatcha mean?" he asked.

"He's in the trunk," she calmly explained as she slowed for a light.

"Huh?"

"Don't worry," she said. "He's dead." She gunned the car onto the Bay Bridge entry.

"Goddamn," he screamed. "You got a dead Indian . . . " He couldn't finish the sentence.

"Yeah," she said. "I killed him."

"Well, fuck me," he whispered, as he slumped in his seat. "That makes it a whole lot better."

"Yeah," she said, smiling at his reaction. "It's better."

*   *   *

March 24, 1974

As I'm writing this, Wynona and I are in this little motel somewhere near Reno. She's sleeping now, as she should, because killing a man can take a bit of energy.

How's that for irony and understatement?

It was a good thing I had some dirt on my supervisor, that I'd seen him one day with a pretty young clerk in flagrant violation of his vows to his wife, who runs the bakery and with whom he'd just purchased a new house that could, I'm sure, be split in half by a disapproving judge. I have to hand it to him, though, he's got some nerve. I made sure he saw me see him in the act, and since that time, I've had pretty much a free run at work in terms of schedules, days off and missing stock.

This morning was no different; I called him at the store; I

knew he'd be there because they were doing inventory. I told him an emergency had come up and that my father (I made the old jerk useful) had a stroke in Seattle. I said I'd be gone a week or two. No problem, he said, my job would still be there. I told him that with me gone, it would be easier to account for inventory. I don't think he appreciated the humor.

We just kept heading east on 80, past Vallejo, then Sacramento, then just this side of the Nevada state line. We got to Markleeville, south of Reno, about ten this morning, and scouted out a site. It's pretty desolate, pretty cold. She said she and Frank had been to Markleeville once before, after they'd first met in Minneapolis, and thought about settling here. She couldn't, she said, because she missed the Badlands, missed home.

Frank told her that all of his relatives had either died or moved away, and that nothing tied him to Markleeville. Shit, he said, maybe he'd grow to love the Badlands, too.

I asked her what was the difference between a rancheria and a reservation. She shrugged. "California thing," she said.

She picked a spot at the base of some foothills and said we should return later, after sunset. Until then we should go into town, grab a bite, check into a motel and catch some sleep.

We did all of that, with an hour or two in-between for some 21 and slots at one of the casinos, plus some nice bathtub play in the motel. Actually, the stopover at the tables paid for our room and then some. Wynona knows her cards and never gives a hint; she'd hit high, against the odds, and still beat the house. Spooky. Within fifteen minutes, she'd picked up an extra three fifty.

"A good sign," she said.

We got back to the spot outside Markleeville after seven, when it started to get dark and very cold. She got a flashlight and told me where to dig. The ground was hard, so hard I thought the shovel would break. But I was careful, worked slowly, and eventually managed to go down about three feet. At the same time, I could see Wynona lighting sage—it grows wild around here—and (she told me later) praying. She'd show up by the grave, then walk off again. Finally, the grave was ready, and she and I dragged the body, which had been wrapped in a blanket, over to the site and laid it to rest. I took out a flashlight and looked at Frank. He was young, maybe about my age, and kind of handsome. That, plus, he was in the bush, a brother in arms, no matter how odd the current circumstances. How'd it come to this? I almost felt sorry for him.

I filled up the grave, and covered part of it with some of the huge rocks and brush that were all over the place. When we were done, Wynona lit more sage over Frank's grave. Eyes closed, as still as a steel post, she prayed while I stood to the side.

Praying Indian way isn't me. I'd be faking it.

Finally, she stirred. "You're home, Frank, hope you find some peace," she whispered, as we turned toward the car.

*   *   *

ROAD TRIP, FROM RENO EAST

"Why can't we go back?" Rico asked. "Why do we have to keep goin'?"

"'Cause we have to," Wynona answered, as her eyes blinked at the sunrise glare. "'Cause we should, you should."

"Ah, come on," he complained. "I didn't mean it."

"Don't matter, you still did it."

"It was just a reaction, you know, that's all, and I'm sorry . . ."

"Sorry ain't good enough," she answered, as she pulled the old Pontiac into a rest area. "Fact is you killed a man . . . "

"But he caught me by surprise." He paused, agitated. "Shit, Nona, don't that count?"

"Shoulda let him be, he couldna hurt you," she said. "Shoulda just got in the car and drove off, I told you not to hit him, ennit."

He put his face in his hands. "But, you know, ah, when he was lying there in that grave, then suddenly, like some vampire or somethin', he began blinking, then he sat up, and . . . "

In his mind he could still see that moment, the highpoint of a string of moments, each one linked, more tense, more terrible than the other. He could see the first shovelful of dirt fall onto Frank's face, recall thinking that this end was a shame, such a shame, but for him, also very convenient. No more Frank, no more competition. Then, as particles lodged in the corner of Frank's right eye, he thought he detected a blink. No, he'd told himself, impossible, flashlight vision playing tricks.

So he continued shoveling dirt. But then another blink, then both eyes open, then Frank's struggle to rise.

He remembered raising the shovel to rekill the dead. Remembered, as well, was her scream saying "don't," and the feel of her clutching at his arm, and him shrugging and throwing her back in order to swing down at Frank's forehead as hard as he could. In his mind, he felt the impact, the collapse of bone, and heard again the death groan that sounded so much like those he'd heard outside of Hue.

"Nah, uh-uh," she answered. "You'd raised the shovel, and I told you to stop, to just let him be, this was a sign. Him still bein' alive wasn't an accident—his time hadn't come, and you looked at me, then looked at him, then you hit him anyway." She stared at her companion and shook her head. "Uh-uh," she said. "You didn't listen."

She paused. "You murdered him, pure and simple," she said. "There's a difference between killin' a man and murderin' him. I need help, sure, I wanted to kill him, but you need it more."

"Where we goin'?"

"To get some help."

*   *   *

March 26, 1974

Damn, I must've slept through all of Utah, a corner of Idaho, and most of Montana. Wynona's been driving for a good part of that way, doing ninety-five, often more, over flat, endless stretches, night or day, it didn't matter, the speedometer didn't move much.

I'd offered to drive, and actually did for a bit in Nevada, but she said I drove too slow—just like a city boy, always riding my rear view mirror, checking for the flashing light—but out here, the cops were few and the attitude was different. Pedal pressed fully to the metal was the rule, or get the hell out the way.

I'd have never thought this old bucket, its insides ragged and torn, could rip up the road like a Porsche. I wondered how it could sustain this pace. When I was awake, I just held my breath and kept my left arm draped over the seat, my fingers searching for any sort of grip. I just knew that in the coldest, most desolate spot, the engine would sputter, or its axel would break. Since I figured a breakdown or some horrible, bone breaking accident, was inevitable, I spent most of my time in denial by sleeping in the back seat. We'd passed miles of desolation and, the way my life has gone, I figured the old heap was just searching for that spot.

During all this time, she spoke twice. Once, she said, almost to herself, that she wished she had a gun. I asked why. She smiled and said that when she was a kid, she and her brother would cruise the highways late at night and shoot at signs. It was a good way to kill hours on the road.

Then, somewhere in Montana, in the middle of the night, she spoke again and told me a secret. The last time she was back home, Frank and his pals had rebuilt the engine, replaced the shocks, and driven from New Town all the way into Dickinson just to get some new Goodyear steel belteds, all four, all top of the line. It was early spring, and in Dakota, early spring means late snow. It was snowing that day, but not a blizzard, just enough to dust the roads and cover the spots of black ice, nature's tricksters that lured careless drivers into ditches and grilles coming at you.

Still, he'd made the trip to Dickinson, and returned that same day after sunset, right before a blizzard hit. She'd appreciated what he'd done. That was his gift, his way of apologizing, and it got him a night with her and a promise that she might think about it. That Frank, she said at the end of her story, was good when he was sober, but the problem was he wasn't sober enough.

She spoke in her usual monotone, a way of speaking that says that's the way it is, thought maybe you should know that. She didn't even glance my way for my reaction, like maybe I'd be mad that she had something good to say about her ex.

I have to admit, the comment made me uneasy, given what we've just done, and what I'm starting to feel for her. And sure, I have to admit, maybe I was a bit jealous when I heard her talk, although it's hard to be jealous of a dead guy. Still, Frank deserved his end—his shallow grave near Markleeville—and I don't feel one bit of shame for helping to stick him in his new and very shallow home, no doubt before his time. He should never have hit her. Maybe it's a learned thing, I don't know. I know that as mad as I've been—those days of rage and hopelessness—I never struck a woman. Maybe it's because Dad, for all his faults, never hit Mom. I never saw it, I don't do it.

It's an irony, though, about old Frank. Imagine surviving the bullets and bombs and the mines—ours as well as theirs—only to come home to get killed by an ashtray. Hope the coyotes don't dig his dead ass up.

*   *   *

ROAD TRIP, WEST OF BILLINGS

The old Pontiac, front windows open, cut through the night; its driver leaned forward, her brown eyes wide and focused on the dividing line and the headlights of oncoming big rigs, destination Boise, and later, Spokane. Wynona knew this road by heart, its turns and twists. She had a little more than half a tank. If the gas gauge was right, this meant two hundred miles, a bit more than two hours, maybe even less, if she really gunned it past the rare trooper drinking coffee, smoking cigarettes, and trying to stay awake.

She whispered a prayer, but not to a Christian god. In the mirror, she watched her lips move. In the mirror, she glanced at the object of her prayer, a man she cared for, maybe even loved. Rico was asleep, but she knew that sleep is sometimes the gateway to death, that in sleep things sometimes happen, and as she drove, she prayed this wasn't the case. But she felt it might be and, as her eyes welled up, her hands dampened and shifted on the wheel; her grip tightened, strangling the life out of something that wasn't even alive.

A hundred now, the speedometer read. She stepped harder on the pedal. Faster, she thought. Faster. She couldn't go fast enough.

She glanced back again. His eyes were partly open but he was still asleep. His lips were moving, as if in conversation, but he made no sounds. Go away, she thought. Go away. Go to your tribe, your ancestors. Leave the living alone.

In the mirror, his expression had changed. His eyes, still open, were frightened, uncomprehending, his face full of lines and deep furrows. His lips were still moving, but faster this time, though no words could be heard. She could feel his heartbeat, fast and frightened, like a flushed, hunted buck that had bolted into the open and would keep running, its killers in pursuit, until its heart stopped beating. Back home, she'd seen it happen and thought it might be happening now. Ahead half a mile was a rest stop. She sighed and released the pedal, then slowly tapped the brakes.

It was almost dawn—a good sign, a holy time. She needed to stop now. Otherwise, she knew she'd be bringing home her new lover's body, and that wouldn't do.

She pulled into a space on the edge, away from the street lamps over the small brick building housing restrooms and water fountains. Others were gathered there, couples and their half-awake children, solo travelers stretching and bending to shake off the night. She fished in her pocket and smiled. Still there, she thought, and walked away from the car to the farthest corner of the rest stop. There, among a small stand of firs, she faced to the east, toward the sunrise, and lit a small stem of sage she'd gathered near Markleeville. Eyes closed, she held the burning sage in one hand and coaxed with the other the smoke that purified and protected to touch and cover her head, her body, and her feet, front and back. She extended her arms and whispered a greeting to the sun, then

turned to the other three directions, before bending to leave a cigarette, its paper ripped open, atop which she placed the charred,
still smoldering stem.

She returned to the car and peered inside the rear window. He
was still there, still breathing, but also still trapped in his perilous,
fitful sleep. This time his eyes were closed and his lips were still,
but beads of sweat had begun forming on the left temple, the one
she could see. She imagined where he'd wandered, to what dangerous point his soul had strayed. She opened the rear door, then
reached into her pocket for another stem of sage. The tips of her
fingers told her there was one, a tiny one, and she sighed in relief.
Then she pulled it out and, one foot in, leaned inside the car—her
protection from any sudden breeze—while she lit the small leaves
of the nearly bare stem. As the smoke started to rise, she guided
the lit sage over his body, head to toe, while she whispered prayers
she'd learned as a child.

She hoped it would work, and maybe it would, but there was
no way to know. Glancing at the sun, which was higher now, she
knew she'd done her best, but knowing that brought no comfort.
She jumped in the car to resume her race home.

ROAD TRIP, JUST WEST OF DICKINSON, NORTH DAKOTA

Mouth foul, eyes full of crud, Rico finally woke up and, realizing
his state, took his sleeve to wipe first the eyes—and the oil that had
pooled in the pores of his face—then the corners of his mouth.
"Got any gum?" Rico mumbled, as he leaned forward and stared
into the rearview mirror.

"Damn, I look like shit, bad road food, or somethin'."

"Yeah," Wynona said. "Or somethin'." Through the mirror,
she watched him watching her. She saw his reflection slowly shake
its head as the corners of its mouth turned slightly upward.

"Yeah, that burger shack back in Nevada, knew somethin' was
funny, like they didn't cook the meat," he said. "Maybe bad mayo,
who knows?"

"Maybe," she said, as her eyes stayed focused on the road. "It's in my shirt pocket . . . "

"Huh?"

"Some gum."

"Oh yeah," he said happily, as he reached across to pull out a green stick and, as he did, the crook of his index finger paused to caress her right breast—through denim and thin cotton—and a nipple, formally dormant, now came to life. "No bra," he whispered. "Nice."

"Chew the damn gum," she said, her eyes still on the road. Through the mirror, she saw him lean back, unpeel wrapper and foil, then pop the stick into his mouth. He chewed hard, first one side then the next, like this was the required first step before moving on to other, more pleasant ones.

"Better," he said, as he clambered over the seat and sat next to her.

"Better," he cooed, as he kissed her right cheek, then targeted an earlobe with nibbles and gentle electric licks, then lower, the nape of her neck, for more of the same. His touch was soft, softer than any man's she'd ever known, and his softness weakened her.

"I'm driving," she said, her statement describing an act, which he knew was present tense and uttered not in protest, but because she thought she should. Undeterred, he lifted her shirt to lick and bite her belly with every intention of moving south.

"Hmm?"

"Nothing," she said softly.

*　　*　　*

March 27, 1974

After days and nights that never seemed to end, I finally talked Wynona into pulling over here, right in Dickinson. I'd told her we weren't racing through Baja, and did she remember she was driving a Pontiac? Then I added that this wasn't some sort of endurance test, and that whatever awaited us wherever the hell we were going, would still be there when we arrived.

She looked at me, her eyes bloodshot, and just nodded; we went straight to the motel yesterday morning, and haven't left yet. Although exhausted, we managed to hold off sleep for a precious, delicious moment . . . Our lovemaking was so imaginative, intense, and after we came, she just collapsed with her head on my chest. For awhile, we didn't speak, then I felt a moistness on my chest. I glanced down; both her eyes were brimming. I asked what was the matter. Tired, she mumbled.

Nona's curled up, as she's been since yesterday, back turned to me and sleeping like a cat. During the night, though, she thrashed about and when I awoke, she was talking, but not to me. Who was she talking to? I wasn't able to pick up too much of what she said, other than "it" would be okay. Then she nodded her head, curled back up, and hasn't moved since. I was tempted to wake her, but I figured that whatever was in the back of her mind needed to be brought out and played through, at least at some level, even if she forgets it the moment she awakes.

That's what I learned at the nuthouse. Dreams, the nutcase docs told me, even the most horrible, violent nightmares, were good, a way for the subconscious to release repression, otherwise too much pressure builds, too many hidden memories of things too awful to consciously revisit. It was the brain letting off steam. The nut docs said I should view dreams this way, that they couldn't kill me and weren't even meant to be literal. Dreaming, they said, was natural and often symbolic, and that even nightmarish scenes often stand for something else.

Dreams are a mechanism used by the mind to survive. I had to bring them forward and out in the open to integrate them, to become whole. Dreams can't kill the dreamer, the nut docs kept telling me. Damn, once I realized that, I was home free. I still dream, but when I do, it doesn't shake me, not even the dreams from the bush.

When I dream, and it's a bad one, I make myself a cup of coffee, then I try to recall every detail, to grasp what it is that my subconscious is saying, all the while realizing that everything I've done, I've had to do.

In daylight, over coffee, I've learned to stare that dream, that motherfucker, right in the eye and tell it to do its worst. Given what I've gone through, I'm clean. Through this post-dream process, I take away a dream's power to terrorize me or beat me into a puddle on the floor. Dreams are just symbols of the past. They have no power or reality of their own.

Wynona hasn't talked much about Frank, what she did to him. I see it as a righteous kill, a pure act of self defense. Still, it's got to be hard to accept that you killed someone you once loved, especially your spouse. I guess that right now she's just dealing with it through dreams. Maybe I should talk to her about that and tell her what I've had to go through. I know from my time at the nut house that some folks have a harder time with dreams than others, and those that do end up staying there.

I hope wherever we're going, someone can help her. I don't know much about Indians, but I know we're in the heart of Indian territory. Maybe a medicine man knows something that the nutcase docs don't.

Chapter Nine

Thick brown hands folded, eyes half closed, the old man sat quietly at his kitchen table; it was clean and bare except for a cup halfway filled with stale, black coffee and an ashtray full of matches and crushed butts. Except for his breathing, and an occasional blink of an eye, he was as still as the dark pine wall that surrounded him. He heard a car approach, then the door open, then footsteps —two pairs, he knew, drawing nearer. He began to stir. About time, he thought.

"Uncle Bernard," a young woman said.

He turned, just slightly, in the direction of the voice. "Nona," he said evenly. "I've been waitin'."

"I know," she said. "This is Rico."

"Hello," he said, and nodded in Rico's direction. The old man studied him, his dark eyes showing neither approval nor dislike. He then turned toward Wynona. Theirs was a wordless chat.

"Ah, Rico," she began slowly, "why don't you wait in the other room."

"Sure," he said, and walked slowly into the small adjoining space that served as the living room. It was late afternoon and, in

III

the Dakotas, a time when the cold comes quickly. He walked over to a potbellied wood stove in the corner and rubbed his hands over the flat surface. Warm, he thought, but not warm enough. Nearby was some dried, split wood.

"Go on and feed it if you like," Wynona said. He looked up. She and her uncle were quietly talking and—judging by the expression—a frown, a grimace, a dismissive movement of his hand—he knew they were talking about him. Wynona handed him a packet of tobacco, which the old man accepted. Rico saw Bernard, his face solemn, roll his eyes. He thought he heard him sigh.

Rico then turned to his task of stoking the fire. With a thick wooden stick, he carefully opened the hot stove door and slid in a piece of wood, tinder dry and quickly consumed.

Rico focused on rebuilding the fire; he tried to look busy, like that day in the bush when he was on point, and he knew in the way that men on the edge knew, that death was again near. His buddies had sworn by him. Rico, they said, could hear a bird blink. A sniper had marked him, was tracking him. But where was he? In the tree line on the horizon, or buried in the elephant grass nearby and to his right? Where?

So he just walked and listened, knowing the game that had to be played. The sniper wanted him, but he knew the sniper wanted the platoon more; a dead man on point was just one pair of eyes; the body would surrender more. On that day, his right ear had saved him, detecting an odd rustling in this dead afternoon air. It had come from the grass—a slight turn and a confirming corner of his eye glance. A glint. He hit the ground, scrambling for cover while screaming and pointing where the fire should go.

When the volleys finally stopped, the Marines pulled out the top half of the body of a girl—so young, not more than sixteen, seventeen max—and the shattered remains of her rifle. Young, he'd thought, impatient, careless. He'd imagined her waiting in the heat, just waiting, checking to see if her breathing was too loud. He thought that maybe she'd tightened—her muscles in painful rebellion—and she'd corrected, but had stretched too far. Who knew? He shrugged and walked on.

Here, away from the bush, he was relying on his right ear again, the one that had saved him, and while his intuition was conjuring the darkest images, his hearing was careening toward a wall of language that he couldn't understand. Wynona and her uncle were talking in Indian. And although he knew that words weren't all of communication, without them, he was left with grimaces and movements of the hand and an intuition filling quickly with dark images.

*   *   *

A gentle tap and a soft voice awakened him. "We have a lot of work to do," Wynona said softly. Rico had fallen asleep on the floor, as close as he could next to the potbellied stove. The fire, once raging, had long since died and, as he opened his eyes, he began to shiver.

"Damn," he said drowsily, as he shook off the chill, then blinked several times to make out the slender candlelit form of his lover. As Rico adjusted to the light, he could see she was barelegged and barefoot, and wearing a simple blue print dress.

She grabbed him by the elbow and helped him to his feet. "Over there," she said, pointing to the candlelit kitchen table and what appeared to be a bundle of red cloth.

"What?" Rico mumbled, as she guided him toward a chair.

"Prayer ties," she said, without further explanation. She raised a pair of scissors to the candlelight, then reached for a nearby tin of *Bugler* tobacco on which sat a roll of string, none of which he'd noticed at first. "Watch," she said.

"Prayer what?"

"Watch," she repeated. Without another word, she cut a corner of the cloth into a one-inch square and held it between her thumb and forefinger for Rico to examine. She then put a pinch of tobacco on the tiny section and rolled it, much like a cigarette, before tying both ends. "Your turn," she said.

"Why?" he asked, as he tried to stifle a yawn.

"Because it could save you," she said bluntly. "Each tie is a prayer, and you'll need every one of them."

Rico shrugged and, despite his skepticism, did as he was told. "There," he said when he was finished. Rico smiled, satisfied he'd finished what she'd asked. "Now, baby," he purred. "Let's you and me go find someplace to sleep and, well, you know." Hearing those words and their lovely implications, Rico could feel himself harden.

"Not so fast," she said in a cold water tone that shriveled his ardor. "You need about 349 more ties, or about six feet to tie together and form a circle."

"Wynona," he protested, as she began walking away.

She glanced at a white plastic clock on the wall. "Almost seven," she said.

"How long," he sputtered, then surrendered his protest when he saw her standing with her hands on her hips—a woman who wouldn't be moved. He tried again. "Uh, how long this gonna take?"

"Four hours," she said as she stifled a yawn. "Maybe more."

"Huh?"

"It takes that long."

"Where you goin'?" he asked, trying hard not to whine.

She laughed. "I'm still tired from the drive, so I'm goin' back to bed," she said, still laughing. "Like any normal human being."

*　　*　　*

Eyes closed, Rico leaned back in his chair until he heard his neck crackle and pop from his straight line stretch that veered left, then right. Satisfied, he then sat up and extended his arms to make small circles with his wrists, all the while opening and closing thumbs and fingers numb from the task he'd somehow managed to complete. He looked at the table and the now completed circle. In the hours it took to cut and bind, he used an old Marine Corps trick by disconnecting himself from the tedium and running a film of lovelier scenes. He knew that for Wynona and her uncle, making this circle had some connection to their, not his, beliefs, but in his head, as he snipped and tied square after square, he was viewing another reel—of him and Wynona nude or partially clothed in as yet untried positions. That kept him going through this time that seemed without end, as did his hope that by completing the circle she'd finally give him a taste.

Wynona's voice halted his reverie. "He's waiting outside for us," she said flatly. "Keep the boxers, get rid of the rest." She handed him a thin cloth robe and a pair of rubber slippers.

"Huh?"

"Put them on," she said sternly. "We're going to the sweat."

"Why?" he asked, his tone skeptical. Somewhere in the past, he'd heard or read about sweats, maybe in *National Geographic*— the Japanese did it, same with the Russians and Swedes, cold weather folks all. It was invigorating, a healthful, social, sociable custom. He hadn't known that Indians did it, and he wondered why her sudden insistence. Still, he did as he was told, and quickly shed his pants and shirt.

"Why?" she repeated his question. "Because you need to be pure, you need to be strong."

"For what?"

"For what you've done, for what you'll be facing," she said, and looked at the lines of confusion etched upon his face. "Look," she said impatiently, as she took his arm. "He'll explain." She opened the door to the dark, thick and still and broken only by the dim light of a fire in the distance. "Let's go."

He hesitated. "What's that?" he said, pointing to the glow.

"The sweat lodge, the first step."

"To what?"

"Your healing."

"For what?"

"Look," she said angrily. "Do you want to keep living?"

There was something about her tone, about her. It made no sense, but neither did his time in the bush. His intuition told him she was right; he had to go. In the bush, intuition had saved him. Maybe it was working to save him now. But save him from what? No matter, that quiet little voice told him he needed to go, and so he would, goddamn the logic or its lack.

He was almost out the door, when she pulled him back by the sleeve and held him for a moment. Fiercely, she pulled him onto her. "We'll make it," she whispered.

Make what? he wondered.

*   *   *

He wasn't sure what he was supposed to get from the sweat, but at the start, and to be polite, he practiced the art of mime. He prayed as Bernard had told him to, and followed Wynona's lead, closing his eyes when she closed hers. If she looked up, he did too. Somehow, he'd managed to last through all four rounds, the rounds representing the directions, each round growing hotter. By the third round, he was panting and wishing there were fewer directions, maybe two at the most.

By the fourth round, he was just hugging the ground, looking for a cool spot on the flattened grassy floor. Head spinning, he'd abandoned any pretense at prayer, and was just hoping the ceremony would end before he fainted or died.

He made it, but just barely, as both Wynona and her uncle had to help him from the lodge. But on the way back to the house, he began to feel stronger as the cool air met his hot, wet skin, that gentle collision awakening him, invigorating him, spurring recall, however briefly, of the strange and faint sound of women's voices speaking, but not in English.

Must've been the heat, he thought.

At Bernard's, they sat for a meal, a simple one of dried corn soup cooked with dried venison. To his surprise, he ate his portion quickly and, just as quickly, asked for seconds. In his rush Rico didn't notice Bernard pour a spoonful of soup into a small porcelain bowl on the edge of the table, nor did he hear Bernard say that this portion was for the ancestors. Bernard shrugged when his words weren't heard—but Rico didn't notice that either. He didn't see Bernard, bowl in hand, leave the room for the potbellied stove where the fire was roaring once more. "Ancestors, please help," Bernard whispered, as he emptied the soup into the stove.

Rico, his head buried in his bowl, missed everything important. But he was full and feeling better, much better and, at the moment, that was all that mattered.

The sound of a door slowly opening, then closing, and Wynona's voice broke the silence. "He's waiting outside," she said simply. "Bring the prayer ties, you'll need them."

*   *   *

It was still dark and quite cold when Bernard and Rico began silently walking, guided only by the old man's small flashlight. For the first five minutes or so, they walked over land that was grassy and flat, before gently sloping upward. A stroll, Rico thought. A snap.

Twenty minutes later, the terrain changed again to add several degrees of difficulty. Rico knew they were now on a trail, a steep, rocky one that punched at his feet through the worn-out soles of a ragged pair of black Converse sneakers. Rico slipped twice, the second time cutting his hand and knee, before finally reaching their destination. Christ, what he'd do for love, Rico thought, as he—now hot, hurt, and out of breath—set foot upon a smooth, level surface.

"Be still," Bernard said in English, a language that twisted his tongue.

Bernard and Rico were standing in the center of a gray clay butte. Dawn was just beginning to break, and for the first time since the meal at the house, Rico saw Bernard clearly. Over his thick parka, the old man had donned a buffalo robe, the sight of which was oddly disturbing, the sacred vestments of an intangible realm which, in turn, conjured in Rico memories of recent warmth and comfort, of hot corn soup, then a tangent of thought that drifted to a question: an Indian last supper? He shuddered. But whose?

Slowly, Rico began turning in a full circle. To the west, a small cluster of houses, their lights flickering on. They'd come from that cluster, he thought, less than two miles away. Wynona was there now; he wished he was with her, his body pressed against hers. Cold at the start of this journey, he was no longer that and, in the dark, had shed his bulky outer coat and two pairs of gloves that Wynona had given him. They were now lying in a pile beneath some brambles by the edge of the butte.

Bernard pointed with his eyes at the pile. "Rico," he said, using the younger man's name for the first time, "Get 'um."

The sound of his name, of familiarity, comforted Rico as he searched that dark, serious face, hoping that maybe in the corner of an eye, or in an upturn of his mouth, he'd find more traces of comfort.

He'd survived the bush, its noise, death, and fear, but those sorts of dangers he understood. They were tangible, expected. The enemy could be killed. Standing here, though, in the cold stillness, where he heard himself breathe, he wasn't as sure. In combat, he'd never run, but he wanted to run now. Bernard had just used his name, a small comfort; that was a start, but Rico needed more.

"Ah, Uncle Bernard," he began.

"Bring 'um," Bernard repeated flatly, cutting him off. He pointed toward the pile.

"Okay," he said, and complied.

"Put 'um there," Bernard said, and pointed to a spot roughly in the center of the butte. "Stay there now."

Bernard approached Rico and, using the younger man's body

as a windbreak against an early breeze from the east, he bent slightly to light a long stem of sage. "We'll smudge," he said, and cupped his hands to guide the smoke over himself, then over his companion. During the ceremony, he whispered prayers in Indian.

"Follow me," Bernard said in English, as he walked toward the sunrise. He looked straight ahead and resumed praying. Rico resumed not understanding.

"Indian?" Rico asked.

"Mandan," Bernard mumbled, without turning.

Facing the sun, Bernard, eyes closed, cupped his thick hands and protected the small flame. In the same fashion, he then turned toward the other three directions and, after the fourth, he reached into his jacket to pull out a small leather pouch from which he took a pinch of tobacco. He knelt on one knee to place it carefully on the ground, atop which he lay the remains of the still smoldering stem. He rose and faced Rico, who could see that both of the old man's eyes were brimming and a tear, building near the bridge of his nose, was beginning to fall. It streamed down his cheek, and others quickly followed, but he did nothing to stem the flow. "Powerful," he said.

"Rocks," Bernard said, and pointed to clusters that dotted the butte. "Bring 'um here."

Rico then set out to gather the rocks, all the while keeping an eye on Bernard, whom he knew was watching him closely. Bernard signaled with his hands that they should be brought to him and placed at his feet, which Rico did accordingly. "More," was all he said.

Rico kept bringing rocks of all sizes until Bernard, satisfied, looked at him and nodded. The younger man sighed and mopped his brow which, despite the cold, had begun to glisten. Bernard tapped him on the shoulder, a sign that said watch him. He pointed at the rocks, then each hand moved in an arc, two opposing arcs, joined at the bottom and top to form a circle. Clear enough, Rico thought, he wants a circle, but where. He glanced at Bernard, who was pointing to the center of the butte.

"Rico."

He looked up. Bernard's hands, his fingers straight and extended, were making the same circular motion again and again, starting at the top then joining at the bottom, the points of his two index fingers pressing together for emphasis. Bernard was standing toward the east, his back to the sunrise. Rico blinked.

"A circle," Rico blurted. "Don't leave an opening."

Through the glare, Rico saw the old man's head bob. He thought he might have even seen him smile, but the moment didn't last. Bernard turned quickly and, as Rico returned to arranging the rocks, all he could see was Bernard's back and thin wisps of smoke. All he could hear were prayers offered in a language he couldn't understand.

*   *   *

The circle was done, at least for the moment, and Rico glanced at the old man for approval. Another quick bob told him it would do and Rico smiled and dabbed at the moisture on his brow. A flicking hand, bending inward at the wrist, beckoned Rico forward, and he walked toward Bernard until he was facing him, maybe two feet away. Bernard extended his arms and grasped Rico firmly on both shoulders. His eyes told Rico's eyes to look into his, to not waver or become distracted.

"English is hard," he said slowly. He then began speaking softly in Mandan. Slowly, as he continued speaking, Bernard's hands fell away, and his left reached into a coat pocket to pull out a small leather pouch, which he balanced in the palm of his hand. The old man opened the pouch and placed his right index and middle fingers, wetted with saliva, inside. He withdrew his fingers, which were now coated with a mash of charred wood, flowers, and clay and began spreading it on Rico's face.

"Paint," Bernard whispered. "Look fierce." He then resumed speaking Mandan.

For the next few minutes, Bernard carefully painted Rico's

face, sometimes taking time to study his work—from this angle or that—until he just stopped. "Good," he said in English, before stepping back.

He returned to speaking Mandan, his words punctuated by movements of his hands, which Rico followed. Some of them told him to close the circle from within with the prayer tobacco ties, while two hands extended, each index finger pointed, said he had to stay there. Rico nodded.

"Once you're inside, you can't leave," Bernard said in halting English. He paused. "Do you need anything?"

Rico shook his head. "No," he answered. "How long I gotta stay?"

Bernard held up four fingers.

Rico chuckled. "Oh, four hours?"

Bernard shook his head, a simple nonverbal reply. Rico felt his jaw drop. "Days?" he sputtered. "Four days?"

This time, Rico saw Bernard's confirming nod, and a stare so focused, dark, and fierce, it told him not to argue, don't even complain. As he resumed speaking Mandan, Bernard took off his buffalo robe and motioned for Rico to turn around; he felt the weight of the garment as Bernard draped it over his shoulders. A nudge at his elbow spun him around to face the old man, who then handed him a large bunch of sage and several lighters and matchbooks. Next he made lighting motions—thumb moving up and down, index finger and thumb striking against a palm. Rico nodded; he understood.

Bernard then folded his hands together, fingertips pointed and joined, and looked skyward—a Christian sign for a Christian man. Damn, Rico concluded, Bernard must think he's dense. "Pray hard," the older man said in English. "The Creator, the ancestors."

Bernard then reached into another leather pouch, a longer one, and pulled out a feather. He handed it to Rico. "My dream," he said, and sadly shook his head. "The eagle is very strong," he said, before beginning an elaborate pantomime, which started with

Bernard pointing to the center of the circle. Outside the perimeter, he adopted different poses, human and animal, that Rico could make out—a beautiful woman shaking her hips, beckoning; a dear and welcoming friend; a wolf or a bear determined to scare him away. Bernard just shook his head, his right index finger thrusting at the center of the circle.

"Stay," he said. "Stay."

"Your dream?" Rico asked.

Bernard slowly shook his head. "Not good," Bernard answered in a tone that made the younger man shudder. He sighed, then patted Rico's shoulder, before pointing first to Rico, then to the circle. "Go in now," he said quietly.

Once inside, Bernard's hands instructed him to take the last step. "Time to close," Rico mumbled, as he carefully spread the prayer ties in a circle with himself in the middle. Although he still wasn't sure what he was doing on the butte, he figured Wynona or Bernard or someone would eventually explain it. For now, he focused on the immediate—just like in the Marines. That meant doing whatever he was doing right—no questions asked, no answers given, until later.

Again, he looked at Bernard for approval. The old man watched him, then, without comment, began slowly walking away.

Task complete, Rico separated a stem of sage and lit it. He cupped the smoke and, as he'd seen, guided it over himself. He wasn't sure what he was praying for and started with simple things, that he not be harmed as he sat here two miles away from the woman he loved. Praying was foreign to him, but he still hoped he'd done it right.

At the edge of the butte before the start of the trail, Bernard turned to look. "Good start," he mumbled, knowing full well that here, on this butte and with this ceremony, a good start was sometimes just not good enough.

*   *   *

"How's he doing?" she asked, her tone anxious.

He shrugged. "Started out good," he answered in Mandan. He walked slowly to the kitchen where she was sitting and pulled up a chair. "But, you know, my girl, it will be hard, I just can't promise."

"But he's Indian," she protested. "His mother's side, Yakima . . ."

Sadly, he looked across the table and answered with a tired laugh, soft and gently mocking, unintended. He had to turn away. "Ah, my girl, if that's what you want to think, and if it makes it easier, I guess there's no harm." Then he paused. Maybe he'd been too harsh. When her father, his younger brother, had died, he'd practically raised her. He'd known her since her first breath, had heard her first word.

"It's more than blood," he said, his tone more careful now. "It's belief, a belief you and I've been raised with over years. We've practiced it, we've lived it. It's our nature to think this way, to believe. It's as real as our skin. He hasn't had that chance. And now this same belief, this way of thinking, he must accept, absorb over hours. I know what he's done, I've seen it—the war, the violence, Frank's murder. He's not entirely to blame. Your friend just isn't whole. Still, he killed a man and he must recognize and be sorry for his role in that, but now I know his heart. He lies, even to himself, and lying is so easy, so enticing, and if, in the beginning, it succeeds, it can become a way of life. I know, I've read him and he plays games to escape the horror, and I know his past is something he didn't ask for, didn't deserve. But telling the truth is still better; at the worst, you die once. Your friend has already died several times."

He looked away. "You want to know if he'll make it. I don't know," he said softly. "You know, I know his people, the Filipinos. My unit went to the Philippines in 1944. A tragic, devastated place, but they fought the Japanese bravely and afterward, they tried to rebuild and they tried to pray. It saddened me."

"What did, Uncle?"

"The prayer."

"Why?"

"They'd forgotten how to pray."

"Why?"

"Too many churches, too many priests," he said, and frowned at the memory. "Like us."

He then gestured with his hands, fingers spread, up and down, a visual syncopation with his words. "For your friend to survive, he has to unlearn, to forget, to pray as we do, as his ancestors once did. It will be difficult to strip that away in such a short time."

He knew what he was saying. He understood its impact. Bernard needed a break but, more important, Wynona did, too, and he reached into his pocket and pulled out a packet of tobacco and some papers. As he rolled a cigarette, he pondered what to say next.

"My girl, I did my best, but healing is a hard ceremony, very hard," he said haltingly. "The tricksters, his demons, they'll all be waiting."

He looked at her, and the tears—just starting to fill her eyes and break her heart—also began breaking his. He had to look away.

"But Uncle," she said, her voice unsure and scouting a barren verbal landscape for hope, any sign, however tiny. "You've healed others . . . "

He sighed. "Indians," he said, as the fingers of his left hand drummed the table top. "Believers like us." He watched her shoulders sag, her eyes drop.

"I'll go back, my girl," he said, his fingers still drumming. "I'll check on your friend."

She managed to smile, a tiny upturn, the most she could muster. "Thank you, Uncle," she said softly. "When?"

"After sunset," he replied, then added: "It's very dangerous then. He'll be hungry and weak. He'll need me."

*   *   *

He'd set out early enough, an hour plus before sunset, enough time, he figured, for a sixty-one-year-old man to reach a place and keep a promise. Before leaving the house, he'd grabbed his old felt hat and a long black scarf—protection against the cold on the butte.

As he approached the trail leading to the butte, he began to quicken his pace. His mind started churning, images flashed and dug into his body a deep pit filled only by despair. By the foot, by the yard, he forced his old, heavy legs to move him faster, to somehow mock the tethers of gravity and age. He prayed for speed, he prayed also for protection, not for him, but for his niece and for the young man he was going to see. The grade increased midpoint to the crest; he saw her tears and said a prayer. He leaned forward and pumped harder. The trail narrowed; he felt the young man's fear. Another prayer, this one not to stumble, to just keep going.

Finally, he reached his destination, the edge of the butte, and managed to walk a few steps before falling face down onto its cold clay surface. The young man was still there, still in the circle, but standing with his back turned, his hands outstretched and moving, as if in conversation. With his sixty-one-year-old arms, the old man pushed himself up, but his triceps began to quiver, then collapse, as he tried to raise himself once more.

Head spinning, again he felt his arms give way as he gasped for breath—like a bass flopping on a mud bank, he thought. He wanted air, the air on this butte, but just like a tease, it seemed to be dancing away, to fill leaves or lungs other than his. He could feel his chest tighten and could hear his own gasps for air. His eyes blinked—darkening when open, dark when closed. But in his mind's eye, he saw the younger man begin moving toward the edge of the circle; he saw him raise his foot and knew its downward movement would put him outside. He wanted to scream, to stop him, but couldn't. Desperately, he managed to whisper a fragment of a prayer.

"All my relations."

Sixty-two years, he thought, a nice round number, was just a month away. He liked the thought, but knew he wouldn't make it. He could feel his body shutting down, growing numb, unresponsive. Once more, his eyes blinked—dark when closed, dark when open.

*   *   *

"Marites," Rico whispered, as he stumbled through the dark. Arms outstretched, he'd broken the circle, reaching to grasp a woman he'd loved, still loved. Logic had told him this couldn't be, not here on this butte. How did she find him? He knew she'd left, but had hoped she'd return. That hope had faded as the nut house days raced to fill full calendar pages until one night he awoke in tears. The tears, he thought, told him the truth—she'd never return.

But here she was. Smiling and apologizing for being gone too long. He heard her voice, that convent school undulation that he'd mocked and missed and yearned to hear again. And tonight he had, though, as he told himself, he really hadn't, at least at first. When she first appeared, he just stood up and stared as his mind raced through a checklist of logic—hunger, heat, exhaustion, sorrow—that could trick the mind.

She wasn't real, he thought. He'd forgotten his meds, maybe that explained it. But the longer she spoke, the more he believed, and the less he recalled another voice telling him to beware, to stay at all costs within the circle.

"Come," she told him. "Come back to the city, back to our life."

Back to our life, he thought, as he stepped outside the circle to the sound of laughter, a man's voice. He shook his head. Impossible, he thought, he was imagining. He was alone.

"Back to our life," four words that enchanted and lured, then trapped him. Four words that made him forget his new life and other words said to another who loved him just as much. Had he been Indian, he'd have seen through the ruse. He'd have seen an open palm and bent, nimble fingers—a trickster's hand—inside the hand puppet vision, moving limbs and lips to make the right gesture, to say the right words.

Failing that, he was now on his own, unprotected in the hostile dark. Marites was gone, an imagining, he told himself, brought on by exhaustion and thirst. He was outside the circle, and was glad of that; he'd cast off Bernard's words and their shadows of gloom, and wondered why he'd even consented to this ritual, this superstitious ordeal, that had no place in his past and, he decided, would have none in his future. The answer was clear before the question was even asked. He'd done it, he knew, for Wynona; she was convinced, she'd insisted.

The way he now saw it, he'd just gone along. He'd tried it on, it didn't fit; he had Indian blood, sure, but that was it. He shrugged —no harm, no foul. He would tell her he loved her and would respect her beliefs, but his didn't include cold spring visits to North Dakota, or sitting on a butte in the middle of a rock circle. He practiced saying it aloud, then added he was proud of his Indian side. He'd study the history, part of which was his; he'd embrace Native causes. He just couldn't believe the way she and her uncle did. He smiled; it sounded reasonable. Surely, she'd understand.

But first he had to get to Bernard's house, maybe two miles away. During the day, he knew that the distance between the circle and the start of the trail was fifty yards, more or less. But in the dark, when the moon was covered with clouds, human sight was useless. He walked slowly, a half step at a time. He counted them, eighty half steps, maybe forty yards, but so hard to tell.

Conscious of the edge, he then slowed even more and took smaller steps, then dropped to his hands and knees. One hand then the other pushed out to feel for the end of the butte and the start of the trail. He reached out again and again, confident he could feel his way to the point where the butte ended and the trail began. It was an awkward motion, eventually tiring, then painful, but all he could find was smooth, flat surface. For how long he'd searched, he had no idea. Finally, knees and back aching, palms turning raw, he sat and drew his legs up and toward him. It was a windless night—for that he was glad—but still so cold he could feel his teeth chatter.

Huddled within himself, he suddenly longed for the thick buffalo robe, but had no idea how to find it. He needed light, and glanced skyward—the moon was still hidden. Suddenly, he cursed himself, his stupidity, and reached into his coat. Matches, he thought, he had them, and lighters, too. He tried the matches first. He had a book left. He struck one, then another, but all suffered the same result—a brief flicker, quickly extinguished. He tried cupping one hand and placing it close to his body. He tried shielding the tiny flame, but the change in position made no difference. Next were the lighters. From his pocket, he pulled out three and tried them all, shaking them when they failed, then trying again only to find more failure. They seemed to follow the same sad script of sparks and promise, but no lasting flame. He shook his head. Just a run of bad luck, he told himself, nothing more or less.

The search for the trail and now, his dashed hopes for light, had joined to drain him of his last reserves. He was too tired to walk, too sore and tired to crawl. Sleep, he knew, was dangerous and, at the start, he fought its pull. He slapped his jaw and ran in place—tricks, he knew, that might fend off sleep and keep him safe. Soon, though, he stopped feeling the sting, while his legs grew too heavy to move. Helpless, he surrendered and lay on the ground, both hands between his legs, his body curled into a ball. The wind, which had waited until then, now howled at his back, its chill slicing through his clothes to tickle every nerve. He didn't know when dawn would come, but when it did, he hoped he'd be there to see it.

*   *   *

Startled, Rico sat up. From a fitful sleep full of hypothermia dreams, he'd awakened to a sound, but just what, he wasn't sure, other than that it was sharp and loud, a single discordant note in a vacuum. The noise was so loud, his eardrums still rang. While seated, he spun in a circle, trying to find its source hidden in a color starting slowly to change from black to the darkest shade of gray. Patience, he told himself, he'd survived the night. Eventually, the gray would lighten and permit him to see the contours of the butte and the way off, the way back to the house where Wynona was waiting. Dawn would eventually come—a small comfort for the present—as a sudden gust numbed him.

If only he could just hang on; it couldn't be much longer. Slowly, he forced himself to stand and stretch cold, stiff muscles. Then, he began to shadow box, slowly at first, then faster until both arms were pumping like pistons, throwing hard punches as fast as he could for as long as he was able. It was, he imagined, the last thirty seconds of the last round, with the fight even and reckless aggression the factor crowning the winner. In his mind, he also saw his opponent, a collage of enemy faces from Seattle to Hue to California.

Steal the round, he told himself as, eyes closed and teeth gritted, he punched furiously. Sway the judges, break a sweat, see the dawn.

He slowed only when his shoulders felt on fire, and a film of perspiration began coating face, forehead, and neck. Satisfied, he resumed slowly probing with his right, while shuffling around in a small, tight circle. The gray was lighter now, just a bit, but not light enough to see the edge of the butte. Worse, the wind was starting to dry his sweat. Knowing this, he doubled his pace. He danced and shuffled—stutter steps and quick, sudden pivots—while his hands began flying in hard, fast ten-punch flurries.

This time, he told himself, he'd just keep going; he'd mock exhaustion and pain. Shadow boxing, he'd greet the dawn.

As he moved and spun, he suddenly saw the outline of someone, likely a man, judging by its stocky silhouette. He was standing maybe thirty yards away in the dark gray distance, facing him. His hands were at his sides. Rico stopped suddenly and stared, then bent to catch his breath. He rested his palms on his knees, while never taking his eyes off the human outline.

"Who's there?" Rico asked, as he gulped in air.

The outline said nothing; it made no move.

"I said, who's there?" Rico repeated in a rougher, more demanding tone. "You deaf, man?" he added, hoping to prompt a reaction. Again, there was no reply, just silence, but that was reply enough.

He straightened up, just in case, and placed his lead foot, his right, slightly forward. Next, he shrugged his shoulders and shook his wrists and hands. Loose, he thought. Fast. Just in case.

In any fight in the ring or in the street, he'd learned to always strike first. But the ring and the street weren't the same; he'd seen boxers lose outside the ring because they didn't understand the difference. On the street, there were no rules, no referee, no judges' scorecards, just like here on this butte; he knew too well that street fights never went the distance; the winner walked away, the loser often didn't. This would be a street fight, not sport, and he was getting ready. In an eyeblink, he could shift from apparent calm—like quiet conversation designed to lull—to a fast-moving attack in the form of hands and feet and, upon drawing closer, sometimes elbows and knees and once, a head butt. He smiled faintly at the memory of the head butt—so unexpected, so effective—an impromptu surprise even to him. He'd delivered it at close range because he was pinned against the wall of a downtown Stockton bar. The unorthodox blow splattered the bridge of his opponent's nose and ended the fight.

"Come on closer," Rico said, his tone deceptive, inviting, and get in range, motherfucker, he thought, as he shifted into position, checked his balance and flexed his wrists. If the outline accepted his invitation, he could check his hands and any weapons they might be hiding. Better yet, he'd be walking onto Rico's sucker punch, a simple lesson in physics pitting forward movement, care-less and unguarded, against coiled, focused, and explosive energy. In Rico's experience, one-punch energy always won. He rolled his neck and heard it crack, a good, relaxing sound. He was ready to fight, less so for what happened next.

"Rico," a voice said in a tone both strange and familiar. Rico whirled around, not sure of the source. Logic told him it must have come from the outline, now more distinct as the minutes crept closer to dawn. Yet, he just couldn't be sure; his name had seemed to float to him disembodied, then descend from all points and from no point at all. His spoken name came in a tremolo form with no direct line between sound and source. In the bush, he'd developed his hearing and could trace sounds, especially those out of place; he could pinpoint direction. Here, that skill failed him.

Get a grip, he told himself, as he stared at the outline. Odd sound aside, he knew it had to be the source. To believe otherwise would be to accept the unthinkable—that he hadn't just imagined Marites, that her appearance wasn't just a product of hunger and fatigue, that he'd entered a world he couldn't understand. In the moments after he'd broken the circle, he'd explained away his lover's appearance and was satisfied. He didn't want a new expla-nation now.

Rico began to get angry, convinced that the silent, still silhou-ette, now adding colors and texture, had somehow distorted his voice. He was just playing games, Rico thought, ventriloquist tricks.

"Motherfucker, quit fuckin' with me," Rico screamed angrily, as he opened and closed his hands. The outburst comforted him.

Suddenly, the outline moved; right hand extended, index fin-ger wagging, it beckoned Rico to come forward. Rico blinked and stared again. A finger still beckoned. At first, he'd wanted the sil-houette to come to him, to enter his trap. For Rico to move forward meant worrying about other things, like balance and position. Too much movement meant risk. Still, he took that first step to break this maddening impasse. All he wanted was to find the trail and leave this butte; if he had to go through someone—this silent, mysterious doorman—he would.

Slowly, carefully, he took another step, more a half step really. He could whip flesh and bone, any size, any form, he reminded himself, and that was all that faced him now. As he drew closer, the form in front of him slowly began to take shape, to turn into a man and show details like his height (slightly taller than him) and weight (heavier). Solid, Rico thought, and noticed next his thick shoulders and big, powerful hands, like Sonny Liston's—the sort that could squeeze or pummel a man to death. His face, though, Rico still couldn't see, even as he drew closer.

Rico might have pondered more carefully this oddity, but he had other, more pressing concerns. He'd fought men like this before, big-browed neanderthals genetically blessed with thick bones. They were slow but tough, hard on the hands, and very hard to knock out. He was recalculating his offense—five punches now, not one or two—to be thrown before those anvils at his wrists could be raised in anger.

Ten yards away, and Rico still couldn't detect any movement by the outline. He slowed for a second, cutting his already short stride by half. He could now see part of his face—the eyes, the shape of his nose—while an old style felt hat, its brim pulled low, and a long black scarf covered the rest.

"Who are you?" Rico demanded, as he inched a step closer. There was neither reply nor movement. "I said, who are you?" he repeated with all of the menace he could put into his voice.

Then came the sound of laughter, loud and mildly mocking and, like before, the sound seemed to float disembodied then descend from all points and from no point. Rico stared at the still, silent man and saw not a twitch, not even the blink of an eye. "Stop that," Rico howled at the man, although his howling hid a nagging fear telling him his anger might be misdirected. "It's your goddamn tricks, you motherfucker," he sputtered. "That's all . . ."

Like all humans, Rico was a creature of habit, one of which was when cornered, attack. On this butte, hemmed in only by sound and space, he was cornered.

Rico rushed forward, oblivious to balance and position, factors that once were important just minutes before. Position and balance no longer mattered, or at least he wasn't thinking about them as he closed within range, his left hand drawn back until launched at a target that showed two eyes and part of a face. Easy, Rico thought, he's still not moving, not even blinking. At the last split second, he closed his left fist tight, anticipating the crash of knuckles upon bone. He hoped his slender wrist, his weakest point, would stay steady and survive the pain he knew would race from hand to elbow.

That pain never came, but another one did, as Rico tumbled forward and to the ground, screaming and holding his left shoulder, its muscles pulled beyond tensile capacity. Ever the fighter, and even as he screamed, he looked around, unable to understand how he could've missed. He searched the butte, now in first light. His target was gone.

Slowly, he rose to his feet, his curses and moans filling the cold morning air, but not enough to block other sounds, tremolo ones, of sorrow and mourning which, like before, seemed to float before descending. Rico shook his head, but forced himself to listen. He was hearing women's voices, not speaking English, but not Mandan either. He'd heard this language before. Maybe at the sweat, or was it in Yakima so many years ago?

Suddenly, he began to recall sitting with the old women at night, and listening to them talk, but not in English. He was intrigued by these different sounds and would try to repeat their words, his lips forming in the way theirs did, those young boy efforts done to encouraging murmurs and peals of gentle laughter. He hadn't thought of the old women in years. Yet, what he was hearing now sounded like the voices and the tones he'd heard then, but so much sadder. Their sorrow touched him, and he had to shake his head.

Nah, he finally told himself, and laughed. Too strange, too goddamn strange.

With his good right hand, he pushed himself to his feet. His left arm hung limply at his side. He could see the start of the path and began walking toward it, but was stopped by the sound of his name.

"Rico," the voice said in a tone both clear and familiar. It came from behind him.

"Bernard?" Rico was relieved. Wynona's uncle had finally come to check on him. Good thing, too, he thought. He was in bad shape and could use a lift to the local doc. For a moment, though, he wondered how Bernard had reached the plateau without being seen. He chuckled to himself, recalling the westerns he'd devoured as a kid: stealth, an old Indian trick.

Then again, maybe he'd never left? He turned to find him, but found nothing instead.

"Uncle Bernard?" Rico said, his tone less than sure.

"I tried," the voice said sadly. "But I'm too old. You should go, quickly."

"Bernard?"

"Go."

"But where the hell are . . . "

"Never mind," the voice said. "Go."

Rico shrugged, and glanced around him once more; he then walked slowly toward the path. At the entry, he paused and turned around, his eyes scanning the smooth gray surface of the butte. He was searching for something, a fragment of logic that explained what he thought he'd heard.

"Go," Bernard's voice said again. This time shorn of comfort and suasion, it was now full of steel and gruff command. The voice spoke first to Rico's spine, jerking his head back and jolting him stiff, while running do-re-mi chords from bottom to top to bottom.

"Now."

Rico shuddered, then somehow managed to compel his

unsteady legs onto the path. He stumbled at first, then fell head-long over dirt and rocks and loose scrub. Nothing to grab, nothing to break or even slow his slide. Even as he slid on his belly—the end still not in sight, the speed picking up—he was oddly relieved. Although pain seared his bad left shoulder, and he began to feel his extended palms and wrists grow raw, he knew he was safer sliding downhill than he was on the butte.

He was afraid, but it was a normal fear, one of physical harm, the sort he could understand and, given recent circumstances, even welcome. Just then, his body veered off the narrow path and careened toward a ledge, smooth as waxed tile and sloping downward. His fingers grasped and clawed, but still found nothing to cling to to break his speed. He closed his eyes; it was all he could do.

Eyes shut, he'd leave this world. Eyes shut, he thought he heard voices again, of women crying, of old women calling his name. Then laughter, a man's voice, he thought, as the ground gave way to air.

*   *   *

MINOT HOSPITAL, MINOT, NORTH DAKOTA

When he awoke, he was trapped in a mesh of tubes and gauze. It hurt him to breathe, like a good heavyweight had just pounded his ribs. It was a familiar pain, but one he could accept. But his legs, he couldn't feel them. He panicked; he knew he'd survived, but what parts of him hadn't? He began to thrash, to seek movement. His fear had narrowed his vision, obscuring the sight of someone else.

"You're a lucky man, Rico," the doctor said. He'd been standing at the side of Rico's bed. "A ten-foot fall, some broken ribs, a cracked kneecap," he said, then smiled. "No permanent damage though, obviously nothing fatal."

Rico managed a weak smile. "Thanks, Doc," he whispered. It

hurt him to speak. He beckoned for the doctor to come closer. "How'd I get here?"

"I wasn't on duty then," the doctor began. "But from what admitting told me, a friend brought you."

"Bernard?"

"No," the doctor said slowly. "That wasn't the name."

"Wynona?"

He shook his head. "Wasn't a woman's name, as I recall, but that's not important. What matters is you're here and you'll make it." He shrugged and turned toward the door. "Got other patients," he said lightly. "But I'll ask."

Rico sighed and tried to relax as much as he could. As he lay there, questions flooded his mind. He wondered how long he'd been here. Who'd been the good Samaritan? When and how could he contact Wynona? Did Bernard even have a phone?

Suddenly, the doctor appeared briefly in the doorway. "'Frank,'" he said casually, before turning to walk down the hallway. "An Indian guy, about your age. He's the one who brought you in," Rico heard the doctor say. "He said you were friends. Real good friends."

Chapter Ten

April 10, 1974

I'm back home, back in Frisco. I'm still sore, but my ribs have healed, and I'm able to get around, just a bit slower than usual. The meds help. What happened in Dakota was because I was off my meds, nothing more, the docs said. But now, I'm good, back on schedule and I just have to do a better job of staying that way.

My old job's gone, but hell, that's no problem. There are all kinds of supermarkets around here eager to hire folks who can work any shift. Talked to a manager yesterday, a Chinese dude, and he said, sure, any time, give him a call.

Thank God for Buddy. I'd called him after about a week in the hospital when I couldn't take it any more, and he said he'd come get me. Just like that. Man, I almost fainted. I'd started out by asking him to wire me some bus fare, a loan, and he said he'd just dropped a hot new rebuilt into his rig and was more than eager to try it out. Gas shortage? Hey, he had his priorities, and he figured a country cruise would be perfect, only this one would cover four states. No sweat, he said, he'd be there.

I told him not to tell Mom, I didn't want to worry her. She's had a hard enough life, and there was no sense in me adding to it. Of course, he understood.

And just like that, he was in Minot. That Buddy, now he's doing it right. He'd taken a quarter off school—burn out, he said—and was working odd jobs and reading, just for the hell of it. He'd saved enough from the past two summers up in Egigik, working the cannery, that he felt comfortable taking a break. School would still be there next quarter, he said.

I checked out of the hospital and before heading back to the Coast, we drove by Bernard's. No one was home. I tried calling her, but I didn't even know Bernard's last name. I don't remember if he even had a phone. I left a note for Wynona on the door, telling her I was going back to Frisco. In the hospital I'd had a chance to think about her and what had happened on that butte. Just another strange day in a pretty strange life. I'm sure now that the hunger and cold had created the mindfuck that helped put me here in the first place.

I'm mad at myself as I'm writing this. I know now I should never have even gone up to that butte, but she was so goddamn insistent. Over the last few days, I began resenting her for sending me there in the first place. That hoodoo stuff she swears by, it hasn't done me a damn bit of good and lying in that hospital bed was proof. I figured that if being with her meant believing in superstition, I'd be better off alone.

After writing the note and pinning it to the door, I told Buddy to drive, fast.

As we sped away from New Town, Buddy reached into his pocket and handed me an envelope. It had a grand and some change; he said it wasn't all his. He'd asked around, hustled our old Pinoy pals, maybe ten or so, since grown up—married, working full time, the usual. They were watching a fight at his house, drinking bourbon and a truckload of beer, and talking about old times. Buddy then told them about me, then he passed the hat. At the end, the hat was full—cash and checks. Buddy said they swore on a bible not to tell their wives or girlfriends.

Christ, some of these guys I haven't seen in years, since before Vietnam. But Buddy said when they get together, they still think of me, talk about me. Jimmy, who's driving full time for Metro, said he remembered the time I'd backed him up; Tony, who just got hired as a cop, said the same thing. I guess me being a hothead finally paid off.

Later, Buddy and I started reminiscing about our families, about the old neighborhood, about Vince and Jimmy, our dads. They'd known each other a long time, and were close friends since 1918, even before they came to America. They'd worked the same hot fields, the same dead-end jobs. Old Jimmy's still alive, and still married to the same woman, a Mexican lady from San Jose. Buddy and I are mixed—and maybe that's why we're so close. I got curious about a number of questions, empty spaces in the narrative. Like why his parents lasted and mine didn't, and what Jimmy might've told Buddy about Vince.

Buddy began telling me stuff I already knew—that old Vince was tough, independent, respected by the other old timers. Jimmy really missed Vince, and whenever he saw me, he saw him. Buddy then went off on a tangent that must've lasted through most of Dakota, and told me a Vince story I'd never heard before.

My dad was an orphan back in the Philippines. His father and most of his uncles had been killed by white soldiers, Americans, in 1901, during the US campaign to conquer the islands. My grandfather and his brothers were part of a small guerilla band—mostly close friends and relatives—on one of the Visayan islands and when the Americans found their village, they killed all of the men, almost everyone actually, including my grandparents, Dad's mom and dad. Dad and an older sister, Carmelita (my aunt), were raised by Nanay, an older woman who'd survived the slaughter. As Jimmy had told it to Buddy, the handful of survivors either knew well or were related to those who'd been killed.

In the massacre, Nanay lost her entire family—her husband and three children. She'd managed to survive only by being very still, which meant lying motionless under the bleeding body of her

dying husband who was still alive. For an hour, she didn't move,
didn't react to her husband's moans and whispered prayers. She
just listened for other sounds, like the shuffling of soldiers' boots
and voices she didn't know saying words she couldn't understand.
When these sounds stopped, she stood up and spotted Dad and
his sister, the only other survivors.

She grabbed them and they began walking into the jungle, until
they reached a village so remote it was untouched by the Americans. That, Buddy had said, was where Vince was raised. But
Vince wasn't his real name, or at least it wasn't his first one.
Nanay had given it to him. It was the name of her oldest, a teenage
guerilla killed by the Americans. It was the same with Carmelita;
she was named after Nanay's youngest dead child. The girl was
seven at the time. Buddy said Jimmy didn't know Vince's real first
name.

According to Jimmy, Vince was a good son who tended to his
adopted mother, even when she began losing her mind. She'd bab-
ble on about the day the Americans came, then wonder aloud why
the Christian God and the native spirits had deserted her. Near the
end of her life, when Dad was about sixteen, she began to confuse
Dad with his namesake, her own dead son, and to curse both God
and the spirits. To please them and protect themselves, the gueril-
las had worn special amulets around their necks to deflect American bullets, but the amulet didn't stop the bullet that pierced her
husband's chest. She'd saved that amulet and, on the day she died,
she gave it to Vince and told him to always remember that in this
world, humans are on their own: birth, life, death, nothing more.
Nanay had told him she was going nowhere, at the worst to nothing, and given the life she'd lived, she didn't expect the other side
to be any better.

I've never seen the amulet; he's never shown me.

After Vince buried Nanay, he drifted north, toward Manila,
looking for work. He found a job, but it wasn't steady. In a small
furniture factory on the outskirts of the city, he met Jimmy who
said he was saving for a one way ticket to America. Jimmy told

him an uncle was working as a contractor in Seattle, and asked if he wanted to come. Vince said no at first, he hated Americans, but then he got laid off. He then told Jimmy he'd join him just for a while, a few years at the most, enough time to work and save and return.

Then Buddy told me something I'd never heard. Jimmy had told him that Dad used to have this hard-to-control temper that was always inviting trouble. A hard look, an odd stare could set him off. One Saturday night, he and my father were in a card room in Stockton when Dad, without saying a word, just hauled off and nailed this Chinese gambler right between the eyes. According to Jimmy, the guy was dead before he hit the ground. Dad left before the police could arrest him. He left the States and returned home. He lucked out. Since the victim was just a dead Chinaman, the police weren't in a real big hurry to solve the crime.

The temper part didn't surprise me. I'd seen flashes of it—but always directed at strangers. That still made me pretty careful around him. The interesting part of the story, though, was something I never knew. According to Jimmy, Dad was in Manila in 1940, a year before what seemed liked the entire Japanese Imperial Army came down for a visit. He was looking for work when he bumps into a cousin who'd just finished basic training with the Philippine Scouts. As usual, my father was broke, and this cousin said he would talk to his sergeant and get him signed up despite his age (40). With war on the way, even an old man would do. And besides, his cousin said, the Scouts were elite—well paid, the best —and sometimes you needed connections to get in.

When Buddy told this part of the story, he got excited and started cracking up. The Scouts, he said, were a cavalry unit. My jaw dropped when I heard that, and I looked at him like he was an idiot.

Cavalry—an image that didn't easily fit my memories of the old Pinoys I grew up with. But then, Dad was good at the track, and maybe his time in the Scouts explains it.

"Like in 'Rin Tin Tin?'" I asked.

Buddy laughed. "Yo, Rinny, and that little white boy . . . "

"Rusty?"

"Yeah," Buddy said. "Him, too."

"Gotta reexamine that entire John Wayne paradigm," I said. "Flips blowin' bugles and yellin' 'charge' and shit like that and ridin' ponies instead of bettin' on 'em . . . "

"Or roastin' 'em," he added. "Paradigm?"

"Yeah, word I picked up in a lit crit class . . . been lookin' for a place to use it."

Jimmy told Buddy my dad got assigned to his unit just in time to fight the Japanese, first in northern Luzon, then on the Bataan peninsula. And get this: Dad rode in the last cavalry charge of the U.S. Army, right there on Bataan.

Good golly, Miss Molly. I was stunned, stirred, proud, even. And I wondered for a moment if Vince would have been proud of me—a lance corporal U.S. Marine in an integrated U.S. Marine Corps. During our years together, he never said much about his time in the military—at least not about his time with the Scouts. But maybe I should have guessed, or asked. Buddy's storytelling stirred an opaque memory of Dad at my bedside—I was three or four then—singing a lullaby about me playing a soldier. "Come along my soldier," I think it went, "put away your gun, the battle's over for tonight . . . "

Yeah, I know, corny, and I'm glad no one else will read this. But that was our ritual for awhile. The tune is pretty—I can still hum it—but I can't remember the rest of the lyrics—probably because I was out right after he'd sung the only line I can still remember.

After the war, my father apparently stayed with the Scouts, who were absorbed by the regular Army. That's how he ended up in Seattle at Fort Lawton. It's also how he met my mom. She was a civilian employee. They started dating and got married. I came along and my father left the Army. According to Jimmy, life after the Army was still too hard—too many doors stayed closed, too many insults stayed the same—like the sacrifice on Bataan didn't count.

Uniform on, uniform off, you're still just a monkey.

Jimmy said Dad burned his uniform, got rid of his medals, cursed this country and swore he'd build us a house on the beach. Dad often said this land suffered too much from amnesia, but I didn't know what he meant. Life was too hard. He told Jimmy he wanted to "live like a king," and he knew he could do it back home, but not here. He wanted a better life for us. So he kept working odd jobs, whatever it took, and kept saving for that day— but it just never came.

Then he changed his plans and left without a word. Vanished. I guess he just decided to go home alone.

I then asked Buddy why. He said he didn't know, but Jimmy figured it had to do with Mom. Their marriage was doomed from the start. She was Christian, a devout Catholic full of compassion and belief in a loving God, all of which he rejected. Jimmy had known Mom before she got married, and he said that in all the years he'd known Vince, she was the only woman he'd ever loved. He loved her so much, he'd even married her in a church, a Catholic ceremony, but had sworn to his friends this was his first and last concession to religion.

I can still hear Mom and Dad argue about how to raise me and my sisters. Baptism, communion, confirmation, the whole sacramental list, plus Catholic school—Vince would scream and yell, but he eventually relented, except on school. He just refused to pay for it. The other ceremonies, though, were free and true to his word, he never attended a single one or, for that matter, set foot in a church again.

On the matter of religion, Nanay had taught her lessons well.

I remembered Mom and Dad arguing one day. She'd invited the parish priest, Father Olson, over for lunch. Father Olson was an old white man. Dad was home that day, and when he heard about it, he just stormed out of the house and took me with him. He was so steamed he'd turned colors and became a much lighter shade.

According to Jimmy, Dad's hatred for priests went back to the

Philippines. He thought they were frauds, agents of a deaf and blind God. He'd known them back home—the foreign missionaries, Spanish and American, all white—and had learned their history. He'd concluded that their beliefs were hypocritical—a pious sham to take land and money from the great unwashed. America sent teachers after the fighting to teach the savages how to wear shoes and practice democracy. He attended for awhile, then just dropped out. The lies—like the Americans had freed them from the Spanish—were just too much. He kept hearing Nanay's stories in his head.

For Dad, poor Father Olson had three strikes against him: He was white, he was a priest, he was both. Dad would've beat him just for fun.

Then there were the hard times Dad faced when he arrived here—the racist insults, the countless fistfights—which just confirmed Nanay's passed-on hatred for whites in general. Jimmy figures Vince just gave up on anything American—including his family—and returned to the Philippines. He's probably right.

I remember that afternoon, just Dad and I, as he drove down to the lake. He kept driving until he began to cool off. Although we didn't talk much, mostly because he didn't like speaking English, the silence didn't bother me. I loved him. And besides, I'd found out from most of my Pinoy pals that their dads were the same.

On that drive—I was thirteen then—he gave me one of his rare lectures, the last one as it turned out. He told me that to make it, I had to be strong, tough. Filipinos got no breaks in America, he said. That's why he'd shown me how to box, how to take care of myself; he knew it would come in handy and that enemies would come to attack me or to take something valuable away. (I remember when I'd beaten someone at school, rare before he left, and the teacher would call our house; if Dad answered, he'd just laugh and say the beating was the parents' fault; the other kid should learn to fight better.) Never mind this pray-to-Jesus-and-turn-the-other-cheek stuff, he told me, all bullshit. Hit first, hit hard, don't worry about the rest. He looked at me as he spoke, rare for him, like this was a fatherly duty, a bit of wisdom he had to convey.

I remember I had an odd feeling as we were driving along. He'd reached his limit and was leaving. See ya, my first-born pal, I'm off to my little grass shack. Blood of my blood, you're now on your own.

That drive, I'm sure Vince figured, was goodbye enough— tearless, oblique, man-to-man. He probably figured I'd eventually understand.

I didn't understand.

But he'd left me some things, an attitude and a skill. He'd taught me the basics of boxing, so, I guess joining a gym was the next logical step—months of training and the amateurs first, then, if the war hadn't come, an earlier pro career. A form of therapy, I guess.

But therapy only went so far. By the time I was sixteen, I'd lost control and began picking fights in school. After class, when I wasn't suspended, I'd go to the gym and train until they turned off the lights. I fought in a bunch of novice smokers and won most of them, more on anger than on any high level of skill. My main regret was Dad wasn't there. I'd fought a lot because this was his gift to me, and because I think I halfway expected that word would some-how reach him, wherever he was, and that one night, I'd just glance and he'd be there, standing in the shadows, smiling and proud. At every match, I'd always glance around, but he was never there. For awhile I just stopped boxing. I picked it up again, just before the Marines, and while my moves got better, the drive and discipline had disappeared.

Mom was so different from Dad even at the start, an oddly matched pair. Now it's clear, a dynamic was always in motion: the more Dad hated religion, the more religious Mom became (Jesus, she always said, would change his heart).

Jesus didn't hear her. Maybe he was loaded. Religion, though, wasn't all bad, at least not in the case of Mom. She was patient and truly kind and had a lot of white friends, especially those from the parish. Some even came to the house, but never when Dad was around. Buddy added that Jimmy thought the differences between Mom and Dad had made Dad's leaving pretty much a sure thing. Having kids, though, just kept putting off the departure date. As Buddy told it, Vincent couldn't stand the thought of growing old and dying in a land full of enemies, tended to by a woman who spouted superstition.

I asked Buddy why his folks had stayed together. They, too, were so different from each other, maybe even more so than my own parents. His mom was like mine; she lit candles and always prayed the rosary, but her husband was a rascal. I knew old Jimmy and had heard Dad talk about his booze swilling, woman-grabbing days, and knew they weren't entirely in past tense. Although he got dressed up and attended Mass each Sunday and even sometimes served as an usher, I figure he did it mostly for show. Yet, they'd survived and, even more amazing, seemed happy together. Why?

Buddy shrugged and peered into the sunset as we neared the Montana state line. He was quiet for awhile, at least ten miles into a new state. Maybe he couldn't answer the question.

"Nanay didn't raise Jimmy," he finally said.

*   *   *

April 15, 1974

I started work today at a small market on Polk Street. Right now, I work as needed—no benefits, low pay, bad shifts—but it's better than nothing. Buddy's gift bought me some time, but it was beginning to run low. And because I got back too late, I missed registration. No school, no GI Bill.

Sure, I miss the money, it would've been nice, but to tell the truth I miss class more. I even miss hearing bad poetry and listening to part-time instructors ooze encouragement and impart misplaced hope. Over the last few days, I've come to realize that since leaving the nut house, the life I'd been living—full-time school, full-time work, full-time woman—left no time for anything else. Yet, the world's just kept on spinning, and time's just kept on keepin' on, whether I've noticed or not.

I don't recall much of this year—the one reporters call "momentous"—especially not the first nine months, when the only thing momentous was my dense personal fog. In the heart of this town, buried in clutter, suspended and still in constant human movement, I'd managed to reduce most of my existence to monologue and shadows. No one was the wiser. I was a Carmelite, physically present but also removed. But somehow, I'd managed to do or say just enough through school and work to get by.

Now I'm clear of all that madness and when I'm not working, I have time, and I've been filling it watching television, from the news to the soaps. I've also resumed reading books, politics and history. I'm reading Halberstam, The Pentagon Papers, stuff that makes my heart hurt. White man ego, false assumptions, downright lies—the gasoline that fueled this war. The secret operations, the Gulf of Tonkin incidents, the resolution, McNamara's slick haired, horn rimmed lies—it's all there, all documented. Halberstam's hard-to-read, frustrating; each page fills me with rage, but I have to keep going to find out why the men who run things could so easily doom a generation.

Because they can?

We were throwaways, acceptable losses.

I found myself also getting mad at Halberstam; he was too late by years, by thousands of tours of duty already served. Too late for me, too late for Jerome. The lessons to be learned from these pages of history? Who knows? No one I know does.

In addition to books, I've even fallen into the habit of two, maybe more morning dailies over coffee.

Nixon's in trouble for the Watergate affair and the odds are he'll fall farther than me—a comforting thought.

The reporters have stopped covering Hue. I guess it isn't news anymore. But the killing, I'm damn sure, goes on. It's become just a war between colored folk, theirs and ours, but I guess gooks killing gooks doesn't count. So, No Hue Today (now that's a headline I want to see), not even a sentence on Vietnam. Damn, was it that long ago, like some ancient Greek war that no one remembers or cares about?

What was the sacrifice worth anyway? On some days when I was there, I used to fool myself that what I was doing really counted. Now, it seems like everyone wants to forget.

Mr. Old White Man President (Eisenhower, Kennedy, Johnson, Nixon—take your pick), was it worth Jerome King? Jerome who? you might ask. You know, Jerome King, I'd reply politely. Now that was a patriot, one of you, at least by race. He was just a stupid cowboy, loved by no one but his horse, his folks, and me. All he had was a toothless honky tonk future, full of Okie dust and wind, bad wine, and retarded music. But Jerome, he believed you guys.

Surely, Mr. Presidents, you must remember him. He crossed the Pacific whole, a proud teenage Marine, but returned disassembled, like Humpty Dumpty after the fall, his cold left arm the only limb left—barely. From the climate controlled comfort of the Oval Office, you sent my friend to die . . .

What my time in did was to allow me the luxury of reexamination, of change. You know, Mr. Presidents, when Kennedy got it in Dallas, my mother cried. She just couldn't be consoled. Her eyes flowed with rivers of Roman Catholic tears. Mine did, too, but they wouldn't now.

Now, here's a change. If Dallas was tomorrow, I'd jack Lee Harvey good and grab that piece of shit Carcano. I'd aim and squeeze, then save enough for the rest of you. That Oswald, though, was a piece of work. He just didn't do enough. He was an ex-Marine; the Corps trained us well. Semper fi, motherfuckers.

I'm rereading now what I've just written. It's here on this page. I can see Jerome's Gomer Pyle face, pale and wide open. Goddamn the bitch for dying. Can't write no more about him, at least not today.

Ten minutes later. Rereading again. I'm tight as a knot. Maybe the fog was better.

*   *   *

NEWMAN'S GYM, SAN FRANCISCO

"Kid, that boy was strange," the old man turned slightly to his left and mumbled to his companion, someone just as old. Kid was a Mexican, an ex-fighter judging from his cauliflower right ear, the scar tissue above his left eye, and the ring name he'd taken at nineteen and had kept for half a century. The two were where they always were at five in the afternoon on all days except Sundays— seated on old folding chairs set twenty feet back from the main ring. As usual, a handful of fighters, amateur and pro, were going through their skip rope, speed bag, heavy bag paces.

"Didja see 'im?" the old man asked.

A heavyweight—a massive and muscular black man—was pounding the snot out of a nearby heavy bag, the biggest in the gym. The stream of rhythmic thuds of leather glove on hard leather surface made mumbled conversation difficult. Kid was hearing only those sounds, that sacred, percussive music, a fighter's Gregorian chant; he closed his eyes and nodded his approval to the beat, then nudged his companion.

"That colored boy's good, Ira, good power, kinda loopy punches, but he's got a good trainer," Kid said slowly. He pointed with his eyes to a short white-haired man overseeing the heavyweight's work. "Old George can fix the loops."

"Nah, nah," Ira said. "You didn't hear what I said." He then leaned over to address his friend's good ear, the left one.

"Whatcha say then?" Kid replied. Out of courtesy and habit, he made himself look at his friend, but kept an admiring eye on the heavyweight who, at his trainer's command, started throwing quick, multipunch combinations. The bag swiveled and bent in this final fast sprint to the end of a three-minute round. "Steal the round," Kid heard George yell and nodded again.

"Nice," Kid said.

"That new boy, a Filipino, I think," Ira began.

"Good fighters," Kid interrupted. "Fought a few in Stockton, or maybe that was Bakersfield. Lessee, '36 or '38, anyway, before the war." He shook his head. "Long time ago," he said sadly.

"Nah, nah," Ira said impatiently. He was still leaning across his friend's body, still talking to his good ear. In this awkward pose, his lower back was beginning to stiffen, but he was hoping to finish his story soon. "That Filipino kid, a featherweight, had come in a few times," he said. "You seen 'im, you liked 'im."

Kid blinked his eyes. "Oh yeah," he said. "Good hands, smart footwork, fast, reminds me of, ah, anyway. He knew his way around a gym."

"Well, not this one no more."

"Whaddya mean?"

"Didn't ya hear?"

"Uh-uh," Kid replied.

"Well, yesterday, before you got here, he was sparring with another pro," Ira explained. "It got hot real fast, a little outta control 'bout midway through the first round, like they was fightin' for a belt. Then, in the second, the Filipino nails him good and knocks him right into the ropes, and George calls a break." He paused. "But the Filipino ignores him and just keeps goin', and it took George and a couple of fighters to finally pull 'im off."

"That so?"

"Yup," Ira said, pleased he'd finally finished his story and could straighten himself. "He got eighty-sixed right after that. He just walked out, kinda wide-eyed and blank. He still had on gear— gloves and headgear—and walked right down the street. The gear was the gym's, but no one said nothin', no one stopped him. I guess they figured they were lucky just to have 'im leave." Now finally erect, Ira paused. "Ain't never seen nothin' like it."

"Nothin'?"

Ira shook his head. "Nope," he said firmly as the gym bell rang and the rhythmic thwacks on the heavy bag resumed.

Kid chuckled. "Well, let me put it this way," he said slowly, as he touched the scar tissue above his left eye. "This game thrives on desperation, and it's too damn hard for most guys that's sane. You don't see no future senators here, do ya? From what you told me, he ain't too different from what I used to be." Kid shifted in his seat to watch the heavyweight.

"So, whaddya think'll happen?"

"To the heavyweight?"

"Nah, nah, Kid, to that crazy Filipino."

"Shit," Kid replied, never taking his eyes off the heavyweight. "Death row, a championship, maybe both. Pros get paid to try to beat each other, sometimes to death." He paused, thinking back to the times he'd tried to kill another fighter, or the reverse. "Cold-blooded killers and champions got the same sorta mind, you know," he finally said.

* * *

April 16, 1974

This morning, I'm more than halfway through Halberstam, same with The Pentagon Papers. I went to the library (can't afford to buy books), and picked up more on Vietnam. Fire In the Lake and everything else the librarian would allow me to carry at one time. Filled two knapsacks. Hell, I don't even recall the other titles. All I know is that here on my living room floor, I'm surrounded by books, reading two, sometimes three at a time.

It's not like I'm busy with work or anything. The store hasn't called recently and although I'm low on cash, there's enough for next month's rent. I've got some canned beans and fresh fruit; in the bush, I lived on less. I'll check for more shifts later. I've got coffee for a few more days, but damn, I just learned I'm out of toilet paper. It's a good thing the library's nearby. I figure I can go shit there and, for even greater convenience, I'll snatch a roll or two—public money at work.

An oddity. There's a pair of sparring gloves and headgear in my bedroom, but the stuff's not mine. I remember going to the gym and working out light—calisthenics, bag work, skip rope but no sparring, nothing too heavy.

I needed a break and the old routine felt good. I must've grabbed the gear by mistake. I'll bring it back later. I've got books here piled up and begging to be read.

*   *   *

RED APPLE MARKET

He was an odd sight—short, slender, and wearing a blue stocking cap over hair that was starting to grow long. A brown elf, she thought. He was sitting on a crate of oranges near the produce section. Occasionally, he lifted a sandwich to his lips and nibbled, but mostly he just focused on a book.

Curious, Birdie drew closer. *Thunder Out of China*, the title read. His eyes never left the page. At his feet, open and face down, was another book. She bent to examine its title, *Fire In the Lake*, which conjured in her Texas mind an image of oil floating on the Gulf and flames reaching to tickle the stars.

"Fuck," she heard him whisper to himself as he, brows now knitted and still oblivious to her, put down *Thunder* and picked up the book that reminded her of her Houston home.

"Rico," Birdie said softly. "Break's over, honey, and we gotta hustle and finish these aisles."

For the first time he looked up, a sheepish smile she found attractive softening his dark, serious face.

"Damn, Birdie, back to the chain gang, eh?" he said, as he rose and carefully placed both books atop the crate. He sighed. "Break's too short. Guess I can leave 'em here."

"They're safe," she assured him. "No one reads, least not in English."

"I do," he answered.

They'd worked this odd, after-hours on-call shift for the last four days. They both needed the cash, but he needed it more.

She'd arrived in Frisco on her eighteenth birthday, more than four years ago, hoping to find hope, or at least a city that wasn't Houston. She found instead a city full of other desperate vagabond kids growing old before their time. She'd tried to love, but that magical summer had long since passed, leaving full-color photos suitable for publication, but no forwarding address. In its place were cold nights in a park or in doorways, and the necessary barters—of body, sometimes of soul, for a warm spot and a meal.

Concrete, she'd come to learn, was concrete, whether in Houston or the Haight, and assholes were assholes, despite the long hair and ragged uniforms. Frauds, she'd called them, Nazis in rags. Even here, in the city of love, they'd take her last dime.

Those first few years were hard, but what made it hardest was watching her friends—or those who claimed to be friends—leave her by overdose, by insanity, by abandonment. Still, she stayed and wanted to believe that Frisco was better than Houston, but even that small shred of faith was beginning to disappear. The turning point involved a man, someone she'd once fucked and was thinking of fucking again, this time for free. At a party, she'd heard a rumor—one she'd loudly denounced—that he routinely tipped off the cops and was handsomely rewarded.

She'd continued to believe in his innocence until one day she saw him in a black and white, wearing dark blue and driving, not being driven. He pulled up to the curb and rolled down the passenger window. He smiled. She smiled. When'd you get outta the academy, she'd managed to ask.

Since then, she decided to get a regular job, open an account, acquire credit, become a rat, join the race. She'd keep running, even if in place, until she could figure what else to do. Through a friend of a friend, she'd found a cocktail gig, which brought her a luxury—to sleep alone, not six to the floor.

The prospect of a fatter account brought her here to Red Apple Market. Aside from the extra cash, this dark, studious man was an added benefit. He intrigued her. He was handsome, on second look, not first, and looked Mexican, maybe Indian—in Texas, there were plenty of both—but not quite either. He was hardworking and friendly enough. He was odd; he read books. After their first night of work, he waited with her outside for her cab. During breaks, though, he kept to himself and read.

But it wasn't just reading, she thought. He seemed to absorb entire pages of text, like some better than standard double ply rolls she'd just finished stocking. She'd asked him as they stood outside that first night if he was a student. He just laughed and shook his head.

Earlier, she'd asked him why he was reading so much. He said he wanted answers. She'd then asked what he was (Indian or Mexican, the politely unstated part). His answer surprised her. A survivor, he said. Finally, as the cab pulled to the curb and she opened the door, she asked if he wanted to fuck her. Her mind replayed the reel. He just smiled that sheepish little smile, the same one he was smiling tonight.

Thanks, but not tonight, he said, he still needed to find answers.

Actually, the proposition had not been so crudely put—it never was—but the implication had been sufficiently clear. His response, or lack, puzzled her. Men had never refused her invitation, not since she was fourteen in Houston. Was it the family minister or his son, or both, on that boozy, star-spangled July 4th church picnic? In equal but wholly different ways and on different tables in different parts of the park, her mom's famed chicken wings and her youngest daughter's breasts, legs, and thighs had stolen the show.

Birdie was Texas long legged, lean and firm, and very good looking, with full brown Priscilla Presley hair, but not piled so high. She'd been named Elizabeth Louise, shortened of course to Betty Lou before her name took its current form. This was because her parents had decided that Betty Lou was too common—one on every block, at least in Texas. Plus, her dad hunted doves in season and out, and her nickname honored what he loved to shoot.

The time since Texas had seen her round out the angles, and that was to the better. Each morning, her mirror told her that. In fact, her beauty and the fact she loved sex were the main reasons she'd left Texas in the first place. There, she could've married and with her good looks, jumped over her family's modest trailer-park status, and landed in the middle of three perfect children, the best private schools, and country club Saturday nights.

But at what price? Marriage to a banker, an oilman perhaps? And what about monogamy, the brimstone Bible Belt admonitions against those whose sins were original, causing them to stray and sin again? For them (for her) the hail of rocks was stacking off-stage, pebble and stone, and preordained to fly their (her) way. Surely, a frightening enough thought to dry one's juices, but becoming Harriet and having to forever fuck a sexless stumplike Ozzie was also scary. A life of perpetual missionary, once-a-month polite sex—two strokes, can't let Ricky and David hear, cum, shrink, dry kiss, good night.

Scarier still, one dick only until the end of time. What if it was small or pink or, God forbid, both? She'd shuddered at the thoughts and shuddered so much that right after high school, she just left Houston and didn't stop until the Pacific touched the rocks at Ocean Beach.

Then, there was the other way—somebody's, everybody's girl-friend, mistress, whore, good while it goes, but only until the tits sagged and the cheeks expanded and sank below the smooth wooden surface of a bar stool. Free love Frisco, she'd heard, was different; it offered a third alternative to women like her; the choices in Houston were one too few.

Frisco was an improvement over Houston. The way she'd figured, almost anything outside of Houston was an improvement over Houston. Since arriving in town, she'd had her share of men, of men and women, of women. But oddly, in this diverse town, all of her lovers—her one-night stands, her two-night relationships—had been white. It was just an old habit, residue from her Texas past, where white women fucked only white men, a custom enforced by gossip and violence. It was safer, she knew, to fuck a married white minister (and his son) than a barrio boy or anyone darker.

Since working downtown, thoughts of lovers had largely disappeared; she'd come to enjoy her solitude, her new sanitized existence, her growing checkbook. Lovers took attention and, more important, time, which cut into money, which she'd finally realized she didn't have enough of. A car, she figured, would be nice. So, even though the offers still poured in—at the lounge mostly, but sometimes, when she walked down the street or waited for a bus—all were refused. But tonight, she wanted to make an exception, to give herself a gift—like a certain diffident co-worker, maybe wrapped in a ribbon, but not much else.

Her friend and hoped-for lover was now just finishing up canned fruits, arranging them so the labels faced the aisle. She glanced at his arms, extended to the top shelf, and watched his sinewy triceps lengthen and contract. She forced herself not to stare, and to appear to be busy unpacking small bottles of oregano, bay leaves, and other spices. These, in turn, spurred the odd image of lovely sauces made by her last lover, a North Beach Sicilian, who'd beaten her once, but had fed her well and had fucked her even better.

She'd stayed a month and had made it that long because of his two Cs, his cooking and his cock, but one afternoon, those letters suddenly vanished when a drunk Muni driver hopped the curb and pinned the Sicilian under his right front tire. Her lover survived, but just barely. She'd tried caring for him at first, hearing the twangy refrain of stand by your man in her head.

One night, while asleep on the couch, she had an epiphany. It was easy for Tammy to sing that song. Her man was ambulatory, Birdie's was a gimp. She awoke laughing, relieved. It was deep and moving, like what she'd heard a philosophy student ex once describe at a party in the Sunset. She closed her eyes. Na-me-ho, she began chanting, and wished she could remember the rest.

The end of the relationship officially came on a warm Sunday afternoon. She'd told him that helping him pee and wipe his ass "just wasn't her thing." Good luck, she said, as she left him outside his apartment and walked west on Broadway, while he, wheelchair bound and hobbled by casts and a brace, struggled to catch up. Furiously, he spun the wheels but never made it. In his effort, he'd suddenly found himself in the middle of a crosswalk, but against the light, which in Frisco is a free fire zone, the worst place to be at the worst time. A Datsun nailed him and just kept going.

She'd heard the screech, then the crunch of metal on metal. But she never stopped, or even looked back. She still didn't know if he survived.

Dead or alive, though, she would still sometimes think of him and although she couldn't remember his face, she could see, with unusual clarity, every fold and vein of his always hard cock, from the tip—shaped like a helmet—to its thick, bushy base. They'd eat and fuck, and sometimes the reverse. Once, a dream of hers had combined the two, as her lover's appendage rose slowly from a plate of pasta marinara to open the gates of heaven.

Sex, for her, had never been so good and, she feared, it would never be again. For the most part, though, she tried not to think of it, and when she did, she'd just change the tape—to her job, or a new Mustang she'd seen in a showroom on Market. That would usually work, especially the car, but usually isn't always. During those few unguarded moments, she would yearn not just for his size, but also his endurance, his brute energy. In this time of abstinence, she'd pondered the source of his power and concluded it stemmed from color and geography. He was swarthy, the darkest of her lovers, still white, but just barely, and from Sicily, an island close to Africa where no white girl from Texas would go unattended.

She looked at the bottle of oregano and fondled it; her palm was starting to moisten. She then glanced over at Rico, who'd moved farther down the aisle to stock cereals. She smiled.

He was darker than the Sicilian, much darker. She wondered if he could cook.

*   *   *

They were standing outside after work. Rico was smiling, glad for the end of the shift, the last workday for awhile. He could return to his reading; his two books were cradled in his right hand.

Oh, he knew sauces, Rico assured her, but tangy Filipino ones full of cloves and garlic and pepper like his dad used to do. Filipino? Sure, Filipino, he said, you know, from the Philippines.

That near Africa?

He laughed. Close enough, he replied.

"You look like a schoolboy," she said.

"Wish I was," he answered. "The first time around, I wasn't too good." He gripped the books tightly and jabbed them to make a point. "The next time, though . . ."

They were waiting for a cab she said she'd called, but hadn't. She glanced at her watch. "Damn, it's almost three." The store was now dark; it had closed five minutes before, and with it, easy access to a phone. There was a booth across the street but as everyone in Frisco knew, its purpose was form, not function, an urban mirage—its coin box jimmied, its cord severed, its coin slots jammed. Worse was its outhouse use by the bums on the street, one of whom was just zipping up and walking away.

"Where you livin'?" he asked.

"Diamond Heights," she answered.

"Damn," he whispered. "'Cross town, uphill, too."

"How 'bout you?" she asked, knowing full well he lived nearby. Earlier in the week, he'd casually mentioned he'd walked to work. For a moment, he didn't reply. She didn't know why. Maybe he was married or had a woman at home? Hell, maybe he had a man? It was time to find out.

"Well," she said slowly. "I better get goin'." The sound of her words was perfect, resigned but gritty, better than she'd hoped. She then turned, but not too quickly, so as not to miss the expected, which came before her first step toward home.

"Wait," he said.

Again she turned, but even more slowly, in order to hide her smile. Look surprised, she told herself, as her eyes settled on Rico's.

"Well, ya know, I don't live too far." His free, non-bookholding hand was lively, all five fingers expressive. She noticed. "It's a slum though, a real shithole." He paused. "Don't get many guests, but hey, it's got a phone. Call your cab from there."

He shrugged. She smiled and shrugged. "Okay," she said. "That's real sweet," she said in a tone that let him know the high dosage of sweetness.

"Hey, it ain't like I can just let ya walk all that way alone," he said.

"Honey, it's still sweet," she repeated, same tone. "Which way?"

He pointed toward downtown. "Not too far," he said. "Ten blocks or so." He smiled. "That's the good news, the bad news is the Loin's rough." He was now speaking slowly. "So make sure you stay real close."

"Hm," she purred. "I most certainly will."

*   *   *

They walked several blocks in silence as he examined every shadow and questioned every sound. On this night, the streets seemed empty, but he knew too well that the dark hid intent, a blade or worse. And so he walked slowly, without a word, despite the puzzlement of his companion, who wondered just what to say. Why was he quiet? What was he thinking?

"Rico," she began.

At Sutter, the intersection was well lit and free of traffic, human or otherwise. He began to relax. "Oh, I'm sorry," he finally replied, and turned toward Birdie.

"I'm starting to get hungry," she said. "They got a Denny's? Even a Sambo's?"

He shook his head. "Nothin' all night, least not around here," he said. "Hold on, we're gettin' close." His head suddenly swiveled toward a noise, a clanging that seemed to come from a mid-block alley across the street. "A cat, nah, two cats," he mumbled, then relaxed. "Anyway, I'll go fix somethin' up real quick."

"With a sauce?"

He laughed. "Sure, Birdie, so damn good it'll make you cry."

She'd love to cry. Birdie then smiled and as she did, the tip of her tongue skimmed left to right to left. This was a tiny movement, reflexive and quick and, in the dark, impossible to see. Thoughts of a hot meal, a new sauce had triggered it, but only in part.

*   *   *

The rest of the trip was almost without incident, but not quite. A block from home, in the heart of the Loin, a huge, straggly haired white man, maybe twice Rico's size, stood blocking the sidewalk. Rico had spotted him; he was hard to miss. Arms waving, he faced them and growled curses at the sky and in their direction. With his free hand, Rico motioned for Birdie to get behind him. With his other, he handed her his books.

Rico veered into the street; Birdie followed; the man did, too, still growling, still waving. Rico sighed. "Fuck this shit," Birdie heard Rico whisper. "Don't move."

She then saw Rico walk up to the man who towered over him. Rico began cursing him—motherfucker this and that—then jabbing a finger into his chest. She was amazed. With each jab, the big man gave ground and Rico moved forward. He then motioned for Birdie to join him and, as she did, she couldn't believe her good luck.

Animal, she thought. Dangerous like her Sicilian, just smaller.

"Whatcha say?" Birdie whispered, as they walked past the man, now quiet and calm.

"Nothin' I ain't said before," Rico replied. "I just told 'im I ain't in no mood, and I'd just as soon kill 'im tonight. His choice." He paused. "Even drunks and psychos can make choices."

Finally, they reached the entry to his building. Rico inserted his key. "Sometimes junkies nod out in the hallway," he said evenly. "Just step over 'em." He smiled. "No big deal, you get used to it."

As they walked up the stairs and then through the hall—her eyes peeled for prostrate human forms, on this trip there were none—she wondered what else her new friend might reveal. He was a mix of clashing skills and instincts—a lover of books and a fierce man of the streets—and that made him interesting. No, she thought, the term was too neutral, too removed. Entrancing? Well, maybe not yet, but there was always the future, starting with the first second after now.

Finally, they were inside his apartment—small, spare, and tidy, except for the books piled and scattered on his living room floor. "Gotta pee," she said.

"Gotta cook," he said, and pointed to the bathroom. He then headed the opposite way.

"Bay leaves, bay leaves," he mumbled, as his search through a drawer was broken by the sound of his name. He then walked to the bathroom and could hear running water. Rico knocked on the door. "Birdie?"

Suddenly, the door swung open. Birdie was standing and facing him, her ass and both hands resting against the sink. Her clothes were neatly folded on the toilet seat.

"Well darlin'," she said, smiling. "You got an extra towel?"

*   *   *

He had an extra towel, quickly draped, more quickly removed.

Skin upon skin, they were voracious, soon bathed in sweat, full of yearnings and regret, hidden and known. For her, a release, for him, a chance to forget. For her, a chance again at love, another one, the others had all gone so badly. Was she lying to herself once more? She didn't know. For him, a break in his search, his consumptive obsession.

Finally, they unlinked and muscles that had pressed them so tightly, suddenly uncoiled—relaxed and released—and forced them apart, each wondering what words could be said to a stranger.

He opened small. "Nice," he whispered, a placebo word. He was staring at the ceiling; she was, too.

"Yes," she answered, then topped his opening with a smile. He matched her and smiled back. They were even.

"You hungry?" he asked, searching for an excuse to rise. Anxious to help, she nodded. "Got some pork," he added, as he walked to the kitchen. "Marinated in garlic and vinegar, other spices, onions. Potent."

As he searched for a pan and utensils, she drew her legs up and rested her chin on her knees. She could see him from where she was and liked the sight. He was lean, wiry, no fat seen—a dark, lovely vision—now standing and in full view. Birdie knew she was wanting him too much; this was dangerous, she was fighting it, but he was born to please. Was she born to lose? Just what flaw was he hiding? When would he drive her away? She sighed. She didn't have the answers, but what she did have was a lover fixing a meal. He was hers, at least for the moment.

"The sauce," she heard him brag. "Girl, it's gonna make you cry."

She smiled and drew her knees even closer to her chest, before reaching to brush the corner of an eye. "It already has," she whispered.

*   *   *

April 30, 1974

I've been working a lot lately, and haven't had the chance to read as much as I would like. But time permitting, I keep plugging away and uncovering more. Sometimes finding this stuff makes my head hurt; knowledge is making me nuts.

I'm reading up on the history of modern colonization, i.e., rich white folk controlling poor colored folk for profit. Before World War II, so much of the world was governed from London or Paris (I didn't know that) and that included Vietnam, Cambodia, and Laos.

I've been focusing on China, the root of the mess I found myself in. Even China, with her thousands of years of culture and history, wasn't immune. We couldn't see that Chiang, our China boy, was a corrupt, ineffective old bastard, a man separated from the poor. While Mao, that commie devil, had his faults (being a commie devil, for one), he also carried the hopes of the poor, desperate shits that Chiang worked so hard to ignore. For them, a simple decision: fake democracy or a hot meal. I guess the answer depends on when you ate last. (Let's see, in China, Mao had millions of supporters and sympathizers, disciplined and tough, fervent, hardened by war. Question to President [fill in here]: Who's going to win this showdown?)

So, in 1949, Chiang, his army gone, skips to Taiwan, from

which he declares, like MacArthur, he's going to return and finish the job he'd so poorly started. No one pays him any attention, least of all Mao, who's busy being the supreme Chinaman and rebuilding his country in his image and likeness.

Meanwhile, on the other side of the strait, Chiang's loss sent a lot of Americans into shock. He was the sort of Chinese leader we loved—democratic, at least in appearances, open to American control, American investment—the best sort of Chinaman. He was friendly and smiling, his smile wan, a toothy enigma, like the chow mein merchants on Grant. In the absence of answers, we provided our own and filled him with intent and purpose and value, all ours. He was our China doll, a puppet confirming our best beliefs.

And then there was his country. The missionaries, those self-righteous vermin, just loved Chiang's China—half a billion heathens waiting for The Word. They loved his American educated wife; they loved the image of bible-carrying Chinamen, who still carry bibles, only now they're little red ones.

So, because Mao had the bad manners to win and prick (they were all pricks) our best Christian wishes, we pouted and ignored him. He was this silent, malevolent Buddha, the slant-eyed demon—the worst sort—Stalin's junior partner, the newest rogue emperor poised to conquer the world. But was he? We didn't know; the white guys never bothered to ask, so they assumed the worst and sent me over to contain old Mao, who puppeteered Vietnam from the safety of Peiking.

All that time, those stupid, brave VC and NVA, fighting and dying, blowing their bugles and moving forward, defying napalm and our artillery, just to get close enough to kill us—and all for a fat Chinaman, not for Ho, not for their families or themselves. Dumb bastards, they died for Mao and didn't even know it.

I wonder now just how the white guys thought all this up? Was it drugs? Dulles, and later, McNamara and the Bundys, JFK—a rich male Caucasian hall of fame—all top secret junkies? Smoke?

Too weak. Coke? Nah, too mellow, you think of pussy, not war. Must've been manufactured junk, a very bad batch. Or maybe it was just rich white guy, Harvard arrogance, where the world conforms to their delusions. Whatever. They made the call, created the delusion, made it real.

And others paid the price.

It gets worse.

Yesterday, I found articles on Nixon at the library (I need to read more on this guy; he was evil, but interesting). Such an irony—pictures of Dick and Mao, pure Kodak moments—talking about friendship and common interests (like hating the Soviets, the enemy of my enemy, etc.). They're sitting there together smile fucking each other, chatting away like ace boon coons. If the smiles were any larger, they'd have sucked each other off. (I remember hearing about it at the time—Nixon's visit—but I wasn't paying attention to that, or too much of anything else.) It seems to me that chat should've happened earlier, like before I was born, because then I might not have been sent to bite at the old Chinaman's heels.

When I get worked up, I have to step away. I've been gone an hour or so, two double shots to calm me. I sipped and just stared out the window looking at the girls and their cash-paying johns, and at the junkies whose only goal is the next high. Get paid, get laid, get high—simple needs, unexamined lives. Before you know, your hour on earth is up, but the world keeps spinning. Given that, there's something to be said for an unexamined life. Thinking's dangerous, it fucks me up . . .

And when it does, I know it's time to switch gears. Birdie said she was swinging by. We've stayed in touch and have stayed friends. We won't push it; we'll keep it light and not be lovers. Can't handle that now, especially with her. We're too different. Still, I enjoy the company, no drama. It's nice to not think, to just be, and she takes me there.

Still, I catch myself drifting, thinking of the others, sometimes dreaming, asleep and awake, of Marites (back in Daddy's good graces, I assume), and of Wynona who just vanished. My guess? She's back with Frank and her kid, a happy nuclear family. It makes sense.

I need another drink.

*   *   *

Two bodies touch then entwine, bucking and rolling as one. Birdie's low moan he takes as his sign to thrust faster; their syncopation is smooth, their feels and scents familiar. Rico slows now, exhausted, then gently, he kisses her lips, her neck, and both nipples.

On this night he pleases her, as he always does, but tonight, she wants something more. She's silent for a moment; in her mind, she's busy brushing aside his caveats, his constant warnings he's incomplete—his heart, he's always telling her, has a hole and besides, they're too different. Mao, rhymes with cow, he'd told her, not mayo as in-naise. And that's for starters. No matter, she'd said, she was willing to learn, to read, to understand, to pronounce, or at least try to.

What more could she do?

So she practiced. Mao rhymes with cow and, for her, that was progress. For him, too, she figured because one night, he let her feel his wounds, the points of entry and exit, to probe them with her fingers and trace the spiderweb patterns of broken skin; she heard his stories of war and loss. At the end, she kissed his wounds, then caressed them as they made love.

On other nights, she'd asked, Did he love her? Did it matter? he'd always replied.

But she was a believer in signs and finding him was a sign, the best she'd had since coming to Frisco. Tonight, she wants more; he does, too, or so she wants to believe.

Yet, she pauses, the moment's precious, why spoil it with words? The words, though, can't be stopped. They take form.

"Rico," she says. "Do you love me?" For awhile, he doesn't answer, other than to press her close. In the dark, she can't see his face, can't see the softness she thinks he'll use to cushion the blow. It would be death of a sort, but kindly delivered. She closes her eyes.

"Yes," he whispers.

Chapter Eleven

June 10, 1974

Summer school. I'm glad to be back. I've been taking this class on Southeast Asian history. The material's pretty standard—I've already read most of the texts—and the professor's young and almost lifeless. His last name's Burton, a very pale, very thin doctoral candidate from Berkeley whose fondest wish, I'm sure, is to be teaching something else, somewhere else. But hey, he's young, and shit rolls downhill, and none of the other faculty wanted it. He seems nervous and it's obvious students pick up on it; his weakness makes them frenzied, even more willing to poke and jab and agitate. And this class is jammed full of folks happy to agitate, like they've revived the last decade and all the old fights—not-so-old lefties, not-so-old vets, a handful of normal people and me. I stayed for the circus, and dropped this advanced poetry workshop just to make room on my schedule. (Poetry and writing are kind of secondary right now.) I wasn't disappointed—class as guerrilla theater.

I didn't have to wait long. Even before we got to Vietnam, this thick white dude with a ponytail stood up and demanded to know Burton's qualifications to teach this section. Before Burton could reply, he proposed a study session, which he, of course, would lead, then launched this long lefty, flushed faced harangue on how professors had sold out for security and promotion. Where was their voice, their sense of moral outrage, their skepticism when Americans went to "murder freedom loving peoples of Southeast Asia." (Man, that was a giveaway—Comrade Ponytail, Red Guard, Caucasian auxiliary. If he could've, he'd have sent poor Burton to shovel pig shit and pluck hens and publicly confess his failings. And Burton, eager-to-please chump that he is, would've gone.)

Then one little dude, a Mexican from Salinas (infantry, I think) got up and walked over to Ponytail. Without a word, he just busted him in the head; he caught him in mid-sentence. Ponytail went down, and the Mexican went back to his seat, gathered his books and left before security arrived. I haven't seen either of them since. In this class, the new American revolution had a short run.

There've been no fights since, but that doesn't mean the tensions have disappeared. In a way, the makeup of this class is like society—the war divided us even more than we were already divided. About half the class is returning vets. Why are we here? Some to learn, some to vent. It's also a good way to hear what our fellow Americans think of us.

For some, the hurt's so bad they want to believe they'd served some good purpose, that they'd killed for a reason, a moral one. In class, when the question of why comes up (a lot more often than the syllabus says), a couple of them, the believers, will carry the colors and grab at the wind. It's desperate, it's sad, especially now. I'm out of the Corps, they're out of the Army, our country wants only to forget. If the North wins—as it looks like it will—what comfort can we claim? That the war stands only as a West Point or War College lesson: what not to do, a mistake to never repeat. Is that all we get?

My attitude? Fuck the others, my future fellow Americans. Let them die and learn on their own like we did. If I had a son and he was dumb enough to even think about signing up, I'd break his damn leg and drive him to Canada myself.

In class, the believers chant about dominos falling and threats to the U.S.; about the need to win hearts and minds; the need to cross the shining sea to protect fruited plains, spacious skies, etc. You can almost hear the bugle. When they talk like that, my eyes go blank. I can't focus. Still, I bite my lip and don't say a word; believing means too much to them. The other vets stay quiet; it's our show of solidarity, our silent acquiescence.

I understand these guys and their pain, their need to believe they weren't lied to. (The truth, of course, is we were. I know that. Some of the other vets do, too.)

We figure if that's what they need, they should have it. They've already paid a high enough price. One more lie won't hurt.

*   *   *

Through the small window in the middle of the thick wooden door, Birdie peered into the classroom. Her movements were slow, cautious, so as not to be noticed. Rico was there as she knew he'd be, attentive to the lecture. Occasionally, though, he'd sneak a glance across the aisle. Her eyes followed his to their object—a young woman, striking and brown skinned. Birdie's eyes then followed hers. The young woman snuck glances back at him. She smiled, he smiled—both smiles duly noted in the hallway.

Scouting mission complete, the spy withdrew from the window. Her guts were churning as she walked away from the door toward a chair across the hall. She sat down and crossed her legs at the knee. Her top foot, the right, began pulsing up and down. She glanced at her watch. The pulse quickened. Students began filling the hall. She glanced at her watch—a minute until the hour—she stared at the ceiling.

Inside her head, bitch and motherfucker words danced a tango. She glanced at her watch, twenty seconds now, and thought of him, that night, when he'd said that word. It was magic. It wasn't that long ago, a matter of weeks, but since then, he'd been dancing away: making excuses, not answering his phone.

Baby, I got school. Or, Baby, I gotta go to a meeting. What sort? An anti-Marcos group. Who the hell's Marco? No, it's Marcos, Ferdinand Marcos, the Philippine dictator the U.S. backs. The Philippines? Yeah, the Philippines.

Shit, she thought, when she first heard of Marcos. Another fucking leader, another fucking country, another fucking name. Mao rhymes with cow, then Ho rhymes with Joe, that had been hard enough.

She'd last seen him three days ago when she'd spent the night. She'd asked again if he still loved her. Sure, he said. She wasn't convinced. Since then, she'd concluded that love, when spoken by him, had a different meaning; his was stipulated (a new word she'd learned and that worked nicely here)—as in, I love to fuck you, I love you because you're convenient and willing, or I like you a lot and you'll do until something better comes along.

As she pondered the nuances of definition, she bit her lower lip. Suddenly, the door opened. As expected, the two walked out together—he and his still smiling friend—not touching, but close enough. She rose and walked toward them, inserting herself between them.

"Another meeting, Rico?" she asked

"Birdie," he gasped. "What, ah, damn, this is ah . . . "

Before this moment, she'd wanted to suspend belief and quash her instincts. His blush told her otherwise. A wandering man? It had happened before, but before, she'd just shrug and walk away, knowing full well there was always another. But he was different.

He cooked; he never beat her; she was never afraid. Plus, his dick sang a lullaby to her heart. Before the last few days, she'd been dreaming babies, lovely mixed blood ones of different shades. They fell gently in her mind, from top to bottom then off her screen, like soft spring raindrops. They smiled as they passed—I'm yours, they seemed to say—but no more. Their voices were now silent. It was clear the dream hadn't been shared.

"Sweetheart," she heard his smiling friend say. "Who is this rude . . . "

Birdie thought her voice was odd—lightly accented, melodic, foreign—as she hurled her right fist, knuckles forward like her dove-poaching daddy had taught her, through the air. She felt the impact of four knuckles on bone, and watched his head snap back. He looked more surprised than hurt. Daddy would've still been proud.

One down.

She whirled quickly in the direction of the voice, her rival, and punched once more. Birdie wondered how sweetly she'd smile missing a tooth. The thought pleased her as again she felt knuckle strike bone, then a sharp pain above her ear. The sensation was familiar, but so long ago. In Houston, a Mexican chick had hit her there, a lucky, looping desperate punch, but no matter, Birdie still dropped. She could feel it again as she fell back into the arms of someone. Rico, she hazily hoped.

Through her dimming vision, she could see her target bleeding from the nose and sitting on the ground, her blue bellbottomed legs spread open. Someone was holding her down. Black hair, brown skin, another goddamn Mexican, Birdie thought, which pleased her. Before going black, Birdie stared at her mouth; she was curious. Open, bitch, she thought, say something, anything. She'd wanted to gap her smile; it would please her if she had.

"Get them outta here," Birdie heard someone say.

*   *   *

Her name was Carmen and, as Rico applied an icepack to the right side of her nose and cheek, he studied her face. It was narrow and well defined, but not European, not that sharp, and except for the swelling, quite nice, lovely, in fact. And no, Birdie had been wrong; they hadn't fucked, but they'd thought about it and had stopped just short. He'd noticed her from the first day of class and had picked his seat accordingly. At the end of two hours, she'd smiled at him and said something in Tagalog. He knew the lilt. Convent school, familiar ground, he thought.

He smiled back and said he didn't speak that shit and she, still smiling, replied that well, she was mistaken and please pardon her, but she'd thought he was Filipino and he clearly wasn't, at least not a pure one. He laughed and had said she was correct. He was born here, a U.S. citizen, and she was free to marry him for her green card, so she could bring over her fish-kissing relatives, themselves a huddled mass.

Better be nice, he'd told her, you can start tonight. Coffee perhaps? And did Immigration know where she was and that she was planning to overstay?

Coffee led to more coffee, to study sessions, and even to a meeting. (He hadn't lied to Birdie; he did go to a meeting and sat next to Carmen, as close as he could.) Those attending were mostly Filipinos, mostly immigrants, and their topic on this as well as other nights, was Marcos, what they could do to topple him. Rico, new to the gathering and trying hard to be polite, feigned interest through a drumbeat of lefty incantations: Mao says this; Ho did that.

They were ragged and motley, purposely so, Rico thought, the first clue being the coats on the coat rack—fleeced levis and nice leathers—tres chic, tres Huey, tres new—the second being their hands, so soft and well trimmed, unmarked. Marcos, they ranted, was a fraud and his promises to the poor, the peasants—that he needed power to control the rich and bring social justice—were lies, all lies.

Rico, his eyes beginning to roll, didn't know the Philippines, but he did know something about peasants, having watched or killed them for almost a year. Fuck it, he thought, and just started in. Just what were the promises, Rico asked casually. Land reform, someone replied. Land for the landless? Take from the rich and give to the poor? Yes, that's what he said. The answer came from an earnest young woman across the room. He sounds like Mao, Rico said, and stretched. He, still casual, then added offhand. By the way, anyone know any peasants?

The meeting quickly broke up with Carmen escorting Rico

out the door. They walked briskly to her car, a new Corolla, and each step brought a jab to his ribs.

You—jab—just—jab—can't—jab—behave—jab, jab, jab.

He nodded in agreement. Nah, he admitted, just can't. At that point, he kissed her; she kissed him back. Let's go slow, he said, I'm seeing a woman.

She shrugged. So what's that got to do with me? She paused, then kissed him again.

"I guess you'll be seeing two," she said.

*   *   *

Rico thought in structural terms—the building tension, the climax, the inevitable denouement. He and Birdie had reached the third stage, the point where all questions are answered. Close the book, return it to the shelf. Rico hoped he and Carmen were just at the start of a long, lovely drama. Maybe this one would have a happy ending?

He turned on the small bedstand lamp. Gingerly, as he and Carmen lay on their sides facing each other, he inspected her bruise; with his fingertips he brushed it softly, like a man showing through touch he was willing to love. She kissed each finger, each kiss inviting comment, and wondered what he might say.

He didn't know. The years since Vietnam had been hard ones. Hell, he thought, even the years before weren't easy. His mind flashed images: of Marites choosing comfort (not rich enough?); of Wynona choosing Frank (not Indian enough?). Was he the problem, the reason for the end, or were they? He just didn't know. He was sure, though, that he was changing; unlike before, he had to know why. It had started with books—on China, on Vietnam— but why was dangerous. Once unleashed, he couldn't control it; why went beyond others, his original targets, Kennedy and LBJ, their arrogant-old-white-man lies, to boomerang back to him and pose the same question. Why?

His search had freed devils others couldn't see. Birdie had tried, but she could never come close. At heart, Birdie was an optimist, her recent assault aside. She could never grasp, as did he, that for some life was a dump, a cesspool—the longer you lived, the stronger the stench. The war was just the worst of it, at least to this point. For him, and others like him, he'd concluded Vietnam was just the last paragraph of a black prologue. More grief, he'd come to believe, was on the way.

Maybe Carmen would be its bearer. But why?

Was it circumstance? Was it fate, some virulent strain of original sin? Did God damn children, some children only, before they were born?

His mind flew to Buddy, his lifelong ace, whose family was larger and even poorer than his. But God loved Buddy. His ticket got punched; skip jail, friend, his card read, your lucky life, your longshot pony's come in. Collect cash, live normal and happy, be calm, keep on keepin' on.

Buddy was like his brother, more loyal than kin. That much he knew and the knowing brought him comfort. Still, sometimes it was hard for Rico to resist the dark temptation, the urge to compare—Buddy and him, little kid pictures, the same little kid dreams. When did his stop? Why? But when he'd surrender, he'd begin to resent, then begin to feel shame.

A touch stopped his reverie. He was relieved. Carmen, who'd moved closer, was tracing his bruise, a smaller one, in the corner of his right eye.

"It's discolored," she said softly. "Does it hurt?"

"Nah," he replied. "Shit, been hit harder, a lucky punch. I wasn't ready."

She giggled. "We're matching," she said.

"I'm a boxer, you know."

"No," she said, her tone unbelieving.

"No, really," he said firmly. "I got gear, I got clippings . . . "

She smiled and raised her hands. "Okay, okay my new lover's

a boxer." She paused, and stared at him, her look serious. "Just not a very good one."

*   *   *

As Rico would discover over the next few days, Carmen was like that. She was smart, independent, irreverent—a nice balance to his moody ways. She could make him laugh, usually at himself.

The next afternoon, they were sitting in his kitchen. The sun warmed their hands, which joined on the table, their arms surrounding two glasses and a half-empty bottle of red. She told him she'd gotten her glibness from her father, a fast-talking Filipino-Indian from Fresno.

Filipino-Indian? Rico asked, surprised. Yeah, she answered, a Western tribe. He smiled at the irony. What were the odds?

What kind? he asked. Let's see, she said, he told me a couple times—didn't know much himself, his mom had died at birth—it's a small one, but, ah hell, I'll remember it later . . .

At eighteen, her father had joined the Air Force and was sent to the Philippines. He'd wanted to escape the fields and hot, nothing Fresno. Near Clark Air Base, he'd met her mother; they married, and she was born a year or so later. During the next twenty years, the family moved from one assignment to another, which included a couple of stateside stops (ninth grade in Tacoma, junior year in Sacramento) and two long Philippine tours. (Her folks were still there—her dad now retired, her mother running the business, a little bar outside Angeles.)

More often than not, their gypsy life meant she was the new kid in school. Being quick, being smart and funny helped her fit. The movement and change helped her read situations, read people and adjust. Talking, she'd concluded, was better than fighting, though she could do that, too.

"Like you, for example," she said, her lilt now full of sarcasm. "I read you that first night in class."

"Whatcha mean?"

"Oh, Rico," she said, and rolled her eyes. "I saw you walk in. American born, obviously. So confident, full of yourself, animal. And cute. I saw you see me, hmm, like you knew me. Just a feeling. To you, I was familiar. Did I remind you of someone? Someone close? A Filipina? Immigrant maybe. Just maybe. American born, immigrant, the greater the difference, the stronger the attraction. I guessed what you'd do next and played the part. I became what you thought I was." She folded her arms and shook her head. "You're so obvious, poor boy." Her sigh was exaggerated—air loudly pushed through her lips followed by a smirk.

"You'da done me right there if you coulda, and ya know what?" She paused to build tension. His brow, already furrowed, furrowed even more. That reaction, fully expected, tickled her. She chuckled. "I'da letcha," she said.

"Huh?"

"I said . . . "

"Nah, nah. Not what you said, how you said it, I, uh, the Tagalog, the accent," he sputtered. He looked and sounded worried, like he was losing a close friend.

She laughed. "Bilingual, baby," she answered, her tone now guttural, raw, the sound of the street. Her lilt and high class affectations were suddenly gone. "Oh, the language is real enough, I was born there." A bigger smile now. "Brothaman," she added.

"But how?"

"My dad, for one," she answered. "What, you think he went to Stanford?"

He laughed. "Nah, guess not."

"That, plus the other Americans—ain't like you can't find one overseas—and my time in the States," she explained. "Public schools, darlin', fulla hostile psycho cholas with ho hair upta here." As she spoke, she hovered her right hand high over her head. "And them black chicks, shit, bitches be lookin' me up and down. Coppin' attitude, talkin' smack, just waitin' for a reason to jack me." She paused. "Know what I'm sayin'?"

Rico knew what she was saying. Still, her transformation had shocked him. He managed a nod, but just barely.

"Damn," he whispered. "But your friends, that anti-Marcos immigrant group, you . . . "

"Sound like them?" Carmen shrugged. "Scammin' darlin', fittin' in. Keeps 'em happy, comfortable; I'm parta the group. Yeah, parta me, maybe, but not all the way. Born there, sure, my folks still in Angeles. Uh huh. But parta this crowd? All the way? Shit." She turned to glance out the window; on the corner, two cops were wrestling with a suspect. A small crowd was forming; the viewers looked happy. Two black guys were passing a joint. "Nice block, kinda like South Sac," she mumbled.

"Huh?"

"Nothin'," she said. "I mean these folks got cash, boatloads, American, not that fake Halloween color Philippine shit. When Marcos took control, he seized their property, squashed their happy little lives."

"So why . . . "

"They all soft, but they useful," she said, her sound getting blacker as she refilled her glass and pointed toward his. "How 'bout you?"

Rico nodded.

"They got deposits overseas, here, New York, Switzerland, Hong Kong, so they ain't broke. Hey, noticed you sniffin' their jackets the other night, not too subtle, my man." She sipped from her glass.

"Maybe not," he mumbled. He stretched his neck—up, then side to side—and heard the small cracks. He was starting to feel warm.

"And yeah, they soft, but they still rich, they got contacts, they talk democracy, what Americans wanna hear. But mostly they pissed 'cause Marcos robbed 'em."

"So what?"

"So what? They wanna fight, so I'ma help."

"Why?" For a moment, Rico flinched: that word again.

"It's personal," she answered. "Marcos is vicious, he makes misery worse. I hate the motherfucker. My hatred's personal. Unlike my friends, though, I had nothin' to start with, nothin' to rob. It ain't about money . . . "

Rico leaned an inch or so closer, his eyes fixed on hers. "What is it then?" he asked softly.

Carmen leaned back an inch or so in reply. She sighed and finished her wine. "Let's put it this way, I'm enjoying now, this moment, you do, too," she said.

He shrugged, unsure what she meant.

"Love the one you're with," she sang. "That's good enough."

"For now."

"Okay," she said. "For now." She paused and gazed at Rico; the corners of her mouth twitched upward to form the trace of a smile.

"Like now, baby," she whispered.

*   *   *

Carmen rolled from side to side, then finally came to rest on her back. Rico reached to feel her body; his hand traced her arm to her belly, where she'd folded both hands. It was late, she wasn't asleep.

"More truth?" he asked, and turned to switch on the lamp.

"Keep it dark," she said.

Again, he was surprised by her speech and tone. It had changed once more, all in the course of hours, and had traveled from refinement to the street to a point in-between. Is this who she was? Or was it temporary—her latest persona just here for a visit?

"Who was he?" he asked.

"A classmate, UP."

"University of the Philippines?"

"Yes," she whispered.

"His name?"

"No names."

"Were you lovers?"

"Yes."

"What happened?"

They'd met through campus politics. UP was a hotbed then. He got recruited, she said, then went underground, back to his province down south. He said he'd send for her, but later. He was good, they said, smart and brave, the best. Like air. Ambush, blend in, disappear. The government had put a bounty on him—twenty thousand dollars, not pesos, a fortune there. He'd told her in a letter, carried by a courier, he was pleased he bothered Marcos so much. The next month, the bounty doubled, then again, two weeks later. Army agents began trailing her. He was captured. Her folks got nervous; they sent her here.

"How'd they get him?"

"Two of his men shot him, then turned him in," she said evenly. "They split the money, took the amnesty, retired from the war."

"What happened to your friend?"

"Imprisoned, I heard."

"Where?"

"No one knows."

"Is he alive?"

"No one knows."

"Are you waiting?"

"Yes."

"For how long?"

"Until he finds me."

"If he's alive."

"Yes, if he's alive, he'll find me. I'll wait until then."

"Why're you with me?"

"Why not?" She was still on her back, her eyes fixed on the ceiling. "Your turn," she said.

For a moment, those two words made an image in his mind. They stopped being words and had somehow become visual, an overbright beam boring into his heart. For that moment, he followed the beam to the door of a vault full of failures, secret and known, recent and lifelong: Marites, Wynona, the war, his AWOL father—in his mind, they were all tied together, an unbroken line connecting dots through the passing of time. In his mind, he was staring at the door, then turning to walk away.

She was honest, obsessed with the truth—but truth overwhelmed him. What would he reveal? Not too much—a corner, a part of a part—lest it be used as a cudgel to beat him once more. (Would this beating occur when she left him?)

Carmen said what she thought the moment she thought it. She didn't ponder, alter, or edit her words. They were spontaneous, combustible—dangerous traits for a man needing control.

He was sure she expected the same of him, and that made him nervous. Again, he saw himself at the vault; again, the door stayed closed.

Too dangerous, he concluded. His heart would stay guarded. He then rolled on his back and stared at the ceiling.

"Not much to say," he said.

"Tell me."

"Left high school, worked, came down here, boxed a little, worked, went to school, pretty ordinary," he said, of a life that wasn't. She didn't reply. Maybe she believed him? Encouraged, he stretched slowly to his full length, toes and fingertips extended. Such a casual, comfortable move—he made sure she noticed before resuming his monotoned lie. "Had some girlfriends, you met Birdie. Jealous? Violent? Sure, but under the circumstances, ah, normal. Let's see . . . "

"How'd you get this?" She was touching his entry wound. He'd told Birdie, but with Carmen he was hesitant. Maybe later, he thought, when he knew more about her.

He laughed and hoped it sounded natural. "Stupid kid stuff, my dad's loaded gun. Typical." He laughed again just in case.

"Typical?"

"Sure."

"Big," she said.

"Large caliber," he said, as much to the ceiling, as to the one lying next to him. "Dad liked to kill what he shot."

* * *

August 2, 1974

We've decided to live apart, and that's likely for the best. I enjoy her company, and she enjoys mine; we're getting closer. But sometimes, she presses too much, demanding—usually without saying—that I open up and tell her. Open what? There's nothing to open. Tell her what? There's nothing to say.

She throws up her hands. Whatever, she says.

We've had a few of those conversations, and maybe I'll tell her, but for now, I'm just not ready. Still, I like being with her. I also like being alone.

Plus, she hates my neighborhood, and I can't stand her anti-Marcos friends. About them, she was right—soft, every one of them. I tried going to another meeting, mostly just to spend more time with Carmen. They were polite in their limp sort of way and smile fucked the stupid pagan. That lasted half an hour until I got up to go home. I even passed up the spread on that huge living room table—missing the meal's the only part I regret. I should've asked for a doggie bag or two.

They didn't want me, I didn't want to be there. By staying and matching them smile for smile, I was holding them hostage, they had to behave. A week's worth of chicken, pork, noodles and rolls could've bought them their freedom.

Later that night, Carmen swung by, doggie bags in hand and crammed full of lumpia, pansit, pork adobo and other treats. When Dad left, he took his cooking with him. Carmen and I sat at the table and polished it off. I told her that her immigrant pals and I had nothing in common, other than pork—marinated and deep fried—the only cultural tie that still binds.

She laughed, then added that the immigrants, even the rich ones, are colonized people tied to America. Almost thirty years after independence, they were believers still in American legends. So when Nixon says Marcos is okay, a swell democratic prince, Filipinos nod and smile and worship the words—their chant verbatim, their tone solemn.

Yes, Bwana.

Then they apply for their visas, destination downtown USA, in time for the holiday sales at Macy's. She sighed. Monkey see, monkey do. They still look up to whites—Americans are white, right? —to tell them what to do. The Philippines, she said, was fucked up that way. Sure, Americans oppress Filipinos, but mostly Filipinos oppress themselves.

She walked over to the refrigerator and opened a beer. Need to drink, she said between slugs when she returned. Can't stand it otherwise.

"Anything harder?" she asked.

"No, just beer."

"Damn," she muttered, and killed the beer.

"Yeah, Marcos is a puppet leading a land full of puppets," she said. "But we welcome him because the Americans have blessed him."

Not me, I told her. American born have no illusions. We're poor, we don't have heroes. No icons, no MacArthur in the sky. We get rid of our presidents.

She nodded her head. It's different here, she said—skeptical, cynical, free of fake legends. Then she stared at me. "You don't believe," she said, pointing at me. "I don't know why 'cause you're not saying, but you've made your own world and within it you're free. You're lucky in a way." Carmen then rose for another beer.

"You fuck me, Rico, and we have a good time," she said lightly, then popped open a Bud and licked the foam.

She was starting to smile a bit too much. Not even two beers, such a lightweight, I thought. "You just don't believe in me, at least not enough," she said. "It could bother me, sure, but it doesn't yet . . . What's it matter to you? I'm a temporary fuck, I'll get over it . . ."

*   *   *

Maybe she didn't get over it? Rico hadn't seen her for three weeks. She'd stopped going to class, stopped answering her phone. No one seemed to know, not even her immigrant pals who shrugged and smiled when he dropped in. As usual, they were meeting; they were chatting about sales and great bargains and planning a revolt they'd have others fight.

Carmen here, Carmen gone, no one knew her anyway—pass the lumpia, please—maybe back home. Back to her lover, he thought.

The first week without her was okay. He didn't miss her, he told himself, and watched his lips form the words in a mirror. To be sure, he worked a few extra shifts, killed time, and made some cash. The second week, though, was harder. He didn't miss her, he'd whisper, but he'd show up at class and stand outside the door as the buzzer rang. No Carmen, no Rico either, as he'd just turn around and head back home. Burton called and wondered where he'd been. Would he please start attending? He'd hate to fail him.

"Fail me," Rico growled, and hung up the phone.

By the third week, no longer able to lie, he buried himself in work, taking as many shifts as his body could stand. Rico worked whenever, wherever, welcoming movement and fatigue and later, glasses full of late night and early morning shots, one after one after one.

On Monday, he'd finished a pint, by Wednesday, a fifth. By Thursday, the bottles, now empty, were forming a line over by the window—glass sentries on review, the tallest ones last. When she asked—if she asked—what would he tell her? Everything, he thought, his litany of sorrows, of failure, these he'd decided to share. If she asked, if he saw her, he'd open the vault and show her his life.

If he saw her, if she asked.

One morning, half drunk but unable to sleep, Rico decided to go for a walk. He stumbled down the stairs and out the door. It was a bright Saturday morning of the third week without her. He squinted. The sun hurt his bloodshot eyes. He began walking in the direction of what he thought was an old Catholic church two blocks down; he wasn't sure if it was, he'd never been near it.

But it was stucco, Spanish style, with a red tile roof and served free hot lunches. He'd heard his neighbors say they were going to eat at Saint whoever or Blessed body part or whatever it was. It sounded Catholic.

Plus, the building just looked Catholic. He hadn't been in a church since Seattle, his sophomore year, when he showed up at a cousin's wedding. But that didn't count; mostly, he'd hung out in the back and waited for the reception. There, he chatted with his buddies, snuck smokes, and laughed at his cousin who was marrying one pregnant girlfriend (four months), while passing on another (two months). His bride to be, he explained, was more pregnant and had seniority, plus two brothers who'd promised to kill him.

Rico smiled at the memory. As he recalled, he'd been at the church, but not inside. It might be time, he figured, to reacquaint himself.

*   *   *

It was Catholic after all. Rico entered the church and sat in the rear. A handful of others were scattered throughout. One old lady, eyes tightly shut, was kneeling in front of a statue, a saint of some kind who'd died a violent, blood-stained death, but whose name he couldn't recall. Two other parishioners—maybe husband and wife—prayed the rosary and looked hopeful and calm.

He was neither. He wondered how they did it, these people of faith, and wished he could, too. Between forefinger and thumb, the beads made their way through the mysteries of faith—their tactile reply to original sin. They believed in God, His mercy, a life after death. For Rico, his goal wasn't so high. A life in this life would do nicely.

He stared at the beads, steadily moving, as if their movement could change a thing. He thought of Wynona. She was like that, a woman of faith, but her creed was another and foreign to him. Still, between them—Wynona and these Catholics—they shared a trait, a belief in the other, however defined. If she was here, she'd understand the pious old woman, the husband and wife. She'd see their hearts, their will to believe. She'd nod and smile. But his own heart? He wondered, what would she see? Rico looked at the others with their eyes-closed faith and dropped the thought.

He pondered for a moment the irony of praying for one lover (or trying to), while remembering another. Ironic, he thought, but not inconsistent. Wynona had faith and Carmen did, too, but hers was of a different sort, rooted in humans, in their will to fight back. For Carmen, God wasn't needed. His name had never been said.

For Rico, though, this was a time to rethink—he'd tried it alone. But alone he'd plunged down, not straight point A to point B down like a bomb marked "born to lose," but slower—always circling, spiraling, catching the occasional updraft that allowed him to float and hope and delay his descent. The delays were the cruelest, a deceit. What was the point? Why linger and sugarcoat the ending? A lousy life, a crummy end—it had its own inherent logic. His life was passing, and there were times he just wanted a quicker pace.

Rico believed he carried a brand, a big scarlet F—fuckup, failure, Filipino, take your pick—and Carmen was the latest in a string of tragedy and unsuccess, a word he'd coined for his condition. Each new sorrow had diminished him, ended the hover, and begun his plunge anew, but faster than ever.

He missed Carmen and his missing ate what was left of his soul. Early in the string, right after the war, he'd told himself that his setbacks had made him strong, more able to endure. He'd come to conclude he was wrong. Defeats invited bigger defeats, made them inevitable. He wanted now to break that string, and understood this might be his last chance. Did he love her? Maybe, maybe not—he hardly knew her—but that was beside the point. He was willing to try, to open the vault and empty its contents.

He'd beg her to stay, to forget his unnamed rival and his doomed revolution. What word did she want? Love? He'd say it (shout it, even), and mean it. He'd lay it all out, a winner-take-all move. He smiled ruefully at the thought. The French had done that in a valley near Laos—a set-piece battle with nothing held back. The winner would take all. Dien Bien Phu, the valley was called. The French were slaughtered.

Still, he was willing to gamble. Maybe faith could change his luck, and this time he'd land on a ledge where he could rest and finally change direction.

Would prayer do it? He didn't know; he'd never really tried. He knelt and stared at the altar, the tabernacle, the crucifix. He saw angles and shapes; he saw marble, gold, and wood, but nothing else. He tried closing his eyes—maybe that would help?—and this time he saw Carmen. They were in his apartment making love. He lingered and savored the moment before sitting back down.

His quest had produced an erection. His sudden hardness surprised him. It had been so long, almost three weeks. Just to make sure, he grabbed himself. Hardness confirmed.

Rico sighed and rose, then walked down the aisle toward dark heavy doors. As he entered the sunlight, he stopped for a moment at the top of the stairs. He sniffed the air and sampled a scent carried to him on a breeze. He smiled. "Meatloaf," he mumbled, and remembered that lunch here was free.

When was the last time he'd eaten? For the moment, he wasn't sure. A day at least, maybe longer. Now famished, he followed the scent to the auditorium. As he filed into line, he smiled. The day hadn't been wasted. Meatloaf and a hard on, he thought, surprising results of his search for faith.

*   *   *

One day's middlin' can be another day's prize. That's how Rico felt as he left the auditorium, his belly now full of meatloaf swimming in thick, bland gravy, instant mashed potatoes, and a handful of canned peas. He'd eaten better in boot, where the purpose of food was to keep recruits upright and moving through the next ordeal. Enough meals, enough ordeals, enough Marines bound for the bush. For recruits, flavor wasn't an option, an item to be ordered. It was the same for the poor.

Still, he couldn't complain. The midday sun, unhidden by clouds, warmed him. A good omen, he thought, as he turned toward home. Plus, the meatloaf—that humblest offering—was an improvement over the booze he'd been sucking, and maybe his first hot meal since Carmen had vanished. He couldn't finish his portion—a nibble here, a few bites there—his stomach had shrunken so. Still, the simple pleasure of eating, once almost forgotten, had just been recalled. The recalling pleased him; he felt alive, almost giddy, as he slowed to where he'd stop just to inhale or to look at others who shared this length of sidewalk—the junkies and drunks, the merchants and cops.

As their myriad colors and forms, their sounds, even their smells rushed to fill him, an odd sensation touched him before moving on. He was happy, he thought, as if that was so odd.

He approached a bus stop bench, built for three but occupied by one, a scruffy young white man who oozed bad attitude and occupied too much space.

Rico sat down and turned toward his companion. He smiled. "Don't."

Convinced he wouldn't, he turned to other matters. Was happiness temporary, a permanent past-tense condition? If it came, how long would it last? Why did it come today? How could he make it stay?

The blue uncluttered sky recalled Vietnam, his killing days, when he'd hated the sun, which broiled his helmet and sapped his will. Over open valleys or fields, or up steep, slick ravines, he would search for an enemy that refused to be seen. Experts at camouflage, they became where they were—twigs among trees or leaves among foliage.

Always watched by those who would kill him, it was one more step, always one more step, and to take that step, his mind had played games. Living and dying, he couldn't control. Sure, he could reduce the risks, but the final call wasn't his. So, every four days, he'd decided to shave, in the same way and, if possible, at the same time. Dying or living, he couldn't control; his schedule for shaving, he could. And so, almost without fail every fourth day, Rico shaved, whether in the field or a Saigon hotel room. Shaving brought him pleasure. In the midst of disorder, it was an act he controlled.

The schedule took on its own life and logic. Four days became his own unit of time; ninety-six hours filled his day, not twenty-four. That was how he counted time remaining, which was always less than that owed by his pals. Twenty days (twenty shaves), he'd told his friends; it sounded better than eighty. Still, he knew he was playing a mind trick, using a stopgap, a way to get by, but for a long time it worked until reality grew too large north of Hue.

There, the trick had collapsed, it had to, but despite the failure, it may still have uses, an awareness brought by, of all things, a meatloaf. It had triggered a run of rare good feelings. Maybe its secret wasn't its taste—none really—but his decision to eat, to act and exert some measure of control. Carmen, he knew, was beyond control.

He'd loved her present tense, for the moment. Wasn't that what she'd said? Like the sun over Frisco, Carmen might appear, but never at his beckon.

Tomorrow, the sun would be gone. Would he mourn its passing? Did mourning make sense? Then why mourn Carmen? Control what you can, he told himself, get rid of the rest. Brave words, logical, the latest mind trick, the best. He sighed and slowly rose from the bench. Maybe for now—with his belly full and the sun warming his face—but tonight, when she'd come to his dreams, how would he fare? He paused, hand shielding his eyes, and stared down the block toward his apartment. He saw colors and shapes, but nothing in particular. He shrugged and began walking slowly toward home.

How would he fare? He couldn't promise.

He just wanted to sleep well, a dreamless, Carmen-less sleep. That was the goal. As he walked, he pondered the means. Did exhaustion kill dreams? Did booze? Should he go to the gym or the bar? Should he run until collapse, until the concrete pounded his joints and fogged his brain? So immersed was he, so distracted from specifics, he passed the entry to his building and the jumble of human forms and sounds—gathered as always on or near the steps—that were part of his building and part of this street.

A car horn jolted him. He looked up. To Rico's surprise, he was at the end of the block, a foot into the crosswalk but against the light. He jumped back in time to avoid a white delivery van whose Italian driver flipped him the finger as he sped by.

Another sound, this one human, caught his attention.

"Where ya been, brothaman?"

Rico knew the voice, knew the inflection. He froze and faced the light as it changed from red to green to amber to red again, then green.

"You crossin'?" The voice was just behind his right shoulder. For that voice, he'd pined and desired—then arranged, minimized, and categorized—once switched on, he'd begun to switch off. The change, either way, was hard. He didn't turn to look.

"No."

"Then why we standin' here like a couple'a light poles, just waitin' for a dog come piss on our legs?" She yanked on his sleeve.

"Got takeout, good Chinese." He could hear the bag shake. "Three dishes plus rice," she added.

"Just ate," he answered, still not moving.

"Need a table."

"Go to the park."

"Say my name."

He didn't reply.

"Fine, be that way," she said. "I'ma wait by your door and when you get off the rag, come on back home." The voice grew more distant. "You know where I'll be."

Eyes closed, he folded his arms and gathered himself. He was still in a sea of motion, as the stoplight raced through several more cycles and pedestrians moved by him. Finally, he stirred—a shrug of his shoulders, a roll of his neck.

He turned toward home.

*   *   *

Rico sat at the table and watched her eat. He was conscious of distance, psychic and physical, and, hands folded—fingers evenly interlaced—he sat at the table, posture erect, like he was at an IRS audit explaining a bad deduction. Short of being a corpse, he couldn't have been stiffer. He listened as she talked; she'd changed voices again and this time Carmen sounded airy, suburban, as she skipped from unimportant this to boring that, in a lunch-with-the-girls singsong and oh-by-the-way tone.

"Hmm, tasty," she said, as her chopsticks lifted a thick, glazed slice of chicken. "I feel like a pig eating alone, you should join me."

He shook his head. "Full."

"Well, aren't you glad to see me?"

He shrugged. "Surprised," he said slowly.

"Oh," she said, her tone disappointed. She pushed away her plate and stared at him. "You know, I thought about you, I wanted to come back . . . "

Another shrug, so tiny and slow, like it hurt him to move. He didn't immediately reply; he was counting words. "Where ya been?" he finally said. Three, at that moment, the most he could spare.

"Canada."

"Watchin' hockey?"

"Funny."

"You should go back," he said evenly, his even tone designed to cut, to be heard and remembered and when recalled, to cut again. He knew what he was doing; he understood the costs. He'd miss her, he knew, maybe badly, but still, he couldn't stop. He saw her longing, felt her sorrow, maybe even her love. He was feeling the same things.

For a moment he paused—this was insane—but he just couldn't stop. It was an execution; he was killing her heart, maybe his, too, but that was a cost he'd accept. Control what you can, get rid of the rest. In the space of hours, he'd become kamikaze; words, distance, tone were his weapons of choice.

All was acceptable; all was fair.

He played a hunch. "He's alive, right?"

Her eyebrows arched, then dropped. She turned away. "Yes," she mumbled.

"In Canada?"

"No," she whispered. "Still back home, but his cousin saw him outside Manila. He'd escaped, he's in hiding, but okay. The cousin lives in Vancouver and called me from there; he gave me his letters." She opened her purse; inside was a bundle of envelopes tied together by a thin blue ribbon. "He called from Manila; he wants me to come home."

"Go," Rico said, his voice still even.

She stared at him, her eyes beginning to brim. "I'm not sure anymore," she said, her voice unsteady. She reached to touch his hands. He didn't react, not a flinch or downward glance.

"Give me a reason not to," she whispered. "Please."

He looked at her, less sure now than before. Her tears were falling freely. He thought at that moment he wanted to hold her and profess his love, to stop her sorrow, to surrender. Instead, he just sighed, but not so deeply she'd notice. His mien, he was sure, stayed constant, impassive.

"Go," he said again.

*   *   *

The shuffling of a chair, a muted conversation, the sound of a closing door, items in a sequence. They'd happened so fast, they collided in a jumble that was hard to pull apart. Sometimes he would wonder if they'd said what they'd said, or done what they'd done. He wanted to remember, frame by frame, each word, each look, move, and inflection, with a he-did-then-she-did precision. A commemoration, an explanation—these last embers of love he struggled to recall as, weeks later, he would lay in his bed, eyes open, unable to sleep.

Then the final image, their denouement—he would remember looking through his window. He would remember watching her walk away, her hand covering her face. That was the worst, the hardest, he'd almost succumbed and opened the window and called her name. He gritted his teeth; the window stayed closed. This end was for the best; she would hurt him again. It was in her nature, he kept repeating, as his heart had moved into his throat. It was his fate, it couldn't be helped. Better sooner than later—his preemptive strike—before love got too tragic, too deep.

He was doing what he'd had to, he was controlling what he could.

*   *   *

He sat up then turned on the bedside lamp. Eyes half open, he fumbled in the headboard behind him until his fingers found their targets—a pen and a small leather book, his diary. Slowly, he stretched his neck to hear the small, satisfying pops before turning to a blank page. He needed to write. There was something he wasn't sure about, words between them that might (might not) have been said. Of that day, he'd replayed the tape many times, all of it. But a frame was missing. Maybe writing would help fill in the gaps, but first, he had to invite company which came in the form of a bottle, a dark one, its top usually off, no glass needed. He took a deep gulp and sighed at the warmth that filled him. In his small apartment, his new best friends were everywhere—on the table, by the bathtub, near his bed. They'd also grown taller—all fifths now, not pints.

He closed his eyes to drift into the past. In his mind, the tape rewound then played once again for an audience of one. Pay attention, he told himself, and took another drink.

*   *   *

August 24, 1974

Before she left my apartment, I had one last question. She was crying and had opened the door, and I asked her out of the blue, I'm not sure why. Her father's tribe. What was it? She was out the door when she answered.

Washoe? Was it Washoe she said? Wasn't Frank a Washoe?

*   *   *

Rico's diary, long since discarded, lay open and at his side as he shifted and tossed. He wanted to sleep, but couldn't as his mind retook the road trip from Frisco to a bleak Dakota butte. An empty bottle of bourbon was lying on the floor. He was too tired or indifferent to search the apartment for more.

Memories of that trip, long since ignored, had started to blur. It seemed so long ago. What did Frank even look like? It was dark; Rico couldn't remember. She shouldn't have killed him, he told himself. He shouldn't have even gone because now he had another tape of bad memories returning tonight, a painful twin bill to haunt him. But the images weren't keeping him awake. It was the laughter he was hearing, an undulating sound that snickered, giggled, and roared.

He shook his head. Maybe it would leave? But even as he grabbed at his temples, the laughing only got louder.

It was a male voice, it sounded familiar. Where had he heard it? Who was the owner? What was the joke? Would someone please tell him the joke?

Chapter Twelve

Rico thought he'd mourn Carmen for months, maybe years, or longer. But his voices made sure he never got the chance. He first began hearing them a day or so after Carmen left—and that was seven months ago. Sometimes, the meds would help, but that's when he'd remember to take them—an unsure bet at best. Even with the meds, he could still hear the voices, but not as often and not as loud.

Over long stretches of pill-free time, there were moments of clarity when Rico knew the voices meant he was losing his mind. The audio was bad, distracting enough to force him to quit school. He thought about checking himself in to the nut house, but that would mean the voices had won. He refused to give in.

Rico learned to adjust, to expect the words and, with sounds humming in his head, to just focus on the task at hand. As the voices laughed and talked, sometimes sang, cans of peas and beans just kept moving to their spots on grocery shelves, each label turned out toward the aisle for shopping convenience.

The video, though, was worse and more recent. The latest occurred the night before last; his aisle, strewn with boxes empty and full, had darkened into a trail, a narrow, muddy slit, like those he'd slogged in Vietnam. Suddenly, he crouched and became still;

at the end of the aisle, where the produce section had once been, the enemy waited to his left, just out of sight. He knew, he'd heard him, he'd get him first. An accidental bump by a coworker walking by jolted Rico and returned him to his Frisco world of canned goods and box-strewn aisles.

"Closin' in ten, Rico," the worker said, without looking down. "Gotta finish this section."

Had the coworker looked down, he'd have seen what Rico had once been and was becoming again—a dangerous man. The coworker, though, didn't—he kept walking to the back, toward produce, and the back room beyond—and that was better for all concerned.

"Rough," Rico mumbled as he slowly stood up. He winced; his thighs and calves ached, his lower back, too.

"Hey man, you need help?" It was the coworker again. He was pointing to a group of full boxes still in the aisle. Donnie was a nice enough kid, eighteen years old and just out of high school. They'd talked during break. He was working and still at home, saving money for college. He'd returned from the back, his jacket in hand. "Shift's over pretty soon," he said, a big stupid smile breaking across his face.

"I'm cool," Rico said, as he began racing through his remaining boxes, grabbing and tossing cans from box to shelf.

"You sure?"

"Yeah, yeah, Donnie, no sweat."

"Well, you know my ride doesn't come for . . . "

"I'm cool," he said without looking up, as his hands whirred right to left. As soon as he spoke, he worried about his tone; it may have sounded abrupt. The kid was nice, an innocent. Rico glanced up, even as cans continued flying to just the right spots on the shelf; he smiled.

"Thanks, I'm okay, Donnie, no really, Donnie, almost done, really." He broadened his smile. "Really."

"Okay, Rico," Donnie replied, and turned. Rico, returning to his task, heard his footsteps. He sighed and increased his pace.

Being alone, getting rid of Donnie, was important. He was back in the present and standing on off-white linoleum—he looked down and stomped just to be sure—not knee deep in mud. Solid. Satisfied, he took a deep breath.

The voices he'd learned to accommodate; when they came, he just kept going, kept doing what he'd started—walking, talking, wiping his ass, a normal façade. To these voices he refused to reply. Sometimes, they called his name; they wanted to trap him with conversation, but he refused to join because he'd seen what had happened to those who did. They were living in doorways or under bridges, they were sleeping in unlocked cars; their lips always moved as they talked to voices only they could hear.

When his voices came, he decided they could talk to each other. They could laugh and cajole, they could insult and scream, curse or warn. No matter, he wouldn't reply.

But visions were a different matter, pill-resistant, more troubling, much harder to ignore. Like if Donnie, fresh-faced and friendly, had become something else—an enemy, an armed enemy drawing a bead—what would he do? He knew the answer and it broke his concentration of hand to hand to shelf. Rico took a break and stood up. The muscles in his shoulders and neck had bunched together. He twisted and turned; the knot didn't loosen. A fresh wet sheet began covering his forehead. Rico wiped it with a sleeve. It wasn't enough, a new sheet began forming; he wiped it again and glanced at the floor. Three boxes left.

He'd finish the boxes and get the hell out. He'd walk home. He'd be alone. He was thankful for small breaks.

* * *

It was three in the morning when Rico finally left the store to step into a cold, cloudless March night. This store was on Diamond Heights, a bit father away than the others he'd worked. He didn't know the neighborhood; before today, he had no reason to be here. He paused to fish in his pockets; the jangle and heft on both sides of his pants stated the obvious—enough for a cab in coin alone. Still, he knew he wouldn't call a cab—the night was clear, the walk was downhill, he was almost always broke.

Rico moved quickly, hearing only the sounds of his footsteps, nothing more, not even the strain of an engine moving uphill. He walked two blocks, then two more, and passed no one. It seemed odd to him, so unlike his life in the Loin, where junkies and drunks kept their own time and often sang hymns to the night.

That's it, he thought, as he glanced at his surroundings—the handsome apartments, the striking view homes—no night songs here. There was no need. People slept when night fell; they didn't hear voices. He imagined that behind each thick door lived doctors or judges or deans, their lives well adjusted, their families well fed and content. He stopped before a stately Victorian, its youth reclaimed by sandpaper and fresh paint. He admired its silhouette, angled and proud, and outlined in black against a full, bright moon. He tried imagining himself inside—reading the paper, or sipping coffee, maybe making love. He imagined himself happy.

He blinked. Impossible, he thought, he couldn't do it.

Rico shrugged and walked on to a vista he'd seen on the bus ride up. It was a small ledge that jutted out. Beneath him were the lights of this rude, cluttered city, his home for the last five years. In that time he'd never seen Frisco from this angle—quiet and lovely, deceptively so. Beyond was the huge black bay cut only by bridge lights touching the eastern shore.

His voices were quiet now, and for that he was thankful. Every now and then, he'd read that some poor soul flew off the bridge. Did water still those voices? Would water still his? Suicide, sure, he'd thought of it. Who wouldn't? Still, he didn't want to die. Once, in a dream, he'd seen his body bloated, pale, and broken. He'd soared off the bridge and had come upon himself—a bone-dry, dream-state witness standing on shore and watching the fall. The witness wondered what could have driven the deceased—such a poor, cold fool—to have taken this step?

Now, he knew.

The visions, he guessed, were brought by the voices to which he'd adjusted and to which they'd replied, "Oh yeah, adjust to this." It was a game of escalation, like the one between Ho and LBJ, a tat for tit for tat. No, he didn't want to die, but to stop the voices and the more recent visions, he just might.

Oddly, the voices were now quiet, no sounds to be heard or visions to be seen. Maybe his voices would push him only to a point, then back away. Maybe they didn't want him flying and ending their fun. If he was dead, they'd lose their host, their source of amusement.

He scanned the expanse of the lights below. After five years, he knew the city's reputation—as a center of tolerance and love, an oasis of art—and maybe it was, but that wasn't the city he knew. His was a place of old needles and shards of bottles once full of tokay, gulped never sipped, or fortified beer for fragile, unfortified souls. Like urban American punjis, the shards were lying in wait to impale the unwary—the uncovered foot, the too thin sole, the unconscious body on the ground.

Still, in this city there were pockets like Diamond Heights, places he'd never explored. Maybe here there were shamans and saints who gathered to heal those who sought them out. In that case, what was the address? When did they meet? Could he get there by bus?

He smiled and sighed. Such a pleasant thought, floating and unreal, a full dimension away from Van Ness, the broad north-south arterial to the east of which was the Loin, his home and destination. He hated the Loin but he knew he fit there. It was like a field hospital full of discards, the gravely wounded and dying. Which one, he wondered, was he? Did it matter? Or did the first lead always to the second? In his building and on his street, humans cried and screamed; they hurt each other; they pissed and puked on the walls. Maybe in this world, perhaps even in this city, there were shamans and saints, but he'd never seen one in the Loin.

A light breeze tickled the back of his neck. He shivered as his hands burrowed deeper into his pockets. Rico knew he needed help; he couldn't survive alone. But absent a shaman, or at least one nearby, who could he call? He glanced at his watch—almost four now. He smiled, as his thoughts drifted to an older home. Buddy was sleeping; a ringing phone would jolt him. Sure, he'd bitch, but he'd answer; more important, he'd talk.

Rico turned slowly toward the sidewalk and resumed walking. He felt light, for him, an odd sensation. Whatever the time, Rico knew Buddy would talk.

Chapter Thirteen

Buddy promised to come down, the end of the month looked good. When Rico finally hung up, he felt giddy, full of hope. The voices were silent, the visions were gone. Even the weather would be nice. He glanced at a calendar on the wall. It was less than two weeks away; Rico could wait.

But after a few days, a new vision appeared and began leaving trace evidence of its visit—newspapers, some several days old, their corners starting to yellow and curl. *The New York Times* was there, same with *The Monitor* and an array of local rags, morning and evening, city and peninsula. First they began covering floor and table space, then the seat of one of two folding chairs before moving to the bedroom and then to his mattress. Yesterday, they took over his bathroom.

Rico was becoming trapped, hooked on their words and the memories they recalled. In Vietnam, old Giap was moving south, an end-game offensive. He'd seen it first on the evening news. He was sitting at the bar, sipping a beer, killing time, just waiting for an empty pool table. Suddenly, there was Rather, or was it Wallace, microphone in hand, reporting solemnly from the field. A close-up now, a casualty, a Vietnamese officer, his chest a gaping red wound. As blood spurted from the cavity, Rico blinked; his hands and temples moistened. Did he know him? He stared at the screen, which quickly switched images, from bush and dust to air-conditioned New York studio.

He started collecting newspapers, all qualities and kinds. He stopped watching the news. Watching hurt him too much. Written words, though, could be rationalized, distorted, minimized, skipped. Their impact—even in describing the most grisly, desperate scenes—was easier to keep at a distance. An image, though, was different, more immediate. For Rico, television made it harder to forget he had once smelled fear or touched the unnatural angles of a broken body, or seen the lines of soldiers running away.

Still, as he sorted through the dispatches, he'd sometimes drift to the sites. Sure, he'd fight it—he knew he shouldn't return—but most of the time he'd lose and see once more the mud holes and plains where NVA regulars were now sweeping and where ARVN troops were breaking and running. Some of the places he'd been to or through, but usually in search of a hit-and-run foe he'd seldom see. Now, though, with the Americans gone, it was clear those hit-and-run days were over. The enemy was swaggering now, showing itself at full division strength in its victory march to Saigon.

Day by day, he traced their movement; day by day they kept moving south. He was obsessed, fascinated by the country's slow death by slicing, each slice a kilometer or more. It was only a matter of time. Yet, he wished that at some point along the collapsing front, an ARVN commander would do the unexpected—draw a line and tell old Giap, "Here, you old fucker, you stop here."

One afternoon, while reading an account in *The New York Times,* he daydreamed himself back into the bush, where he was exhorting a young colonel who smiled as he listened, but snuck glances to his rear. "Fight for your country," Rico heard himself say. "For democracy, or your family, or your comrades who died, or the GIs who came here." Rico paused to wipe his face.

He felt foolish, like a red-faced cheerleader for an army just playing out the string. He shouldn't have had to say the obvious. "Or whatever the fuck you people believe," he added with a growl.

The young colonel, still smiling, finally replied. "No thank you," he heard the colonel politely say. "You have more reasons to fight than we do." He removed his insignia, then his shirt, and threw them both on the ground.

"Well, nice talking to you, American," the colonel said evenly. "I'm done with war. I'm a civilian now, maybe even a peasant—the Communists like peasants—but we'll see." He shrugged. "I really should be going."

Rico, mouth open, just stared as he watched him walk toward the stream of refugees and soldiers clogging the narrow dirt road. They were heading south. Before joining them, the colonel turned and waved. Rico heard him laugh. "The truth is, we're indifferent, we don't really care, at least not that much. The truth is, it's your war. The truth is, you want this country more than we do. Didn't you know that?"

He paused and stared at Rico. "Ask Kennedy or Johnson." The colonel was yelling now; he was waving his hands. "Ask Bob McNamara."

Back in his apartment, Rico could still hear the colonel—his laughter, his matter-of-fact tone. He glanced at his watch: 3:30, the afternoon daily was on the corner rack. Yesterday, he'd have rushed out to buy it. Today, though, it would stay on the rack. Slowly, he began gathering the newspapers that had overrun floor and table and bedroom and placed them in bags for the morning trash run. Today, he would stop buying papers. Even words had their power, one he now knew he could no longer handle.

*   *   *

"Six, left corner," Rico said, and pointed with the tip of his stick to the target. "I'ma love spendin' your money, my man."

Tommy, his opponent, was a stringy haired, soda straw thin

white guy, a good-natured regular who just shrugged and sipped
on his beer. He drank too much and was too often stoned—his
drug of choice, whatever he could cop. He was messed up now, but
he could still count to four, the number of balls he was currently
down. The outcome was clear. Even when he was straight, he was
a lousy shot, and Tommy was far from straight today. A glance at
the table, then—his attention starting to wander—at the TV
above the bar, which was showing the wonders of Ban. Sighing, he
reached to his back pocket and patted his wallet. Inside was a ten
dollar bill he'd soon have to break. He smiled. At least he hadn't
been picked.

A bank shot—bank, bingo—Rico figured, to avoid the clutter.
If he stroked it just right, the cue ball would hit the six, then stop,
and leave him in line for the eight and collecting a double or nothing bet, five bucks in this case. Not high stakes, but enough for a
burger and some beers from the tap. Good thing, too, he hadn't
been working, he was almost broke, it was late afternoon. His
tongue dabbed at the corners of his mouth; he was getting
hungry.

He drew back his stick and lined up his shot. That was first,
then came the checklist—balance, feel, focus. All present, all go.
He visualized the trajectory of the solid white ball that would buy
him his dinner, and smiled at the thought.

"Hey, Rico," Tommy exclaimed, and pointed to the television.
"Goddamn, man, look at this."

Jarred, Rico dug the tip of his stick into the green felt surface
before it struck the bottom of the cue ball, which made it hop then
dribble to a stop.

"Goddamn, Tommy, man," Rico sputtered. "Man, I get
another . . ."

"Nah, nah, later for that," Tommy slurred, still pointing
toward the screen before dropping his hand to fish in his right
jacket pocket. Two joints, a half pack of Camels, life was good. He
smiled then resumed pointing. "Lookit the tube, man, lookit . . ."

"Huh?"

"The tube, man, the fuckin' TV," he screamed. Now, he was flapping his arms for emphasis.

Rico stared at the screen, which was showing a mob of humans—women, men, children—barely recognizable as such. They'd lost all other traits, except the will to survive, as they ebbed and surged, elbowed and kicked each other, and pinned those at the front against the high iron gate of a compound. Some of those at the front, their faces distorted, pancaked against the bars, managed to reach through the openings—arms extended, palms open, fingers beseeching.

"Turn it up," Tommy, still flapping, yelled at no one in particular. "Fuckin' awesome." He then glanced at his friend who didn't move and just stared blankly at the television. Tommy didn't notice the contrast.

"Man, weren't you there?" he asked, his voice loud and rasping. "Marines, right? I was there, Navy, but we were mostly offshore." He laughed. "Nothin' dramatic, no war stories, unless you count bar fights and cheatin' whores out of cash, you know, poke and dash, but you, man, phew, heavy."

"Yeah," Rico mumbled. He was almost inaudible. "Marines," he whispered, as if in prayer.

He then lay the cue stick on the table and, without another word, turned and walked to the entry. He was so quiet, Tommy at first didn't notice he'd gone. As Rico reached for the door handle, he thought he heard his friend's voice calling him back, saying he'd found a spare twenty in his half pack of smokes. Goddamn if he knew how it got there, but no matter. Life, already good, had just gotten unusually better. Dinner, he thought his friend said, was on him.

Without a reply, not even the slightest turn, Rico opened the door and stepped into a cool afternoon light. The breeze from the west, from the ocean, refreshed him, made him glad to be outside.

His guts though weren't right; they whirled and spun, and seemed to descend, to bore deeper and displace parts of something maybe important, a slab of his core perhaps. The faster they spun, the deeper they went, the deeper they went, the faster they spun. He grabbed his abdomen, where the pain was now sharpest, and steadied himself against the grimy fake brick front of the building housing the bar. He tried straightening up. The effort hurt him. Then he tried to walk; that hurt, too.

Hunger, he knew, hadn't started the spinning. A meal, he knew, couldn't stop it.

*   *   *

May 1, 1975

Maybe there's something to it, this notion of original sin. You're born behind the eight ball, and those that make it out front and away are the ones that God blesses. It makes us weak, prone to sin, in need of constant prayer. Mom always prayed, but Dad didn't, and I'm more like him than I'll ever be like her. I never liked prayer, and even now, after all that's happened, I still can't stand the thought. So maybe this mess is my fault, and all that's left is to play out whatever string is left. The only good thing so far is that I made it home alive, but even then sometimes I think that's been a mixed blessing because now I have to remember this date, the one listed above.

I think that's today's date, but I've kind of lost track...I didn't think it would hurt me, but it did. What was it about anyway?

Got a cat the other day, a little black kitty with white paws and chin. Company. Jumped out the window and fell off the fire escape. Panicked and ran out into the street. Got his ass run over before I had a chance to name him. My now-dead cat left me with ten pounds of kitty litter, a catnip mouse and a rubber ball I bounce off the ceiling when I can't sleep, which is often.

Wonder if cats have original sin, too, or maybe the little shit got it from me. Wonder if the condition's communicable.

Tommy came by, and dropped off some smoke, potent Mexican stuff that he said was laced with something, I can't remember what. Been hittin' on it awhile. After he left, I had some other visitors . . . I saw Jerome and he asked me the same thing: What was it about? I couldn't answer, but it was good to see him. Tan and healthy, he looked like a cowboy who'd just left the ranch; he was rawboned again, he was intact.

Where's Trigger? I asked. He laughed. Pissin' in your bathtub, he answered.

Jerome left, then others came by. I knew their voices, now they have faces. Some I think I've seen, others I haven't, at least I don't think so. I'm not sure, I was so tired I couldn't focus. I didn't see Dad, though, same with Nona and Carmen. Same with Marites. I guess that means they're still alive.

I used to be afraid, but I'm not anymore. They came mostly in pairs, but sometimes alone, like a stream of guests at a wedding. They just kept coming. I'd doze for a second, then two more would pop up.

I'd tell them, take a hit, have a chair. I'm sure you must be hungry, no, no trouble really, it'll only take a moment. Mi casa es tu casa, and that goes for my mind. Kill the fifth, why don't you, I can always buy another. Hell, kill me if you like, I just don't care. If I live till tomorrow, that would be fine. If I don't, that would also be fine. Let me know what you think. You don't mind if I sleep? I'd smile. I'm incontinent, you know. I'll dump on the floor if I feel like it. Please understand. Mi casa es mi casa.

After I told them that, they didn't stay around. They seemed disappointed. I know now I've got nothing to lose. Maybe I'm beyond being haunted? Fuck them all, they can do their worst.

I'm twenty-six, but add fifty years and you have my true age. I wonder what'll go first, my kidneys or my mind? I'll be lucky to last the year; I'm lucky to have lasted this long. If that's how it's scripted, I'll just play it out.

Anything left? Loose ends, I suppose. Yeah, I've got a few I want to tie up. I told Buddy once I wanted to write a book, fiction.

Not autobiography, a real make-believe universe with a protagonist, a challenge, a decision. It wouldn't be soft, or have some neat little ending the public can accept (and buy). I could write an ambivalent climax and denouement, a win-some, lose-more set that resembles most of the lives that normal humans live. In my own life, I'd take that in a heartbeat.

Hell, I'd take a woman who'd stay till intermission. Even that would be an improvement.

This diary's been a great place to practice. I've worked on skills here. On these pages, I've told the truth, at least at some level, at least I think I have—and truth is the soul of fiction.

I'd love to get started on my book and just hope there's enough time. My luck, though, I'm probably down to months.

* * *

Last night's dream was the most disturbing by far. First, there was the all too familiar scent, an ungodly mix of blood and heat, fear and tropical decay. Then, the gentlest of flicks, caresses on the nape of his neck. He knew the sequence, understood what would happen next.

"Hey, buddy," a familiar voice said.

"Go away, Jerome," Rico mumbled.

In the dream, Jerome appeared just as he was during the last moments of his life. His remaining appendage, his left arm, was shredded at the shoulder. It somehow managed to stay attached to the rest of his body, but not by much. His death wound—a bullet through his right eye—mangled half his face.

Jerome had appeared like this before, the first time during the chopper ride back, when morphine dulled Rico's pain and he felt his eyelids close. A drugged-out dream, he figured at the time. But there were other dreams, other appearances, so Rico should have gotten used to it. But he could never fully adjust because he hated reliving the sorrow of that moment.

"Go away, Jerome."

Jerome laughed. "You always say that, but I know you're glad
to see me."

"No, I'm not. Go away."

"The power of modern munitions, eh, buddy? Don't worry,
I've just dropped by for a minute."

"Go away, Jerome."

"No te preocupes, amigo. I don't feel it no more, least not the
physical part," Jerome said, laughing. "I learned the lingo in the
cantinas near San Diego. Nah, nah, not the one you busted up . . .
In a sense, you're lucky. I can't smoke on the other side, bro,
damn."

Rico sighed. "So, uh, what brings you here this time, man?"

Jerome shrugged. "A little worried, I guess," he said, and
looked away. "Man, you're goin' the wrong way, and it don't have
to be so. I wanna see ya, but not too soon . . . "

"Ain't your business, Jerome."

"What happened that day makes it my business," Jerome said
calmly, his eyebrow arched on the good side of his face.

Rico had no reply.

"Now gettin' back to why I'm here," Jerome continued. "You
could still do what I wanted to do. I ain't as dumb as you kept
tellin' me I was. I'd done pretty good in high school and wanted to
go to college. Got accepted, too. I wanted to read and study, maybe
English or history. I wanted to do somehin' my folks never had a
chance to do. I'da been the first in my family to go to college, hell,
I'm the first to graduate from high school."

"Didn't know that, man."

"Lotta things you didn't know. But it ain't your fault. Bein' a
Marine and such, you became your uniform, we all did, acting like
we was supposed to, the warrior whatever . . . and you were doin'
the same thing."

Jerome slowly shook his head, the slowness of the shake a sign
of what could have been.

"I liked writin', thought I could, you know, get pretty good at it in college. But no money, honey. So, one day I go talk to this recruiter and he tells me about the GI Bill, so I figure I'll just take my chances and live long enough to collect."

"I'm sorry, man. Didn't know that."

"You didn't know a whole lot, my man," Jerome said calmly. "But I knew you, know you better now. I know you're messin' up."

"Ain't your business, Jerome."

"It is since you put me this way," Jerome said sharply." "This time you gonna listen, whether you want to or not."

"Ah, man."

"That time in Saigon, outta the bush, three days off, we are at an old hotel, Rue somethin' or other. Damn, can't remember its name, but it was nice, air conditioned, the whole bit. Then late at night, you start to scream, talkin' to someone, something, and I walk over and hold ya, cradle ya, tell ya, sweet baby, everything's gonna be okay. And you hold me back. Remember?"

"No," Rico answered sullenly.

"Typical, man, keep lyin' to youself. Still the Marine, semper fi, fee, fo, fum . . . whatever. That's why on that day, I had to go getcha. I couldn' letcha die."

"Go away, Jerome," Rico whispered.

"You still got a chance, maybe not much, but you still got one."

"Chance for what?" Rico asked as Jerome's image disappeared.

*   *   *

Even before opening his eyes, Rico knew where he was. The dead, antiseptic air, the rubber-soled shuffles and quiet matter-of-fact voices, the stiff, cold sheets—all clues, but which ward? Which hospital. For that matter, which city?

He tried sitting up, but couldn't. Finally, he opened his eyes to see his wrists handcuffed to the posts built into the bedframe. He knew where he was—nut ward, San Francisco General. The last time he was here he'd seen a new patient bound the same way.

He was young, a Samoan, bullnecked and strong. Powered by meth and his own brute strength, he decided to leave. Rico watched him flex and try pulling his hands together. The cuffs strained and held, but the bed almost didn't as the frame curved upward, then in. His effort, staccatoed by grunts, was cheered by his ward mates who whistled and clapped and grunted along. The Samoan was stopped by three hospital cops—one on his head, one on each arm—and a nervous young doc who jammed calmness into his bloodstream. They found him a new bed.

Rico didn't want another sedative; one was just wearing off. They had him, the handcuffs would hold. He wasn't Samoan. Struggle, he knew, was useless. Besides, he wanted answers more than freedom, at least for now. How'd he get here (again)? Just what had he done (again)?

He took a deep breath. In his mind, he began forming questions; softly, he whispered to himself, trying out his tones—too grating, too timid, just right. In his experience, docs didn't like talking to loud crazy people—those messy, bug-eyed souls who spoke, often screamed, in riddles and foamed at the mouth. No, he thought, he'd sound normal, bland, boring as a banker—docs loved that. If he asked the right doc, in just the right way, he might hit the jackpot where the doc might conclude he was sane (at least at the moment), so why was he cuffed? He then practiced smiling and looking alert, aware, but no audience yet, not a doc in sight, not even a nurse.

A neighbor, a skeletal middle-aged black man who'd been watching him and was identically trussed, was hugely amused. "Give it up, psycho," he screamed in a black bass voice. "No way."

Rico, still in character, smiled. "Fuck you," he answered politely.

"I'm on thorazine," the neighbor said. "It calms me pretty well, but I just can't take the sun. How 'bout you, you lingering on the border or gone way down south. Hmm, what's your candy, pretty man? Haldon, I'll bet."

"Fuck your mama," Rico said, still polite.

The neighbor just cackled. "I did, or at least my records say I did, or one of me did," he said, between howls. He'd been laughing so hard, tears began gathering in his eyes. "What about you, friend, what do they say you did, or that one of you did? I'm sure you know the *McNaughton Rule,* you know, the one that asks whether you knew what you were doing was wrong at the time of the act and, oh my, those attorneys just get all worked up over that, and the judges do, too, and they say folks like me abuse it."

Another round of laughter, this one running a range of race, gender, and age. "I'm Venus now," he declared in an alto. "The goddess of love, poor human, just what you and the world needs now is love, sweet love." He started humming a medley of sappy love songs. "Well, you know the tune. I love that Venus, *'Oh, Venus, make my love come true,'*" he trilled. "I start singing that before the jury and, bingo, I avoid hard time." The neighbor paused, his smile smug.

"That was my gimmick, what was yours?" he said, sotto voce, and in a way that didn't expect a reply. He stared at Rico, his look curious.

"You're a little brown boy and so cuuute," he began, his lips forming into a kiss. "I'm the goddess of love, that's *looove,* but I'm not really sure what you . . . "

"Filipino," Rico answered.

"No, now I *know* Filipinos, those tight-packed sweeties from Manila, like little caramels. Hmm. Met my first one in jail. It's not so bad, you know, for me it was kind of like being on *The Dating Game,* but with differences, of course."

"Of course," Rico mumbled.

"That's where I met JoJo, he was in for solicitation and possession." He sighed. "My dear little JoJo, but they were all so much lighter than you, not that dark is bad, of course, but . . . "

"I'm part Indian."

"That poor JoJo, he met such a sad end," the black man said in a lower voice. "My name's Mario, or at least that's the most common one. You *must* speak *Tagalog.* JoJo did, and I tell you, hearing it now would just *send* me. I've seen some Filipino nurses, they seem to be all over this place like dog shit in a park. 'Give me your tired, your poor, your Filipino nurses yearning to breathe free.' That's what it says, or at least it should."

Rico ignored him.

"I sure wish one would come by," he said earnestly. "Don't they have room service?"

"You know, I don't really care."

"Well, thank you for asking about JoJo," he said, as tears began falling from both cheeks. "One night Ding Ding—now, he was also from Manila, you people have such lovely names—stabbed him to death, he was such a jealous bitch, they all are, so hot blooded." Tears were cascading now. "Of course, the prosecutor's trying to blame it on me, or at least one of me."

Rico shrugged. "Of course," he said, and smiled. His tone was just right, normal, now if only a doc would magically appear.

"They told me that's why I'm here," he bawled. "But I'm innocent, I miss JoJo, I loved him. That bitch Ding Ding, I know he's setting me up. Wanna hear how he sounds? I sure do . . ."

Mario continued his caterwaul, but Rico had tuned him out. Neck craned, he was scanning the room and the hallway beyond, looking for someone dressed in white who could listen and hear his tone, his precise, coherent diction—proof he wasn't insane, that he really didn't belong here. At the start, he wanted a doc, then later, a nurse, and, as another half hour passed and he grew more desperate, he was ready to settle for far less—in this place, that meant anyone not tied down.

Buddy met that standard. He appeared at the doorway wearing a sharp, black leather jacket and approached Rico's bed just as his friend had begun his closed-eyed protest—its sign, the reddening around his wrists as he arched his back, and strained against the cuffs. It was futile, he knew, even as he pulled to the point of pain, of hard metal edges digging into bone. Still, he welcomed the pain; it was better than just lying still.

"Hey, man," Buddy said.

"Goddamn, goddamn," Rico exclaimed. "When'd you get in?" In reflex, he extended both arms—an intended hug—a greeting stopped short. "Fuck," he said.

"Yesterday," Buddy said.

"Yesterday? But why didn't you stop by . . ."

"I did."

It was Buddy's tone—flat, odd, almost solemn—that Rico caught first, a trigger to another sense. Buddy's cheek was dark, oddly discolored; his nose was swollen. He was breathing through his lips, which parted slightly to show a missing front tooth.

"Blackboard jungle, huh? Didn't know school was so hard," he said, trying to sound light.

Buddy sadly shook his head. "Man, you don't remember?"

"Remember what?"

Buddy edged closer to the bed, an inch or so, but no more. "Man, you don't remember," he repeated, but this time a statement. He sighed and scanned the room, before recounting what had happened. Yes, he'd come by yesterday, straight from the airport. He'd arrived about noon, and then opened the door to find Rico pacing in circles, mumbling to himself. He said he tried talking to him, tried to touch him, the latter a bad mistake.

"I had my bags, man, just lookin' to hang and catch up, and you Sunday punched me," he said. "Damn, Monday, Tuesday, Wednesday, too, for that matter. Kept callin' me *McNamara,* had one hand around my neck, and kept smackin' me with the other." He gently touched the swelling under his cheek, then chuckled softly. "Gotta do a presentation next week. Think I'ma call in sick, flu or somethin' . . . "

"Buddy, I don't know what to say," he said, as he stumbled for words. "I'm sorry, yeah, you gotta know that, but I just don't remember."

"Yeah, that's what the doc says," he said. "You kept callin' him *Lyndon,* called another doc *Dean,* and did they know what they'd done, and were they sorry? And that you'd kill 'em all if they weren't." He paused. "Crazy shit like that. You had 'em shook, man, really fucked up."

"Man, I don't remember," Rico mumbled. "How'd you get away?"

He laughed, his tone morose. "You had me halfway out the window, man, tryin' to choke me and throw me out," he explained. "And I just screamed like a bitch, man. Made enough noise and the cops came and saved my ass."

Rico closed his eyes and became still, relaxed. He was breathing deeply, eyes still closed, trying to see in his mind what his friend had said he'd done. He couldn't. "I don't know what's wrong with me," he finally whispered.

"It's simple, man, you crazy, you was crazy before you went and the war just made you worse. Thing is, you liked it all, man— way too much. Like a berserker, man, Vikings I read about in college who had it in 'em to go into a trance and do the most fucked-up things in battle—and then turn the switch off. Every culture's got 'em and you're one of ours, but you never had a switch. Or if you did, you left it on—all the damn time. Even as a boy. Remember that time with Delbert? Man, you almost killed him. You was chewing his arm when I pull you off. Covered with blood, man, just laughin' and lovin' it. How old were you, thirteen? Wasn't natural. But we covered for you, man, made excuses—all the fellas did. Maybe you was born bad. I dunno." Buddy paused and looked away.

"And if you ask me, that's why your dad split," he said softly. "He couldn't take no more, not from you, not from your Jesus-lovin' mom. Your dad tried boxing, hoping that'd straighten you out, but all it did was make you more effective. Self-defense, yeah, that's one thing, but you just loved whippin' on folks.

"Then one day, my dad says, you turned on your father, man. I ain't never told you that, but I don't give a shit now. You was drunk and high and you turned on him. Laid him out cold, man, just like that. He figured you just born mean, some kinda Nanay

curse. Nothin' more he could do, least that's what he told my dad
before he left. Nothin' more he could do. You broke his heart."

Rico sadly shook his head. "Man, I don't remember . . . "

"Naturally, man," Buddy whispered. "You never remember
the foul shit you did."

Buddy reached into his inside jacket pocket like he was fishing
for a smoke, then stopped. "Damn, no smokin'," he mumbled,
then stared at Rico. "Then in Vietnam, man, it's like you found
home, your Disneyland, a chance to do all kinda psycho shit . . .
like that time you got Jerome killed."

"Huh?"

"You wrote letters, man, tellin' me what you were doin'. Strip-
pin' the dead, man, takin' ears, fingers, other parts. Your goddamn
trophies. Sent me a fingernail once—and I almost puked before I
threw it away. Then after the ambush near Hue, you heard someone moan, a wounded NVA 'bout fifty yards out. You was suppose
to stay put, but it tempted you too much, so you went after 'im."

Buddy paused like each word spoken had its own invisible
weight. He looked away from Rico and took a deep breath.

"You wanted to slice him up while he could still feel it. Laugh
in his face while you showed him his ears—give him one last
memory before the end. You was supposed to stay put, to be disciplined, but you didn't listen. You pushed it, like pushin' it was
the only thing that ever mattered. Then they open up, and your
butt's in a sling, and Jerome goes to getcha, and you know the
rest . . . "

Buddy hissed as he inhaled through his mouth. His eyes were
narrow, focused, full of something, which if not hate, was its closest blood kin. His tone, though, was even, like he was reciting
instructions in a manual.

"Now this," he continued, "a full blown schizophrenic
motherfucker, plus you got ulcers, man, you was grabbin' your gut
and moanin' and they checked you out. You crazy and your diet's
fucked up. Hope you like milk."

Buddy shook his head. "But the good news is they won't hold

you forever. I ain't pressin' charges, man," he said with a shrug. "For old times, ya know?"

Rico nodded weakly. He knew. "Whatcha gonna do?" he managed to ask.

"Go home, standby, headin' out now," he said. "Ain't nothin' I can do to help . . . Got half a mind to jack ya, though."

Rico studied his friend whose right hand had become a fist. He closed his eyes, not sure if Buddy was serious, but halfway hoping he was. "Go on," he said softly. "Man, I owe ya."

"Big time," Buddy said, in a voice that began to sound fainter, like he was moving away. "One more thing, there was this brother, the sergeant on the scene. Said he knew you from the war, and that he might drop by. Said you gotta leave town, go someplace, just don't stay here, too many memories, too many ghosts." He paused. "Good advice, man."

When Rico's eyes blinked open, Buddy was gone.

"Cute boy, pity you tried to kill him, you should've introduced me, and you know I just love you people," Mario said. "I'd have butted—so to speak, ahem, oh, I just love that word, it makes me giddy—into the conversation but you know, there's not enough courtesy in this city. Let it start here." He smiled at Rico and winked.

"You're in the right jurisdiction, my friend," Mario continued. "The state don't execute folks no more. Ding Ding's very happy, and when you finally kill someone, you'll be, too."

Mario then wrinkled his nose and stared at the ceiling. "You know," he finally said. "I just consulted with my departed colleague, Dr. JoJo, and he said the other doctors have it all wrong. You're not a true schizophrenic like I am, you're a sociopath—and no drug can help that. Ooh, I'm terrified. I'm so glad you're handcuffed."

"Shut the fuck up," Rico snarled.

"Such a temper, the trigger for crimes of cruelty and passion," Mario said and blinked his eyes. "You're such a passionate people. I get thrilled thinking about it.

"Can you sing?"

"What?"

"*Dahil sayo,* that lovely Tagalog ballad. JoJo used to sing it to me at night."

Rico lay back on his bed and shut his eyes. Maybe silence would end the conversation.

"Have you ever had a black man?"

"Fuck you, you goddamn freak," Rico mumbled.

"Ah, tsk, you're so in denial," Mario said sternly, as if in lecture. He shook his head and jangled the chains of his handcuffs for emphasis. "Oh sure, you might leave here, our own little upper reach of hell, but you can never leave. Not really."

Chapter Fourteen

The warm air of a clear Indian summer, late September night made it the best time of the year to be at Ocean Beach. Rico thought so, too.

Earlier that day, he'd made up his mind to be where he was while reading the paper—front page until last. While scanning the obits, he'd seen his name through a morning red wine fog. Maybe it wasn't his name, but it was close enough for him to think it might have been—and just thinking that way made it a Yakima sign, his Indian side finally kicking in. He put down the paper, lit a cigarette, and took another drink.

Although it was nearing midnight, hundreds of young people still lingered—many from earlier in the day when the thermostat hit three digits. They clustered together on the sand or in their cars parked along the gravel divide separating the north and south lanes of the Great Ocean Highway. Above the low, continuous growl of breaking waves could be heard occasional peals of laughter and the amped-up sounds of mixed message rhythm and blues —of blaring horns and of James feeling good and Aretha telling born-to-prowl brothers like James not to feel *that* good.

The scene reeked of hot fun in the soon-to-be-gone summertime, helped along with sacks full of liquid spirits and tightly rolled joints.

"Oye, vato," a Mexican about Rico's age called out to him as he walked along the beach. The Mexican was sitting with several other young men and women by a roaring fire. College students, Rico figured. They were laughing and passing around two fifths of Jack, several joints, and a pipe. A woman sitting next to the Mexican called him "Roberto," then giggled and whispered something Rico couldn't hear.

"Come on, bro," Roberto yelled out. "Party with us."

At first, Rico ignored the invitation. He had an idea in mind, a destination. Then he shrugged and turned toward the group. A few more minutes wouldn't change a thing.

"I know you from somewhere," Roberto said, as he handed him a bottle of Jack.

"Been a lotta places," Rico said indifferently. He took a healthy swig, then handed the bottle back. "Thanks."

"I'm pretty fucked up right now, but I don't forget faces," Roberto slurred, as he took a hit from the pipe. "And you look like . . . I seen you in one of my classes."

Roberto, who was swaying slightly, dropped his head and closed his eyes. Suddenly, he looked up, a broad, full-toothed smile on his face. "The day I popped that dude upside his head," he said excitedly. "You was there."

Rico chuckled. He remembered.

"Got expelled for that, but that was cool cuz I just wasn't ready," he said, as he drained the last drop of Jack. "Too angry, man, a time bomb, know what I mean?"

Rico's slight smile said he knew what he meant.

"Army?" Roberto asked.

"Marines," Rico replied evenly and looked at his watch—now after midnight. He shrugged. A few minutes more wouldn't change a thing, he thought, as he sat on the sand.

"It's better now," Roberto said. He explained that after he was

kicked out of school, he left Frisco and went home—to Salinas—
which is where he should have gone first after leaving the Army.
His family helped him put the war behind him, his friends did,
too. They all pulled together, prayed for him, and covered him
with love. They woke him from his night sweats, cuddled him like
a child, and told him he was safe now—he was home.

Then there was Juanita, with her up-from-the-barrio medical
school dreams. Just one more semester at State, Roberto
explained, then they were going to get married, probably next year.
He wanted children. She did, too, but not until after med school.

Juanita was asleep, her head resting in Roberto's lap as he gently stroked her long black hair.

A pretty girl, Rico thought, more Indian than Spanish. He
sighed again. She reminded him of Wynona.

"I told her to be a shrink," Roberto chuckled. "That way she
can always work on me."

Roberto rubbed his eyes and yawned. One by one, his friends
had since lapsed into sleep or lost consciousness, and it was clear
he'd soon join them. He lay down on the sand and drew Juanita
close to him, his front to her back, and wrapped his arms around
her.

"The booze, dope, whatever's left, take what you need,"
Roberto said dreamily.

"Thanks, man," Rico said. "I'm cool."

"You know, man, when I first got out I used to be scared to
sleep, the dreams, the sights and sounds. Even the smells—that
stench from burned flesh—that was the worst. I tried booze, still
do, but that don't work."

Roberto paused. "But it don't happen so much no more and
not recently neither," he said, as he kissed the back of Juanita's
neck. "She's one of the reasons."

"You're a lucky man," Rico said.

"You ever dream, bro?"

"No," Rico said flatly.

A moment of silence followed, as if in disbelief. "You're a lucky man," Roberto finally mumbled, as his eyes began to close.

The party was finally over. Rico stared at the bodies sprawled around a fire that was still going strong, its crackling and the waves breaking upon the beach the only sounds in the darkness. He looked at his watch—just after one—then chuckled softly.

What was the point? Time no longer mattered. He then took off his watch—a Seiko, a long-ago gift from Marites—and carefully slid it into the space between Roberto's belly and Juanita's lower back. He pulled out his wallet containing his driver's license, social security card, and forty bucks—his entire net worth—and slipped two twenties into Roberto's back pocket.

Back at his apartment, he thought about sticking the bills in an envelope and sending them to his mother—he was sure she could use the money—but decided not to. The cash would hurt her more than it would help. He figured she was Indian enough to know he was gone. There was another reason as well. As he sat in his kitchen surrounded by empty bottles, his nothing-to-show-for-it life suddenly shamed him.

He took one last look at Roberto—his face buried in the strands of his lover's hair—and felt a pang of envy. The face looked peaceful, rested—the very best gifts that sleep can bring, but sometimes doesn't. Sure, there'd be ups and downs, but Rico knew the worst was behind Roberto. He'd made it home.

For a moment, Rico tried to imagine himself in Roberto's place, but couldn't. His face never came into focus.

"You're wrong," Rico finally whispered. "You got all the luck, pal."

As Rico turned away, he knew this was the last stop on his road to hell, where the deepest yearnings of others would be answered, but never his. He knew he'd never be happy, he'd never have peace. The voices were getting louder, the visions and dreams clearer.

They haunted him, he knew, because of the wrongs he'd done. But forgiveness requires acknowledgment, sorrow, supplication, and faith—traits foreign to him. The truth was that even now, he wasn't sure what he'd done—not all of it anyway—and even if he did, he wasn't sure he'd apologize anyway.

For a moment, he stared at the ocean and wondered what could have changed it. If Wynona had stayed? Marites? Maybe a son he could teach to box?

Rico sadly shook his head. He now knew that the docs and the full body of medical science had a basic premise all wrong, reversed—the loss of hope was far more fatal than an unbeating heart.

"Control the ending," Rico whispered, as he began walking toward the ocean, right by a sign warning of danger, an undertow. That was the point, he thought. Already dead, he was just discarding the shell.

He'd thought about buying a gun—easy enough to do in the Loin—but decided against it. He'd already heard too much gunfire in his life and he hated the thought of having that sound be the last one he heard. He also considered the bridges over the bay, two of which were within walking distance of his apartment. But he nixed that, too. He'd heard that over the years a handful of jumpers had survived, and with his luck he'd be the newest paralytic addition to a short, pitiful list.

As he'd pondered his choices, he vaguely recalled a magazine piece on how in Japan some women walked into the ocean to erase their shame. An anonymous end, with the body never found. That appealed to him, especially because his mom should never know he chose to end it. The knowing would kill her. This way, she could pray and always have hope he'd just wandered off and would turn up some day.

As he walked into the surf, his stride never lessened, even as he slogged from ankle deep water then up to his waist and beyond. He reached a point where the waves began washing over his chest. It wouldn't be long. He continued walking, or trying to, but it was harder now. He could feel the current pulling him forward and lifting him up—and himself letting go. He fought his instincts, his urge to survive and move his arms and legs, break the surface and fill his bursting lungs with air.

Instead, he closed his eyes and just let go, his only movement guided by the current's flow. Before losing consciousness, he listened for the voices.

Silence—then a fleeting image. A detachment of cavalry was charging fiercely across a jungle clearing. Rico heard the bugle, felt the heat of galloping horses, the sweat and excitement of the riders.

He also heard, or thought he did, the war whoops of Yakima braves echoing off the mesas and canyons of the arid Palouse— out of place in his jungle image, but somehow oddly fitting now. He was riding alongside his dad, urging him to go faster, racing him toward one more adrenalin high.

Rico smiled. He and Vince were blood of blood, father and son, no doubt. A damn good story and an obvious John Wayne–less paradigm shift—too bad he'd never write it. For just one moment, he thought about turning back, or trying to, and wondered if he could still command movement in his fingers, arms, and legs.

Then he opened his eyes to see nothing, not even the bubbles floating upward from his nose and mouth.

At that moment, Rico wondered where the current would take him. Perhaps to Japan, where he could visit the women who'd done this before him, or maybe to his father's little house on the beach. Wherever it was heading, he was going. In this, the last second of his life, Rico knew he'd finally chosen well.

Chapter Last

As she opened the door, she remembered what brought her to this rundown apartment so far from her home. He'd given her a key from their days together. She never returned it, never had the chance to. It had been more than a year since she'd seen him last.

In that time, she'd been warned to stay away. He was too sick, the elders said, doomed to harm those around him, even those he loved. Stay away, they said, now you've got even more to lose.

She'd heeded their advice until one night four days ago when she called up a sitter, got in her car, and began her drive west. Just hours before, she'd been sleeping in the deepest REM valley when suddenly she sat straight up. She replayed the dream—of waves and unending ocean—and feared that this time her prayers and flesh offerings wouldn't be answered. She reached for a bundle of sage bound by red string that she kept in a bowl by her bed. She then lit it and guided the smoke in directions that blanketed her, but not so completely a tear didn't escape. She'd been taught not to cry, but she couldn't stop the single tear that managed to fall. She consoled herself by whispering that maybe she could stop him. Maybe this time there was still time.

But once inside the apartment, she knew he was gone, as each pore filled with the absence of someone she loved. Hers was a quiet sense of loss. She couldn't cry, she had no tears left. There was nothing more she could do except linger for a moment before heading back. Eyes closed, she stood still to feel once more those other times.

She opened her eyes. The apartment was as she remembered. Little had changed, except for a much larger army of empty bottles forming lines and circles on the window sill and floor. But it was a worn, blue leather book lying open atop a newspaper on the kitchen table that drew her attention, drew her to it.

*   *   *

September 20, 1975

I'm not enrolled this term, and I badly miss school. Work at the supermarket just keeps piling up and I keep getting called in—good for the bank account, bad for everything else. I've been staying on the meds just to keep up with this soul-numbing routine.

When class started, I got the instructor's permission and began sitting in on a mid-level workshop. We've been studying the basics of classic fiction—the plot building to an inevitable climax before descending to the denouement.

Sure, I've got real life stories to tell, but fiction, I must admit, attracts me more—and has for some time. I'm at my creative best when the pills stay in the bottle. I'm not so sure everything I write is art, but I believe I can hit a few high notes once in a while—and it's the trying that counts.

But sometimes, when I get like that, there's a price to be paid, and I'm not so sure I—or those around me—can keep paying it.

Still, I'm free when I'm like that—something Vince never was until he left us. Something I haven't been for much of this life. We're all born with expiration dates, and the only major question is what we decide to do until the buzzer sounds.

I've chosen to create a universe, or at least try to, whether anyone else knows it or not. I want to give birth to the characters, put blood in their veins, passion and motive in their hearts. A pen and an empty page—the seemingly harmless tools of addiction.

Wynona once said there are no accidents—and maybe there's something to that. But when I'm writing, I'm free of that and any other fetter. I can even write a happy ending. It's there in my pen—just not for me.

So much of life is beyond me, but here I control the ending . . .

*   *   *

She read and reread the entry. *Denouement?* She stared at the word, unsure what it meant. She shrugged. A French teacher she knew back home could help her find out.

She then glanced at the newspaper, at the obituary section, where red lines circled and recircled the name resembling the name of the man who once lived in this apartment. Off by the date of birth and by a letter—an "o" where the "a" in "Divina" should have been.

She sighed as she studied the cause of Divino's death—a party-too-hearty late-night drowning at Ocean Beach. She also knew that if she closed her eyes she could see the sender—his smirking, snarling, once-familiar face. But what was the point? Hers was a world without coincidence, just signs of what should be done—ignore at your risk. Someone sent the sign and its recipient was Indian enough to understand it. Knowing this gave her an odd satisfaction. She should have been angry, but couldn't summon the feeling.

She sighed again. It was the end of his time—simple as that.

Laying the book down on the table next to two prescription bottles, she examined the labels, and noticed their expiration dates—one current, the other more than three months expired. Both were crammed with pills. Just like him, she thought. Ignore the advice of those wanting to help.

Prolixin, another word to look up when she got home.

As she rose to leave, she pulled a small picture from her jacket pocket. Carefully, she placed it on the page on which he'd written his last entry. It was a color photo of herself with an infant, possibly a boy. The child looked Indian, but not Indian enough. She had wanted to give him the photo. If he were alive, he'd have seen the resemblance.

As she stepped into the dimly lit hallway, she turned toward the door and placed her hand on the doorknob. Standing there for a moment as if studying the door, she felt the contours of the doorknob, committing their features to memory. Finally, she took a deep breath and gently pulled the doorknob. She saw the door move and heard the quiet click of metal sliding onto metal.

"Denouement?" she whispered, as she turned to walk away.

About the Author

Peter Bacho is a former journalist and editorial writer in Tacoma, Washington. He was recently named the Distinguished Northwest Writer in Residence at Seattle University. He currently teaches writing at the Evergreen State College in Tacoma. In his spare time, he is a writer of award-winning fiction and nonfiction books. Among his honors, he lists an American Book Award, a Washington Governor's Writers Award, and the Murray Morgan Prize. His new novel, *Entrys,* is his fourth work of fiction and his fifth book overall.